IN HER ARMS

Volume 1

By Panda

Art by Jake Solaris and Xavier Solaris

TABLE OF CONTENTS

I FOUND LOVE BY MY RUTHLESS EX

A PAINFUL TRUTH

"She's different," the familiar voice filled my ears and my heart. It was the voice of my first love, the man I had married. I assumed he was defending me to his friends, who would undoubtedly be slandering me as a gold digger. My husband was rich, and his friends considered him important, but to me he was just Richard. All the same, they wouldn't believe me, and he rarely defended me. Now I thought I understood he wanted me to stand on my own, but in my absence, he would stand up for me. That illusion was shattered even as it still formed in my mind, "She will never betray me, and she will never go anywhere. Who cares why she likes me. Whether it's my money, or some shared history, she believes in with her whole heart. Either way, she takes care of the house, she's loyal, she does as she's told, and she respects my boundaries. Any way you look at it, she is perfectly suited to running my home and raising my children. Paying her so much attention when we were young and broke instead of running around was the best investment of my life. Plus, young women are so much more fun now that I'm older, anyway, and with her always waiting at home I have the perfect excuse to create distance when I need to. She really isn't like those gold diggers. She's the best tool I've ever invested in."

"You are disgusting, Richard. I'm leaving," with that stern yet silky voice drifting in the air and the weight of my husband's confession still assaulting my consciousness, the door to the private room in front of me opened.

Scarlet stood in front of me. Red pants of some kind of leather clung to her as if painted on. Her black halter top barely covered her ample breasts. Her pale skin almost glowed in the dimness of the club. Her jet-black hair was in a tight ponytail, and her eyes like a predatory cat shining gold in the club lights were fixed on me.

She stormed towards me, the door slamming shut behind her. I never saw anyone inside the room, and I had hoped none of them had seen me. "We're leaving," Scarlet commanded, snatching my wrist and dragging me through the club. "How long have you been here? How much did you hear?" She asked desperately, trying to figure out how bad it was, how hurt I was. Scarlet was my best friend, and the only member of Richard's inner circle that didn't belittle or accuse me. She had in fact come to my defense more often than my husband had.

All my old friends were long gone, stripped away by Richard's paranoia and possessiveness, or, I was beginning to suspect, to systematically isolate me. Scarlet was different, she had been appointed by the board as a condition to get Richard's start-up off the ground. Unambitious, experienced, an insurance policy if he was out of his depths. Now that powerful presence was crashing against me with pressure, I rarely saw her display.

"From She's different," I admitted meekly, and she began to cry for me.

"He's such a bastard. I was trying to protect you, Ray. I figured if you never knew it, it was for the best."

The implication hung heavy in the air. This was not the first time or some drunk rant taken out of context, this was how he always viewed me, and it made me want to puke. Even so, her use of my nickname made me blush and smile uncontrollably. It was a nickname usually reserved for our monthly drinking parties. That's where she had first used it.

"No matter how dark my world gets, you're always a ray of sunshine, bringing joy and hope. Thanks Ray, you're my best friend," she told me before passing out on the bar.

"You'll stay with me tonight," she commanded me, bringing my mind back to the present. I, for my part, just shook barely. My reaction didn't matter. Scarlet had made up her mind, and she was a force that not even Richard could control.

"Bumped into your wife, kidnapped her for the night, so enjoy your conversation and whatever tonight. Don't bother us," she texted as we walked, her short-clipped phrasing leaving no room for compromise. Richard didn't respond. He had been with Scarlet for years, and he knew he was ill-equipped to win an argument with her.

As we waited for the greasy, over-processed Chinese, we loved to get when the world felt like too much, my mind raced with thoughts of what Richard was doing with this unexpected free time.

"Tell me everything." The words came out of my mouth as if someone else had said them, but I was resolved not to wait patiently in the shadow of my own life anymore.

"I'll tell you what I know, but me and Richard aren't that close, and I tend to leave when they start bad-mouthing you. I'll start by saying the cruelest thing he's ever said to me and the most heartless thing he's ever done to you. When I was first brought on to the company, he brought me into his office and said, 'I was told you're a problem solver. No matter what, you'll get it done. My wife, I don't want her to be lonely. I can't have her looking for real friends or developing her own interests. I've invested too much in making her what I need. So be her friend and keep others away,' he said it like it was the most natural thing in the world. It made my skin crawl. I prepared my letter of resignation when I left his office. Then I met you, and the thought of someone keeping tabs on you, helping Richard deceive you, never giving you the friendship you deserved. Well, that made me physically ill. So, I stayed watching over you. Picking you up when he knocked you down became my purpose." The confession hung heavy in the air, and I could feel it re-texturing our entire relationship. She had made a conscious effort to be there for me, but she had known the whole time everything about Richard, and she had said nothing. She must have noticed the hurt I was trying to hide in my eyes. She averted her gaze and began to talk again. "Do you remember the first time we hung out? It was right after we first met, I invited you for drinks while Richard was on a business trip. He took an intern with him. Do you remember the conversation we had that night?" Scarlet asked, bringing the memory crashing back.

"So, your precious hubby took an intern with him. She's been at the company for a week. Seems awful..." she started before my harsh defensive voice cut the younger, less sultry Scarlet off.

"If you just invited me out to badmouth Richard, I'll go. I don't care what his crass friends consider entertainment. I don't do gossip and insults," I had responded with a harsh and finite tone.

"Yes, I'm sorry," I finally responded after what felt like a lifetime.

"It's fine. At the time I understood we weren't close enough for you to believe me. Then, as time passed, I was afraid that if I told you, I'd get blamed for all the time that passed with me being quiet. At some point though I told myself he was a jerk, but you were happy, and disrupting that would be as cruel as he was."

“Scarlet, you are truly a good friend. Thanks. You said first, so is there more?”

“Yes, but are you sure you want to hear it all, and you will not blame me for telling you?”

“Yes, Scarlet, please.”

“I can tell you with absolute certainty he has never loved you. He would brag about the foresight of picking you and the genius in his criteria. Someone pretty enough to be arm candy, but innocent enough to be approachable and loyal. Smart enough to handle all the assigned tasks but naïve enough never to question why she was being given a list of tasks like a project manager. No family to comfort her and no friends or strongly developed hobbies. There was more, but I left whenever I could, and the picture was always crystal clear. Good enough to stand beside him, but insecure enough to doubt that. It cut me to think that’s how he saw your devotion. Almost all business has been delegated for months. He’s cheated as long as the company has been successful, but now he has two mistresses and dates constantly. The mistress are roommates in a three-bedroom house he rents. I know this because I heard him bragging about how he’s looking for someone for the third room. Such a pig. He almost never comes to the office any more just partying with the guys and spending time with his harem. His plan for your future is for you to raise all his children, and he intends to have a lot. That’s the type of pig he is. Not sure how he plans on bringing them to your house, but he is planning for them. I think everything else would be just rude for no reason. It’s just different takes on your personality, appearance, and years of servitude. None of it is nice, and none of it is accurate. I’m really, so truly sorry, Ray. I thought if I could be by your side for support and you never found out... Any ways you do know so what will you do now?”

"Gut him," I said coldly. I was not hurt or heartbroken, I was angry. I had chosen to believe in love, so I had become the woman he was looking for. I was not naturally domestic. I was originally planning to start my own company, but Richard wanted me safe at home, he said. I only understood now he really meant confined to the home. He had gotten rid of all my friends, but they would have been too meek to stand up to him anyways. That's why they had fled from my side long ago, but he had made a huge mistake there. He had chased away all my friends, who were too scared to stand up to him, or even lock eyes with him. Now they were all replaced by my best friend, a woman who openly challenged him and hated him even more than I did.

"Sounds good. I'll help," she responded, and I knew it wasn't just for comfort.

NO MORE NO LESS

It was early in the afternoon of the next day when a messenger arrived with two large brown envelopes marked with a one and a two. I assumed the order I opened them in mattered and opened the one marked with a one. It was a letter from Scarlet.

"Gwyn, the other envelope contains bearer bonds for our new company. I thought about keeping them so your husband couldn't find them, but I know how hard it is for you to trust now. I'm sure learning he wants us to be friends only made that harder, so I've sent them to you. I've arranged a video call with six key funding partners with conservative backgrounds. I will make them all sign NDAs; your identity will be protected. You can present evidence of his fast and loose management style and of him using the company as his own personal dating app. The rest will be up to you, Gwyn, but I have faith in you."

I lit the letter on fire and tucked the bonds in my bag. It hurt me a little that she had sent them, but not for what she had done, but in acknowledgment of what I had done. She had always been good to me. Stood up for me when my own husband wouldn't. Took me out when I was feeling down. Most importantly, stood by my decisions instead of demanding I obey hers. How could I not trust her completely, and yet I had made her feel like I doubted her. Worse that doubt was rooted in him, and it made me furious. My phone buzzed as I finished reading the letter. "8:00 p.m., good luck." Scarlet had everything set up, and I had a lot to do before tonight.

I ran from one appointment to another, making arrangements on the fly. Hair, tailored suit, copies of presentation notes, and even a spyware scan for my laptop to make sure my dear husband wasn't keeping an eye on my virtual footprint. The level of controlling and manipulative I had learned he was, had left me unsettled. I went to Scarlet's place. It was almost six, but I needed to thank her in person and give her the bonds.

"I appreciate the gesture, but I trust you and I would die if Richard got his hand on them. It might have been different if I'd learned Richard asked you to be my friend and all that other stuff, but I didn't you told me. You have always shown me way more care than my husband, so how could I doubt that?"

"O.k. I'll keep them, but be careful; he's already messaged me three times trying to figure out what you're up to. I told him I'd give you back for dinner. I needed to decompress. I think he bought it. Who knows, though? Have a good dinner then a great meeting, and tomorrow we'll see a lawyer."

With that, I was off, and by the time Richard returned home for dinner, I was getting dressed, and dinner was on the table. I usually prepared everything myself, but I had brought in help to give me time to get ready for the meeting. We ate in silence. He didn't even comment on my outfit, which was an elegant sky-blue skirt suit. A huge departure from my usual attire, but I already knew he'd never notice. I hated to admit it, but I was a little sad to be right. He was still chewing his last bite when he pecked me on the cheek and was gone again. Off to enjoy whatever life my servitude afforded him. The meeting came before I knew it, but it went smoothly. Nobody was ready to cut ties with Richard yet. Not until they knew I could deliver.

However, they each gave me one million dollars to get my infrastructure in place and prove I could handle their needs.

With an overwhelming sense of satisfaction, I went to sleep early that night, but my euphoria didn't last long. Richard stumbled into the room in the early morning, the stench of alcohol so strong it made my stomach wretch when he opened the door. He was mumbling, "Stupid girl, why let me buy you so many drinks if you weren't interested. At least I've got my Gwyn."

Before I could even take in his slurred words, he was on top of me, kissing me with force and nothing else. Like an angry child who had just managed to snatch back a toy he had outgrown but wanted to make sure no one else got to enjoy. I pushed him off me, "Ugh, you stink. Go sleep in the guest room. How could you assault your own wife? I have things to do in the morning."

He looked confused and hurt, but he stumbled out of the room without a word. I rose before him the next morning and left immediately. Usually, I would make breakfast and keep it warm till he got up and only head out after he left for the day. Today, however, I was going to prepare my company. Within three months, I would destroy my husband's company and create a firm foundation for me to start my new life.

I met Scarlet, had breakfast, and went to a law firm that would be able to handle all of our needs. The divorce first and legal counsel for the company later on. Then we went to our bank and initiated the wire transfers from our partners, so we had operational funds to start building our company. We rented two floors of a high-rise with a line of sight on Richard's offices and started reaching out to talent undervalued at Richard's company. It was 9:00 p.m. and my phone was blowing up with messages from Richard.

"I had a rough night. Let's have a night out."

"I was thinking, dinner and then drinks with the whole crew."

"We could just do us, if you prefer."

"Maybe low-key at home. Cuddle, watch a movie?"

"Or maybe you're already cooking? If so, sorry to bother you with all these ideas."

"Fuck, I had a shitty day, and you're not even home, and you're totally blowing me off. WTF Gwyn?"

"Sorry, I'm sure whatever you're doing is important. You're always there for me, just today was really hard. Let me know everything's ok when you get this, ok."

His messages became more desperate, and I couldn't help but smile as I read them. I was eating tacos on Scarlet's couch. I told her I didn't want to go back to Richard's house ever again. She had quickly offered me her place as long as I needed it.

"He's being so clingy. If I didn't know his true motives, it would be a little endearing."

Scarlet chuckled, "I hope you're smart enough to see it for what it is by now, Rey, pathetic and controlling."

"Yup," I agreed, a happiness I couldn't control drenching my tone. I was sure he had started to notice his people were fleeing. Taking accounts and contacts with them. He didn't handle failure or hardship well. He didn't have enough practice with them, I suppose. We finished the night with small talk about our plans for the company and our time as friends. We climbed into bed that night fully worn out. So much so that it didn't occur to me to wonder why she had climbed into bed with me instead of offering to crash on the couch like she had in the past.

I woke the next day nestled into Scarlet's shoulder, my arms draped over her waist and one of my legs wrapped around one of hers. I flushed in embarrassment, but the warmth and comfort made it impossible for me to draw away from her. I sighed lightly at the sense of comfort and familiarity of the situation.

"Oh, you're awake," Scarlet said in response to my sigh, and I went from embarrassed to mortified. I braced for her to shove me away, but instead she stroked my hair. "Rey, you've been through so much. I wish I had been a better friend." Her guilt hit me like a sledgehammer to the chest.

"Scarlet, you know you don't get best friend by default. You've always held me up, and the secrets you kept were ones I made it impossible to reveal." I wanted to say something, anything, to make her understand she was everything I wanted her to be and more. I was in awe of how effortlessly she worried about me. How she always considered me, defended me, and paved the way for me to do what I wanted, how I wanted it done. In truth, I saw no world where the word friend was enough to describe everything this woman had done for me or everything this woman had been to me. "Scarlet, are we friends?" I couldn't help but ask as my emotions overcame my reason. As I did, my arms gripped her hips and pulled us closer together.

"Of course, Rey, you'll always be my best friend."

"I see," I responded, trying to hide the hurt and sadness in my voice and failing miserably.

"What's wrong, Rey? Do you not want to be my friend anymore? I can give you the company, and I'll still help you with Richard. Don't force yourself, it will break my heart," Scarlet responded, the hurt in her tone now mirroring my own. I couldn't let her believe that. I hated myself for making her doubt our connection.

"Force myself," I scoffed. "Don't be ridiculous, Scarlet. If it hadn't been for you, I would have heard that horrible conversation and fallen apart. I don't know what would have happened, but I would have never recovered. I just thought maybe we were, you know... um, more. That's all," I admitted and then instantly wished I had been born mute.

"I see. Rey, you just left Richard. You're hurt and vulnerable. I would never take advantage of you like that, Rey."

"Then why did you start calling me Rey all the time? Why have you not pushed me away? Why are you always more considerate of me than you are of your own needs? Why everything, just Why, Scarlet. If you don't love me, then why go to such lengths?"

"Rey, my sweet radiant Rey. Those are two very different things. I've loved you sense that cocktail party for the acquisition of that little tech start-up. You remember? I had gotten drunk after another terrible attempt at finding love. I tried yet again to tell you your husband was a piece of shit, but this time instead of scolding me for bad-mouthing your husband you said," she began and paused for a moment and in that moment, I couldn't help but take over the story.

"It hurts me to see two people I love fighting. Please, for me, don't hate him too much, ok. Then I laid your head in my lap and stroked your hair for the rest of the party. We got weird looks from a couple of the VIPs, but not even Richard said anything to us about it."

"Yup, that was it. I was done, Rey. I knew the reason I couldn't find anyone I loved was because I had found her long ago. So, I stopped dating and focused on your happiness. So, if you ask if we're friends, the answer is yes. If you ask if "I love you", the answer is very much so. If you ask me out, no matter how much it will hurt me and even though it could damage our friendship, the answer is no. Not now, anyways, I'm sorry friendship is all I can offer you for now,"

She explained, still stroking my hair. My fingers dug into her hip, and I began to cry. We stayed like that for an hour. Then Scarlet left for the day.

A PRECIOUS MEMORY

The apartment was cold and empty without Scarlet, and I found myself wishing I hadn't blown Richard off. I didn't miss him, I didn't want to see him, but this new pain was unlike anything I had ever felt when dealing with Richard, and I just wanted to escape. Back to the numb annoyance of being trained to be a tool with no will or emotions of her own. I wanted a reason to bury this ache, but as I opened my phone and saw the three hundred and twenty-seven messages and the fifty-two missed calls, I knew that was no longer an option. I opened the messages and scrolled to the end.

"Divorce, what did Scarlet tell you? I'll have her job and your head for this!" It said and the anger was palpable even through his text, but I didn't care about that I was focused on the threat to Scarlet's job. She didn't like Richard, but she loved her job. At least that's what I always believed, but as I was working through what I could do to help the woman, I now knew I loved, pushed the door open and came into her living room.

"I was too late," the words slipped from my mouth with no thought.

"Too late for what?"

"Richard fired you, because I filed for divorce," I explained, waiting for her outrage. In typical Scarlet fashion, there was none, just a light chuckle.

"He did what now. Do you even know what my job at your husband's company is?"

I did, but somehow with his threat and my concern for Scarlet I had forgotten. Her job was to represent the board, to step in if Richard messed up. As such, she couldn't be fired without board approval. I felt so embarrassed with myself for getting so worked up, "But why are you home then?" I asked, after organizing my thoughts, completely ignoring her question.

"I'm done. I talked to the board members today, that's why I went in. I was only at the company to help an old friend out and keep an eye on you. If you're free, then I see no reason to force it. I was a bad fit and your husband will most likely lose the company at the next board meeting anyway. I also might have mentioned a new startup that would be worth checking out. I've arranged an investors banquet for the end of the month. We need to have everything in place to wow the crowd by then. You focus on the company. I'll arrange the party, deal," Scarlet explained, smiling at me. My heart skipped a beat. I nodded meekly and looked down at the floor.

"I made dinner," I told her, barely able to force my voice out.

We ate in silence and then took turns using the bathroom to prepare for bed. Once more we climbed into the same king bed, but it was different this time. I could feel the heat and the pressure. She had admitted she loved me, and I now realized I loved her, but she had made it clear she couldn't and wouldn't accept my feelings.

"Can we cuddle again, tonight? Please, it felt so warm and safe."

She didn't respond, she just pulled me close and started stroking my hair. Our relationship was strained, but even still we leaned against each other. Our days continued this way: busy days, silent dinners, warm intimate nights. The contrast in her conduct made it all the harder to organize my thoughts and feelings. I knew I loved her. I mean I had known for a long time, but when I first realized it, I had dismissed it. I was married; I had chosen Richard. Even if it wasn't perfect, I would never betray him. He had though, so how do I make Scarlet realize I was sure of these feelings, because they had been in me for almost as long as she had loved me.

The weekend came, and I still had no answer, but I was determined to pin Scarlet down and try to figure this out. "Scarlet, it's the weekend. We're still friends, right?" I asked, a little scared to hear the answer,

"Always Rey. Even when you become successful, marry some pretty boy and forget all about me, I'll still have your back," Scarlet reassured me. The reassurance made me glow, but her prediction for my future made my heart ache. I pushed the ache aside for now and forced all that joy and gratitude into my voice.

"Then we can spend the day together, right? We need to take a break, and friends make sure friends don't work themselves to death," I said with a tight mechanical chuckle.

"Ok," she agreed vacantly, staring at everything but me. I accepted the fact that she was willing to at least go along with it, and I dragged her to her room and threw an outfit at her. It was a sky-blue summer dress with spaghetti straps and matching beach sandals, a small black bikini instead of lingerie, and a copper bangle stamped with four-leaf clovers.

"Go shower and get dressed. We'll head out when you're ready," I declared, faking confidence, but faltering towards the end.

“Sure,” she responded flatly. With that, the two of us busied ourselves getting ready for the day.

An hour later we were both by the door, and while I had picked out the outfit for Scarlet, the makeup and how she was put together was all her, and she had nailed it. My heart felt like it would explode, and despite our awkward vibe lately, I couldn’t look away. Which was made all the more awkward by the fact that she was in the same state. Her eyes had a hunger I had never seen in them before, and they roamed across my body like a predator sizing up her prey.

Eventually we broke away from our trance and I led us to our first stop, brunch by the pool. We ate. I made a point to make conversation. Even if it was one sided and awkward. After we finished eating, we tanned by the pool again, making conversation, but we both were talking now. Our banter returned to something close to its old ease and comfort, and for the briefest moment I faltered. Wondering if maybe I should leave it. We were good again, but if she didn’t accept my next confession, we wouldn’t stay good, and eventually, we wouldn’t be able to go back. However, I hungered for more, and even in the warmth of this banter, there was an undercurrent of unease. So, I steeled my resolve and moved us on to the massage I had booked.

After that, we enjoyed a light lunch, and I had finally gathered my courage. I took her to a little club that wasn’t as high scale as the places we usually went to, but it was nice enough to impress smaller companies and had been used a lot by Richard in his start-up days. We got a private booth in the back. It was quiet and had its own dedicated server. We sat down and ordered drinks, and then I took a deep breath.

“Do you remember the first time we came here together? It was a contract signing. You had been with the company for a couple months. We had started hanging out a bit. Richard’s friends started harassing me. Trying to drive me away before the client arrived. Richard stopped them, and I was so happy at first. Do you remember, ‘leave her alone,' he said, and my heart soared for the briefest moment, 'If you morons chase her off today, we'll lose this deal, and you'll all be fired. Clear!' and like that my heart sank, but unlike normal I didn't have to bear it alone. You, sitting on my right, grabbed my hand and dragged me out of the booth," I started my story, and Scarlet took over at this point to show she did indeed remember.

"You're the worst. We're getting drinks alone. We'll be back for your precious client. I said and dragged you off, determined to tell you what kind of piece of shit your fake ass husband was. We were enjoying our first drink, and I was gathering my courage when an intern showed up telling us the client was there already. We went back, and we signed the deal," she paused. Seemingly unsure of where I was going with this trip down memory lane.

"Yes, we did sign the deal, but not because me and Richard were a great couple and certainly not because of Richard's shrewd negotiating. He was acting as if it was a done deal when the client got there, and he introduced me as his wife. The client was about to leave, and you brought them back to the table. No promises, no bravado, just this calm confidence and a reassuring glare. Richard got drunk and went to the bathroom, I always assumed, to puke. You stayed composed even though you never refused a drink. You made him realize you would always be there as a safety net, and I'll never forget the line you used to seal the deal, 'Gwyn is there and she's my best friend, my only true friend. As long as she's there I will keep this company on the right track,' he was so touched he doubled his original investment, and you patted the back of my hand under the table, and I thought to myself why couldn't I be with her, and this be her company. We would be so happy, but I had made my choice, and even though he was cold and distant, he had built me a good life. I would not betray those vows even if I ached to do so."

A tear rolled down her cheek, and I wiped it away. She was gasping for air. I was worried, but I had to admit she looked adorable, overwhelmed like this. She was always so well-composed. I couldn't remember ever having seen her like this. I stroked her back as she brought her breathing under control, and then a wry smile overtook my face.

"Does this mean you accept my feelings now?" I asked, glaring at her hopefully.

She nodded enthusiastically. "Rey," was all she said before my body responded to her nod, pressing my lips firmly against hers. With that, our day out was over. I still had more planned. A dinner, a moonlit stroll, a hotel suite with a great view and a hot tub in the room, but I couldn't think about any of that now. She had accepted my confession completely, and I could no longer bear the weight of this longing.

I dragged her back to her place and chased her to her bed, raining passionate kisses on her every time I caught up to her. We tumbled into the bed and for hours we were lost in the exploration and satisfaction of each other's bodies. Neither of us had ever been with a woman before, so our exploration was clumsy to begin with, but we learned each other's responses quickly, and we got lost in the passion. Eventually exhausted and sated, we shifted from passionate embrace to passive cuddling. We drifted off to sleep, our world irreparably changed forever.

HAPPILY, EVER AFTER

We stayed in on Sunday. Enjoyed the newness of our budding relationship. Richard had reached out to me a couple more times, but I had grown tired of reading his repetitive complaints and his new tactless accusations. By Wednesday of the following week, he must have been getting desperate as he showed up at Scarlet's apartment. He knocked, and Scarlet answered. We had ordered Italian, and it was supposed to be arriving, so she put on her robe and ran to grab it.

"I see. It all makes sense now, you shameless slut," I heard the scream echoing through the apartment. I rushed to check on Scarlet.

"Gwyn, lock yourself in the bathroom. He's crazy," Scarlet yelled at me, and I ran toward her instinctively. She hugged me and stroked my hair. "Worst survival instincts ever. Love you," she said as Richard approached. I pecked her cheek, stood up, and kicked my ex in his nuts, and he dropped to the ground like his legs were overcooked pasta. I pulled Scarlet to her feet, and we bolted together to the bathroom. We locked the door and called 911.

Richard, realizing this fight was over, stormed out of the apartment. I heard the door slam, but we stayed huddled together until we heard the pounding on the door, "Police! Open up or we'll breach the door."

Scarlet got up, and I followed behind her. We went to open the door. All too happy not to see Richard in the apartment. We went to the police and filled out a report for the assault and breaking and entering. The police didn't look too motivated to deal with it.

Two days later, I saw Richard signing a new deal. So clearly, I was right. The cops had considered this a domestic issue not worth their time, so Scarlet and I hired security. Both to follow us and for the apartment. Meanwhile, I smiled, thinking about the trouble Richard had gotten himself into. I had written the deal he had just signed and used a friend of Scarlet's to deliver it to Richard. It looked like a lifeline on the surface, but it was layered with impossible deadlines and ridiculous clauses he would have never accepted if he hadn't been desperate. With laser procession a month later, his company folded.

Scarlet's friend had acquired the company for pennies on the dollar and given it to us as a wedding gift. Which we were in the middle of celebrating as the news of Richard's fate played on a T.V. above the bar where we were drinking. It was a low-key affair, but neither of us felt the need for anything big. The world of finance was too big and overbearing for me. I was capable, but both me and Scarlet wanted to be able to step back in a way that wasn't possible if you wanted to be successful in this world of endless deals. We sold my company before the investor's banquet even happened and liquidated Richard's. We invested our money across the board. Real estate, start-ups, franchises, and even CD's and 401k's anything everyday people would have access to.

Then we started traveling. I never knew there was so much of the world I wanted to see until I was looking at it with Scarlet. It started as a one-month tour with five stops. All in Europe and all tourist traps. As it came time to leave, we had added twelve stops and four more months. We were in Italy, and the list had become a map of places we had been and places we wanted to see. We finally decided to let go of our home and admit the truth. Our business didn't need us, and traveling the world felt more like home than any place we had ever lived. We were traveling for just over two years when we bumped into Richard again. It was in Vegas on the Strip; he was selling bottled water on the street. We teased him, but we each bought a bottle and gave him a fifty-dollar bill. Not to be generous, but to make sure he knew that we had not suffered in his absence. He did not take it well. Throwing the bin of ice and water on the ground, he rushed toward Scarlet.

"You bitch. If you hadn't told her everything and stolen her. I made her the perfect woman, and you broke her."

I lost my cool. "Dick," I called, and he froze. In all the years we had been together, no one had ever dared to call him that, but we were done, and I couldn't be bothered with his preferences. "Do you really believe it's that simple? Scarlet kept your dirty secret. Until that night at the bar, when I heard everything, you said. I was already leaving, so Scarlet told me everything she knew. With or without Scarlet, this was your end," I told Richard. I knew in my heart without Scarlet I would have never achieved such a total victory over Richard, but the point had to be emphasized. He made me leave. He was cruel and calculating and, in the end, careless.

He broke down crying, and we left. Not the city, just where he was standing on the strip. We still enjoyed another two months in different hotels. There was so much to see, and do we spent longer there than we had anywhere else in our journeys. It was less than six months later that we got news Richard had died. He had left everything to me. Though being honest, it wasn't much. I couldn't be bothered to interrupt our journey to claim it, so I let the state of Nevada keep it.

We did finally settle down. I was almost sixty. Decades of memories beside the woman I loved, but travel was becoming hard on us, and we were ready to take our twilight years at a more passive pace. We adopted a daughter who was twelve and had been adored by her father until he died in a plane crash. I had read about it in the news one day. He was looking for work. She had no relatives, and he had nothing. We flew to meet her and arranged the adoption in less than a week. She had friends nearby, so that is where we settled. Danville was a small historical town In Kentucky, and we couldn't get enough of its charm. We opened a small bed and breakfast. Got Hope a tutor and settled in. Hope wasn't her name when we adopted her, but she was so sad she asked us if she could change her name to Hope so no matter how dark things got, she'd still have to have hope. We couldn't refuse such silly reasoning, and if something as simple as a name change was going to help, I saw no reason to argue.

She did great in school but stopped after high school. She ran the bed and breakfast with us and eventually married. She unfortunately took after me, and a few years into her marriage, I recognized the signs I had learned way back in my youth. And so, Scarlet and I confronted Hope with the truth, then we helped her with the divorce and comforted her afterwards. Luckily, she had us and her daughter. She didn't seem that sad about losing her husband. I couldn't help but wonder if she had ever loved him or if, like me, she had felt the need to choose someone early that seemed like a good fit and a decent man. Regardless of why she was single until her forties. She brought home a man we thought was her son-in-law and introduced her new husband. They had gotten married in Vegas on a drunk dare.

We tried to talk her into an annulment, but she insisted this was different. He helped manage the b&b and me and Scarlet retired.

"We did it right, you know," Scarlet said to me one night. She laid down into my lap on the bench on our porch.

"Did what right love?" I asked stroking her hair. She was over ninety now and still as lovely as the day she saved me from Richard.

“Life, all of it. Gwyn, be happy for me, ok?” Scarlet said and I started to cry. I don’t know how, but I didn’t need to look. Scarlet was gone, but I kept stroking her hair. I couldn’t bring myself to stop. I stayed like that for what felt like forever, but eventually my grand baby, now in her twenties came over and hugged me.

“Grandma Gwyn, I’ll take care of everything. I’ll stay with you forever too, ok?” She asked, with a desperate pleading tone. I wanted to deny her; to tell her she was too young to give up everything for me, but between her tone and my sadness I nodded meekly instead.

We cremated my wife and then I left town with Little Hope, that’s what we called my granddaughter, her name was Hope just like her mom. Me and Little Hope toured places I had visited decades ago with Scarlet and in each city, I would drop a teaspoon of her ashes. I wanted her to be part of the world she loved.

Little Hope’s POV

Grandma Gwyn had been sad since Grandma Scarlet passed away, but she got happier as we traveled and her heart seemed to get lighter as the urn holding Grandma Scarlet emptied. We had been traveling for eight months, and Grandma Gwyn was back to the lighthearted carefree woman I had known in my childhood. We got back to the hotel one day and she laid down on the bed.

“Little Hope, what will you do when Grandma Gwyn passes?” She asked and the question shattered my heart instantly.

“Depends Grandma,” I answered honestly, “If you pass before we're done, I’ll finish your list and add your ashes to Grandma Scarlet’s. If we’re done, I’ll take you and return home. Either way I’ll return home to my parents eventually and watch over them as I did you. Then one day I’ll join you all.”

“I’ll be waiting,” she said and closed her eyes. I called my parents. Then I called the funeral home. I stayed in town until her ashes were ready. The funeral director made a big deal about putting Grandma Gwyn in Grandma Scarlet’s urn, so I had to let them put her in her own. Back at the hotel I dumped them together. They had been separated long enough, and I had promised Grandma Gwyn.

I finished the list of cities and returned to my parents. I have never gotten married or dated much really nor have I adopted. I just watch over my mother and father as I promised.

MY HUSBAND WANTED TO BE POLY FOR HIS MID-LIFE CRISIS

MANIPULATED AND ENTRANCED

My name is Gretta, and I have been with my husband forever, literally. My mom and his mom had been college roommates and stayed close. Me and Jermiah were born mere hours apart and even in the hospital we shared a room. Flash forward to my late thirties and we have been married for fifteen years. We have three kids all at boarding schools and my husband is a very successful sales rep. for something. Honestly, it's not that I don't care, but he doesn't like to talk business, and he says sales are all the same, it's the connections not what you're selling. He never misses a networking opportunity. Meanwhile I'm a free-spirited artist. I've had some mild success, but I've never settled on a style which has made developing a true following difficult. Jermiah has always been very supportive, and I have always given him the space he needed to live the way he wanted. Retreats, business conferences, out of town sales opportunities, even weeks where he just needed to get away and recharge. I would always be there keeping the house together, waiting for his return.

Then one day he comes home from a business conference. He was so proud, he had been a guest speaker. He was telling me about the praise, the jealousy, and the adoration, at dinner. Then as dessert was being brought out for me, he never ate it but never failed to get me something sweet when he first got back, he took a casual sip of his coffee and then a deep breath and his next words stole my breath,

"You know there's a lot of new kids in the office. They have some crazy ideas on how relationships work," he began and I instantly had a sinking feeling he rarely talked about his co-workers and never the next generation, "One of them said something that got me thinking. It's something called polyamorous. They described it as a couple agreeing to date someone together on equal footing. I know before we started dating you experimented, so I thought maybe we could give it a try."

"You want me to watch you have an affair?" I questioned way louder than intended.

"No, I want us to explore another partner together," he clarified like the sole issue was I hadn't understood what he had said.

Wanting to enjoy my meal and having no interest in having an argument, let alone this argument in public I simply said, "We can look into it."

The rest of the night my overjoyed husband found no end to his stories about the conference and about different relationship dynamics. I felt increasingly uneasy watching this man become increasingly animated on topics he had never had any interest in discussing before. The next day I was working in my studio when he called me, still euphoric from the night before, "Babe, great news, but I want to surprise you with it, so I booked dinner for us at eight. Can you wrap up in the studio in time to come?"

I had a gallery show coming up, but I could tell this was important to him, so I quickly gave in, "Call me at four all clean up and be ready by seven."

"Thanks babe."

I was thrilled, if he was excited by something else so soon maybe we wouldn't have to discuss the absurdity of me sharing him with another woman. Four O'clock rolled around in the blink of an eye and Jermiah was right on time. Before I could even answer he was speaking, "I've got to grab something on the way, so I'll text you the address and meet you there. Babe, I love you."

Somehow it wasn't the fact that he was leaving me to get to the dinner on my own, which he hadn't done once in our entire relationship, but the tone when he said I love you, that made me feel uneasy. I got there first and was shown to a private dining room and again my stomach felt uneasy because of the whole situation.

I was there for less than ten minutes when I heard Jermiah's muffled voice talking to someone and then I heard her sweet giggle in response. The door opened and then I saw her. She was tall, tan, and toned. Her athletic build made my breath catch in my throat. Jermiah was right about me experimenting before we dated and this was exactly the type of girl I had imagined having wild carefree adventures with back then.

"Ah and there she is, my other half. I tell you Angelica you are going to love her as much as I do."

"I really hope so Jermiah you've been so great to me."

It dawned on me with that sentence what was happening. The three of us were on a date, but this woman couldn't even be thirty. She was gorgeous, sure, but what could we have in common?

"Sweetheart, this is Angelica. When you said you were open to trying this, I wanted you guys to meet right away."

"So, when you asked last night, you already had a girl picked out. Don't you think that should have been part of the conversation? And I said we could look into it, not I was open to trying it."

"Sorry, Gretta, if he misled you or used coercion. We've only been hanging out, we haven't done anything, but we have discussed the possibility. We actually met at his little conference. He flew me back here, sure me and you would get along, and this would work out. I don't want to be in a manipulative relationship, nor do I want to be a forced third wheel. I'm bi-sexual and have been in many types of relationships. I wasn't doing anything anyway, so I told him I'd love to at least meet you. Couples who have been together since the nursery are rare. Anyways sorry again I hope you two work it out," Angelica said, turning to leave. Before she had fully turned, I was standing by her side. Not even sure when I had stood up.

I grabbed her arm, "No, wait, stay for dinner. He might have done things in the wrong order and been a bit over eager, but we ought to enjoy dinner and get to know each other before jumping to anything, yes?"

She nodded in consent and then sat down, "I'm Angelica as Jermiah said. I'm an artist, freelance, commercial instalment pieces mostly. I like it. I get to experiment with new mediums and styles based on the clients' needs. Jeramiah tells me you're an artist too. Is that true?"

"Yes, I have a gallery exhibition coming up this month. I'm still three pieces short. I was working on one today, but I cleaned up early to see what Jermiah's surprise was. I'm not surprised by you though. Jermiah has always been attracted to lovely things and my God Angelica you are," I blushed as the words escaped my mouth and she blushed a deep crimson.

"So, what do you do besides art, Gretta?"

With that we fell into an easy flow of conversation. We shared a lot of interests and opinions. We both donated art to charity auctions a few times a year and wanted to travel more. We didn't think movies or sporting events were acceptable dates, unless you were past the getting to know you phase. Surprisingly she agreed when I said online 'connections' were killing our social framework.

Immediately after that agreement Jermiah took a photo. Him in between the two of us and posted it all over the place announcing the amazing first step on our new journey. I couldn't help, but muse that was dense even for him.

I told her I didn't drink in support of my uncle who had lived with us growing up and was a recovering alcoholic. She told me that was honorable and would like to honor that at least why we were on dates. Jermiah offered a toast to deeper connections to that idea and downed his third rum and coke.

At that point he was finally drunk enough that he took the reins of the conversation. He made clumsy passes at Angelica and praised our family dynamic. Our boys made him proud, and he couldn't ask for a better spouse. Then he suggested we go back to our place for drinks and to see if we were all compatible.

"I mean, not you. babe. I know you don't drink, but it could loosen things up for the rest of us," he back pedaled desperately as we both stared at him.

Despite his poor display we all went back to our house.

A SPARK AND ART

Back at our house Jermiah wasted no time resuming drinking. He put on some smooth jazz while me and Angelica headed for the kitchen. I made us smoothies with fresh fruit and dug out a little box of imported chocolates. All of a sudden Jermiah wobbled into the room on unstable legs and kissed the nape of Angelica's neck. She became rigid and stared at me as if looking for me to tell her what was going on.

"Ever since I saw you in that hotel, I've wanted this," he slurred and reached around her cupping her breast firmly. I could see the surprise and discomfort on her face, and I reached out and slapped his hand.

"Jeramiah, this is a date not a hook-up. You want her to feel ganged up on. Go shower, sober up and then you can meet us out back if you can behave. I think this might work, but only if you're interested in treating her with respect."

"You're right Gretta sorry," he responded and dragged himself down the hallway to the bathroom.

"So, what do you think, Angel? You want to give us a try?" I asked Angelica as soon as Jermiah was out of the room.

"Your husband was nice to me at the conference, and you seem amazing. For some reason though something feels off. I'm willing to try, but we're going to have to take it slow. I'm not sure he'll be able to accept that."

"He'll be fine. He was the same way when we first started dating. He likes to push boundaries, but he will not disregard them."

"Well let's give it a try then. Can I stop by your studio tomorrow?"

"That would be lovely. Come on I was serious, the view from the back yard is amazing."

We went out to the yard, and I fed her a piece of chocolate and she fed me. We were sipping our drinks when Jeramiah came out holding a steaming mug. Clearly, he had taken my warning to heart.

Then he finally began acting more like the Jermiah I knew. He told us stories. First a story about how some senior partner at the law firm that represented his agency had been taken to the cleaners by his wife after he got caught renovating a villa for his secretary. The wife left, the secretary kept the villa, and the wife took basically everything else. The man couldn't even afford the deposit to move in somewhere and the secretary wouldn't let him stay with her, saying it would be unprofessional.

I realized stories like this were why we were in this situation. Jermiah was a coward by nature and risking an affair was beyond his courage. I was grateful for that though. I didn't know if our relationship would work out, but Angelica was definitely amazing, and I was certainly glad to have met her.

Then he told us a story about a thrapple that loved group activities like bowling, carnivals, and even sports games when they could get enough people together. Said we should try it sometime. Ironically again overlooking the fact that me and Angelica had agreed most of these activities were terrible when first dating.

Finally, he told a story about his boss and how she was an empowered woman who was pushing everyone to their limits, and she had praised him as the example to be like. That morphed halfway through to him humble bragging about everything he thought made him a catch.

At this point I held up the last chocolate and offered it to Angelica, “Angel, I saved the last one for you,” she ate it from my hand, and I leaned in and gave her a gentle kiss on the cheek, “Have a great night I’ll see you tomorrow,” then I turn to face my husband, "Jeremiah, if you want this to work you’ll listen this time,” I said and waited for his eyes to focus on me, “I’m going to shower then I’m going to bed. You can visit as long as she wants. I want you guys to get to know each other as well and there is no reason we all three have to be together just because she’s around that wouldn’t really be equal, would it? However, don’t pressure her. In fact, don’t do anything with her. Three date rule applies. Peck, kiss, then we’ll see,” I told him. Then I walked into the house.

I took a cold shower and then went to a window to see how they were getting along. I looked out just in time to see them hugging and then her leaving. It had been a great night, but long. I went back to my room and laid down grabbing my phone from the nightstand as I did.

“Hope he doesn’t feel like I blew him off. I really like you guys. I was just ready for shower and bed myself. Looking forward to tomorrow. Luv U,” I read her text and dropped my phone. I picked it back up and read the whole thing again; sure, I must have misread it, but I hadn’t so I texted back.

“Thanks, I had fun too. Can’t wait to see you tomorrow. You really are amazing, and I care about you already too.”

Jeramiah came into the room and gave me a kiss on the cheek, "Taking a shower. I like her, but I'm not sure she's that into us," he said casually as he started to remove his clothes and toss them aside all over the floor.

"R-really!?" I stammered out, much louder than I wanted the confusion and disbelief dripping from my tone. He noticed and gave me a hard glare like he was trying to understand which half I disagreed with or maybe he was trying to figure out how my opinion differed from his, I wasn't sure, but I rushed to defend myself, "She seemed to have a good time," I said, but could think of nothing more to add. He went to the shower, and I went to bed. Sometime later I felt him rustling in the bed pulling me closer, trying desperately to start something that would give a meaningful release to his frustrations that had built all night. I swatted at him, "I just told you, three dates. New relationship, new stats. Not saying they have to be together, but you can only be intimate with those you've put in the work with sorry," I said and then rolled over, pecked his cheek and rolled back. He chuckled and flopped onto his back.

The next morning came, and I got dressed in overalls, no under shirt or bra. It was what I standardly wore when I was working on a messy project. They were torn in some places and splattered with paint everywhere. I slid on sandals and was out the door.

When I got to my studio Angelica was already waiting for me, "I was so eager to see this place and your work. Does that make me sound desperate?"

"Not at all. I'm so glad it worked out," I responded, trying to remember the last time someone had wanted to come see my work let alone been so excited they got here before me. I unlocked the door and showed her in. We were greeted by a giant statue made from salvaged metal. It was a dragon with a knight in its mouth and its giant claw crushing his horse. There was red splattering from his mouth and more around his claw where he had crushed the horse. I explained to her I still had it because in my youthful search for authenticity I had used my blood for the red. It had made the health department get involved and selling it would be a hassle and open me up to litigation. She said if it had been her, she would have mounted it in someone's front yard most likely with a water feature probably with a fountain designed to look like magma and a projection that would look like fire. Then she giggled and admitted that even at her age she would probably have used blood as well. I teased her and pointed out that she was still in her youthful days and was free to experiment.

"And if I'm done experimenting?" She asked and I couldn't help but blush. We finally made it to my current piece after all this back and forth. I showed it to her with pride, "This is the current piece. I call it, Pillar of Hope and Torment," I said walking around the eight-foot tall eighteen-inch round pillar that was two thirds covered with random sprays of layered and contrasted colors. Everything from onyx black to pearl white were splattered around it. As you walked around it your body would sway from the joy of first love to the agony of learning your parents had passed and then back, or at least that was the effect I wanted and the one it had started to invoke in me.

She continued to walk around in circles even as I started to paint. I would start by flinging paint with force and letting it splatter than I would use other colors and intertwin patches of the splattered color with the next splatter. I worked till one and the whole time she watched me and studied the piece. When I cleaned up, she looked at me in awe, hugged me tightly, then gave me a full deep kiss.

"I love you. You're so amazing. Gretta, can we work together on a piece sometime?"

I nodded and took her hand so we could go have lunch. She stopped me at the door and said, "I'm taking Jermiah his lunch. Do you want to come with me? I told him we wouldn't have time to hang out. It's a favor not a date, but he still wants me to stop by. He's working late tonight so I thought, could you and I have a dinner date? That will be our third date so give some thought as to what we'll see means to you now."

"You go ahead. You're right he's not gonna have time to talk and if we're meeting up tonight, I should go clean up and wax my legs and stuff," I said trailing off as I realized I was giving away way too much info. With that we parted ways.

PASSION AND PROMISES

It was four thirty and we were going to have dinner at seven. She was already here, because we were going to go for a walk together before dinner. She had her arms wrapped around mine and we were talking casually. Then she turned our conversation toward our relationship and where we both saw things headed, more specifically though how she felt about me. She said, “I have always hunted for love as long as I can remember. Even before I understood its social, or biological function. I always thought, someone who wanted to be there for you. Someone who would choose you, defend you over the rest of the world would be so amazing. I was so desperate to find it I got talked into a lot of weird relationships. Most of them had no interest in getting to know me, but maybe it was good I went down this rabbit hole because you and Jeramiah were at the bottom of it and you, God Gretta, you are everything I’ve ever longed for.”

“I’ll try to live up to that praise. You know I care about you too, right?” I asked, too afraid to admit the truth I loved her already. I was afraid, I loved her in a way that wasn’t like what I felt for Jermiah. I loved the fact that Jermiah had always been there, and I loved the fact that he knew what I needed and let me be who I wanted to be, but for some reason all the things I loved about him over the years as they ran through my mind they conjured the image of a big brother or a roommate not a lover and certainly not the love of my life, but I couldn’t say that. I had three children with this man, and we had been in each other's life for almost forty years. We even already owned side by side funeral plots. That's the kind of couple we were. Even so I reached out my hand and she took it. Dinner flew by in a blur of the type of easy conversation I was quickly becoming addicted to.

"So, Jermiah is going to be late. Want to take a bath together? It's a great bonding activity and it will let us know if we are intimately comfortable and compatible."

"That sounds like rehearsed reasoning, but sure I would love to see you naked," I responded and we both blushed but got in my car anyway. The bath was amazing. It was effortlessly intimate without crossing any lines. We didn't wash each other, but we stole glances and sat close. I saw everything and she was even more beautiful than I had imagined and every time I snuck a peek, she was turning away from me, the hungry predatory glint still in her eyes. After we put on robes, we settled onto the couch leaning against each other, occasionally talking about whatever popped into our head, but mostly we were just present listening to the heavy breathing and racing heart beats. It was obvious we wanted to go further to dive into each other and forget the world, but we weren't ready and then there was Jermiah to consider.

Angelica was kissing the delicate skin where my collar bone met my neck when Jermiah returned home, "Honey great news," he started, but the joy died in the air as he took in the sight of me and Angelica in nothing, but robes and Angelica kissing me the same way he had when he got yelled at on our first date, "So the rules only apply to me?" he questioned, the accusation thick in his tone.

"We had our date with you, one at the gallery, and we had dinner. Why would you assume I would break my own rules? Don't you trust either of us?" I responded, my tone colder than I meant it to be, but his accusation had hurt far more than I thought it would.

“So, can we all sleep together tonight?” he asked, completely forgetting he had started another conversation.

“No, you still haven’t had three dates with either of us,” I reminded him.

“R-right,” he reluctantly agreed as if he was looking for an angle to argue, but couldn’t find one, “Well I have to go on a business trip. It’s right off a lovely beach. Would you ladies care to join me? Sure, we could find time for dates while we’re there and you guys could keep getting closer when I’m not around.”

I was debating when Angelica spoke from beside me, “Only if we both can go and we get a separate room. I don’t think staying in a hotel room together is appropriate for a second date.”

“I get you, but my wife? We sleep in the same bed here.”

“I know and I didn’t say anything before, because it’s your marriage. Gretta told me though you guys agreed to start over. Same rules as me, right? I think she should move into the guest room. I mean even after your three dates she’s going to need her own space. Every knight isn’t going to be the three of us. Sometimes we’ll want to be alone or in pairs of different constructs. If we’re going to move forward, I think that’s what you should do.”

I stared at this beautiful angel leaning against me and responded without a thought, “I agree with everything she just said.”

Jeramiah took out his phone and made a call. He rushed through a speech explaining his situation and then hung up and made another call. Four calls later he said, "You guys could fly out, stay nearby, we could still do dinner dates and see what happens,” he said meekly, almost desperately. Without looking at Angelica I nodded meekly. He was my husband, and he was trying so hard to make this work. I wanted to put forth all my effort too.

"I should stay over. We can go buy new swimming suits and anything else we might need for the trip," Angelica said enthusiastically, "You'll stay in the guest room with me, right?"

Again, without thinking I nodded meekly, "Thanks for making the effort dear. I can't wait," I said as I got up and pulled Angelica to join me. We took off our robes and spooned tightly. She lay behind me and her arm drifted almost magnetically to rest on the bottom of my breast, and we drifted off to sleep. I got up the next day, and Angelica was making coffee in her robe. She bounced over to me when I appeared in the doorway.

"You ready to find something that looks amazing. I want something that makes you melt and makes Jermiah drool. I'll find you something I can't wait to tear off," she chuckled and handed me the cup of coffee.

I took a sip then looked at her, "We probably should get dressed first. Think Jermiah will want to come with us?"

"Notes by the door he had to work for a few hours. Then lunch with clients and he's leaving from the office building. You know I don't think he expected us to like each other. Thought it was a clever loophole to have an affair."

"Yeah, he's kind of lost interest since it's become real and takes work. That's why I put in the rule in the first place, curious if he'd put in any effort, or if he'd just expect us to fawn all over him. I've always been there for him, so I've never seen how he is starting a relationship and honestly, I was curious.

I feel like we're close enough now for me to admit this, but you were never supposed to happen. I never agreed to try it and honestly, I never would have. I told him we could look into it. But if he flew you across the country clearly, he had already made up his mind. For once I'm glad he's a little selfish and kind of shallow. I mean Angel,

Fuck, well let's get dressed and find that killer fashion," I explained to her and reached out to stroke her cheek. Then I took another sip of coffee and raised to my feet, put the cup in the sink and went to shower and dress. By the time I came out Angelica was dressed in a pair of my yoga pants and an old hoodie that Jermiah still had in his closet despite the fact it hadn't fit in a decade. I bought it for him when I was in junior high. he still owned everything I had given him. In that way he was thoughtful. In fact, in many ways he was more thoughtful than anyone else in my life. Still, it nagged at me. The more I thought about it the more I realized whether or not I loved my husband as a lover was as much a question as any of the new relationships. However, the same could be said about him. The ways he showed love were never romantically, but considerate and protective.

I shook my head to break this train of thought and returned my attention to getting dressed, "You know we have to book a flight and stuff any ways so we could always set up the guest room maybe try out the bed tonight and fly out tomorrow," Angelica suggested a mischievous grin taking over her face.

"Let's see how the flight shakes out then we'll discuss everything else."

"You know I'm not him, right? If you don't want to, if it's too soon, if you want to wait for Jermiah, whatever tell me, don't manage me kay," she responded and I swooned, like legs went limp, heart fluttered, and I doubted my existence for the briefest moment kind of swooning.

"You have no idea how much I want to, but Jermiah is still my husband. I can't deliberately delay being with him to stay here with you. Then it becomes unfair to say he's not putting in effort. If we can't get a flight out, yes. Even if we fly out and he's not too busy, we are still sharing a room, remember. I'm afraid that's the best I can give you for now."

She left the room, and I worried that despite her promise of not being him she was just like him, and I should have left it, but I dressed and went downstairs. She was hanging up the phone as I came into the room, "What's up?" I asked.

"Flight is at four thirty well land in time for a seven thirty dinner if Jermiah can make it that would be lovely and I'm sorry for earlier. I shouldn't be trying harder with you then I am with him, and I certainly shouldn't be actively trying to create moments that exclude him. Just, I want you. I dated probably more than I should. I'm adventurous and free spirited. Some would say slutty and easy. I can only hope that doesn't include you, because it's been at least five years since I wanted someone like I want you," she rambled, like if she didn't get it all out now it would consume her from the inside.

"So, you've felt this feeling before?" I asked and instantly regretted it.

"No. I've felt desire close to what I feel for you, and I've felt connection though never as strong as I do with you. I've never felt both for the same person. Also, there's this third thing I can't name it, and I've never felt it before. It's magnetic and powerful and warms me through. Do you ever feel anything like that?" She asked and I nodded meekly. I was beginning to feel like a bobble head.

We went bikini shopping. We kept it pg though our suits were a bit risqué. We got everything else we needed and at two thirty we were eating lunch in an airport cafe. Then we got a couples massage and then we were off to see our boyfriend.

A PROMISE TO CHOSE

We were waiting at a restaurant a short walk from the hotel. It was eight thirty and we had been waiting since just before seven. I was texting Jermiah for the third time when Angelica's phone lit up. She read it and her face dropped then she read it out loud for me, "Hey, love hate to do this to you. I know we haven't been together long, but a great networking opportunity came up. Thought I'd be able to sneak away after a bit, but it's not happening. Can you handle Gretta for me? She can be a lot when I let her down, but you guys seem to really get along. There's a brunch for reps and their significant others in the morning. I checked I can bring both of you as my dates. Thanks, love, I'll pick you guys up in the morning."

"Wow so, that's our man. He begged us to come out here, agreed to meet us then just dropped us," Angelica started to complain. I cut her off. It wasn't that I disagreed with her, but my focus was on the promise of the night instead of the disappointment.

"Angel, I get it, but that just means we can get back to the hotel early. I promise unless it's something like picking up another man at a bar I will let you do just about anything you want with me."

At that she waved the waiter over and asked for a check. I chuckled, “She’s kidding we’re ready to order. Remember Angel you’re going to need your strength.”

We ordered and talked. For the first time in our short relationship the conversation was primarily about Jermiah, but not in a good way. Angelica was curious if his lack of consideration and last-minute change of plans was common. I told her unfortunately it was. Then she wanted to know if I thought he was faithful and I didn’t even hesitate to say yes. She was shocked and I explained how he was afraid of losing everything to the scandal of an affair. The questions continued as did my unflattering answers. Finally, I huffed and said, “Let's change the topic to something happier. Want to go for a walk on the beach after dinner before we head back?”

“No, that sounds very romantic and any other night it would be my honor but it’s all I can do to not climb under this table and devour you here and now,” Angelica said as the waiter returned.

“Might I get you some chocolate and strawberries? Only takes a moment, I can box it to go if you’re in a hurry,” the waiter said, making it obvious he had overheard everything. I chuckled and we both blushed. Then once again I just nodded.

“Can you bring the check?” I added as he walked away.

That night was a blur of fevered passion and unrestrained need. I had been with women before, but never like this. I could feel her warmth radiating through me and my body sought out every inch of hers. Not in discovery, not even in claiming, but as though it was part of my body that had escaped long ago and was only now finding me again. The night lasted until dawn, and we fell into a deep slumber. Not embracing each other but still entangled. We got up with a start as my phone rang.

"I'll be there in twenty. Are you ladies almost ready?" Jermiah asked and I shot upright and tossed clothes at Angelica.

"Absolutely, babe. We're so excited, been up for hours."

I could still feel the pain in my joints and the sticky residue on my inner thighs, but all that would have to wait until after we played devoted girlfriends to my husband. We got dressed in matching summer dresses and tied each other's hair up into ponytails. Sandals and then we did quick make up touches. We were dressed and downstairs in just under eighteen minutes and Jermiah pulled up about five minutes later. Me and Angelica climbed into the back seat saying in perfect unison, "We don't want to fight over who sits next to you, so we'll sit back here."

"You look lovely. My coworkers can't wait to meet you guys."

Interesting I thought to myself. In all the years we had been together I had never been to one of these things. I don't know if they knew he was married, but now somehow, they knew about both of us and knew we were coming. I told myself it was probably just because he had to get permission, but that really only explained why they knew now not why they never knew before.

Me and Angelica chuckled and whispered and after a few moments it dawned on me, we felt more like a couple who had hired a driver and not the thrapple we were trying to be. So, I decided to make an effort to include my husband, "Honey, we saw some great places yesterday. This city is truly gorgeous."

"Not as gorgeous as our girlfriend though," Angelica chimed in, leaning in to suck on my neck.

"Wow you guys sure have progressed. Glad you're getting along. Can't wait until my trial period is over and I can join you. By the way do me a favor, don't mention your silly rule or the fact we're not sleeping together at the party please. I mean we are together which is all I told people, but assumptions were made and it's been great for my image. My image is our money so please? I don't want you to lie just don't correct anyone," he said and now his interest and priorities were crystal clear. It wasn't that he cared more about Angelica, which I honestly could have accepted. She was amazing, but he valued the status of being able to have two attractive, caring, and charismatic women attend to him together gave him in his social circle. Angelica must have understood because her laughter died in her throat and she looked like she almost wanted to refuse to go.

I leaned in and whispered, "Just give him this and we don't ever have to come back into his business world again. He's not usually like this only when he's in work mode."

She whispered back, "He was nice when we first met and he's kept you happy for decades, so we'll do this your way for now."

Jermiah looked in the rearview mirror, "You guys, ok? You went awfully quiet all of a sudden."

"Yeah, just enjoying girl talk. You know how it is," I replied, plastering on my best supportive wife smile. We walked into the banquet hall. Me holding his right arm and Angelica holding his left. It was a tasteful hand clasping his forearm, but enough to announce to the room the three of us were in fact together. Jeramiah glowed as the attention of every man in the room was drawn to our entrance. We walked up to the man closest to us and Jeramiah shook his hand, "Frank it's been so long. How's the wife? This is my wife Gretta and our girlfriend Angelica."

The man's eyes went wide, "They're even more lovely than you said. I can't believe your wife let you have a mistress and so soon after getting married."

"She's not a mistress, we both care for her, and we've been married for a while. It's never come up before but since you guys inspired me to take a risk on Angelica, I thought you all should meet."

"That makes sense, enjoy the party," The old man said, taking his leave and we repeated the process. Introduction followed by awkward clarifications. No one here had known about me before I became the awesome sexy wife that let him keep a mistress.

"Your friends are pigs," Angelica said as we retreated to a small table in a corner to get off our feet for a moment.

"They are very influential people, Angelica babe you wouldn't understand. Maybe Gretta can explain it to you. She's been dealing with my personal and professional life for a long time."

"Sure, sweety I'll explain it to her later," I said, rolling my eyes and Angelica chuckled.

"What's funny?" Jeramiah asked, looking around.

"Nothing, babe, I'm just happy. Come on Gretta, dance with me babe," She replied and tugged me to the middle of the floor. To be clear there was some instrumental music playing lightly in the background, but it was a corporate mixer and there was not a dance floor. That didn't stop Angelica.

"Angelica, does this look like the time and place for your free-spirited antics? These are important people with expectations and standards. Try to remember that," Jeramiah said with a frustrated glare on his face. She went to sit back down and then I chuckled and pulled her back toward the floor. I looked at Jeremiah and surprising myself sided with Angelica.

"Forget it Angel, let's do it. Look at it this way, they know we're real and now you have a good reason to keep us at home. Best of both worlds, yeah?" I pointed out to Jeramiah as a way of an apology.

Honestly, I wasn't sure why, but I was positive I didn't want to diminish Angelica's light for even a second.

We danced for an hour, and no one even tried to approach us. When we walked back over to Jeramiah, we could hear him and the group of men talking, "You weren't kidding. They definitely love each other too. Don't you get nervous leaving them so often."

"No, I'm the glue. I brought them together and they both loved me before they knew each other," I stared at Angelica, and she was already frantically shaking her head no, "I'm the provider and the man. Without me...." All of a sudden, our eyes locked, "Babe, how was your dance? You free spirited types really know how to keep us studious types on our toes."

"Angel, let's leave the men to their posturing," I said, taking Angel's hand and walking out of the banquet hall. Jeramiah followed behind and whispered in my ear.

"Give me five minutes. We can leave together. We'll go have a drink date from here and then maybe I can stay over."

"No," was all I said. He looked at Angelica who leaned in and pecked me on the cheek in response. He went back inside. The vacation was a week long, but we didn't see Jeramiah again. He checked in daily, but as he had warned me when we first became an item these events were all consuming for people who knew how to get the most out of them. I believed him. After all he believed if he simply finished the three dates we would magically fall into his bed. He always glanced over details that didn't suit him.

"I don't know what our future looks like," Angelica admitted on the last day of the vacation. We were sitting on the patio off our room in the bikinis we had bought for the vacation, "I love you, but tomorrow we go back to the real world and I'm not sure I fit in there with your husband."

The choice of words made me instinctively cringe, "Don't you mean your boyfriend?"

"If I didn't? If you had to choose?"

I don't know why but, at that moment, I was sure that wasn't hypothetical, "Can we table this until after the welcome home party? He's always at his best right after these things. He'll make some big deals he'll want to brag about. He'll insist on spoiling us and he'll come home early for a few days and we'll visit."

"Ok, but you have to promise we at least stay in each other's lives if I wait for you and don't demand more than you can give."

"Babe, I will never let you go," I replied before I could think of the implications.

SECOND CHANCES AND TRUE FEELINGS

We flew out before him and arranged a welcome back dinner. We arrived to find him already at the bar and honestly more than a little tipsy, "You guys are here. Great, now we can have this stupid third date and I can finally see what you guys have been doing with each other."

"Wow, super romantic," I said.

"You are not spending the night with us like this," Angelica added, "She said you are your best after these trips. She said to give you more time. I keep waiting for that interested man who flattered me and saved me from those thugs to show back up, but honestly all I see is some desperate corporate drone who thought he found a loophole to have his cake and eat it too. She deserves better than whatever scraps you feel like giving her and I demand more than being a bandage for a broken marriage."

She turned to leave then but I grabbed her arm, "You're not a bandage for a broken marriage you're my girlfriend," I said and she looked back at me as if needing to know where this was going before she could decide how to take it, "We have a table. Go order deserts for us ok, love. I'll be there within ten minutes."

With that she headed into the restaurant, and I glared at my husband, "What happened? You're never like this when you come home."

"I couldn't get away to see you guys which was frustrating. We hadn't been together for weeks even before the dating rule. So, I was sexually frustrated. For the first time since I started going on these trips, I didn't sign a single new deal. That was all bad enough, but apparently one of the interns had seen you guys on the beach. They said you were making out like you were drugged at a frat party and you two were obviously the real couple. I was done. I've been drinking ever since. Telling myself all I had to do was get through three dates, join you guys, and everything would be fine, but everything's not going to be fine, is it?"

"We have two options, Jeramiah. We can stay together. For the kids, for your career, for image. You can date whoever you want, discreetly. If you ever get caught, I will pretend I didn't know and divorce you. Otherwise, we can get a divorce now. I care about you and if not for this dumb Idea of yours I would have gone to my grave as your wife, but now I know what true love feels like and honestly, she doesn't like you and I'm not sure I could survive knowing you touched her anyways. Either way me and her will be sharing the spare room for now. If you want a divorce that's fine. We can even move to my studio. If you want the house to yourself, but I warn you don't be cruel during the divorce. Don't try to make this about her. After all she was your idea."

"So, there is no option where you come back to me?"

"Sure. You go over to the table and get her to let you join us. If by the end of dinner, you can get her to say she wants to try again I'll give you a week. If she says she loves you without coercion or prompting by the end of the week the three of us can try again but know that I love her in ways I had never even known was possible. If she ever wants to walk away, I'll go with her."

"Then let's go talk to her."

We walked over and Jeramiah approached Angelica's side of the table, "I had a shit week. I've been really freaking out about this relationship and stuff. I made no sales at an event that usually takes care of my annual quota all on its own. I was so anxious about having to explain things to you guys I got drunk and acted like an ass. I love my wife, and I've truly enjoyed getting to know you. Would you please let me have dinner with you guys and show you I have some good qualities."

"What do you make of all of this, Gretta?" she asked and I couldn't help but feel like my relationship was at risk as well.

"I'm your girlfriend. I want you to be happy. So, whatever you want, Angel, but I'm not sleeping with him tonight."

"Ok, you gave me Gretta, and you were nice when we first met. I even thought I could care about that man. That's why I followed you across the country. Sit, but if you upset me again, we're done," Angelica explained and pointed at the booth across from her. She patted the seat next to her and looked at me warmly and I slid in looking at the Brownie Volcano Sunday she had ordered with two spoons. We fed each other and Jeramiah ordered dinner. A bloody steak with fries and a Belgium beer.

"So, how's your art exhibit coming? I haven't heard anything about your last two pieces and it's next weekend. Sorry the trip cut you so short on time," Jeramiah said and I could see a flicker of his old supportive best friend energy.

"I talked to the coordinator and got permission to put in a couple pieces Angelica had in storage. It turns out to be a good thing there are several people already on the guest list that are fans. Even one gentleman who has several installations of hers in his office complex."

"Theadore, he was obsessed. I worked for him for six months. Still living off the retainer he gave me to work exclusively for him for a year. He released the retainer when I finished early but let me keep the whole retainer. He's like Bill Gates or Donald Trump rich. He'll probably buy a couple pieces."

"That's great. All your hard work is paying off. I couldn't be prouder of you."

His steak arrived and he devoured it like it would try to escape. As he shifted from the steak to the fries, he looked at Angelica, "I am aware I can be difficult. I put too much emphasis on public image, but I sell my image and making those sales is the only way I know how to make sure what I care about is safe. I hope we'll stay together long enough for you to understand how much this family really means to me."

"I hope I can come to believe and accept that as well," Angelica responded flatly, "Our dessert was delicious, babe did you want some food," she was much more energetic now and the meaning was not lost on me and from the look on Jeramiah's face he understood as well.

"You should definitely eat, babe," Jeramiah prompted and I glared at him.

"If you're not hungry we can go. I'll just grab something from the fridge or grab a burger on the way," Angelica said and then it clicked. We hadn't eaten since getting home. I was on edge wondering how things were going to work out with Jeramiah, even now I couldn't really focus on eating, but Angelica was probably starving.

“Order something, Angel. I’m not super hungry though so can I just share yours.” She nodded and waved the waiter over then we returned to our conversation. Jeramiah lit up at his time extension. I think he thought I did it to help him, but I had to make sure Angelica was taking care of herself.

“So, Angel,” Jeramiah began before a fierce glare from Angelica told him he had once more over played his hand, “Sorry, maybe we aren’t that close. I was just wondering if you’ve looked at doing any installments while you’re in town.”

“Good question, Jeramiah. Babe, I want to know that one too,” I knew if she had started to line up clients then she was planning to stick around.

“Not yet. I’ve been preoccupied gathering inspiration,” she smirked and looked at me. That hunger I was beginning to grave had returned to her eyes.

“I-I see,” my husband stammered. Angelica’s pasta dish came out, and she had the waiter get another fork. I started munching on a bread stick, “My work will be more laxed for the next couple months. My clients mostly invested at the convention, and they will be really skeptical to make any moves until they see how they pan out. I didn’t pull the investments like most years. So, I don’t have as much disposable income as most years, but we could do like a day trip or a long weekend with the three of us, no business. I really want to make this work Angelica. I think Gretta would be happier this way too. Can we please try again?” Jeramiah asked in a weak pleading tone.

“Wow I hadn’t expected you to come right out and ask like that, but don’t muddy the waters. I would prefer to at least stay friendly with you, but I will happily accept whatever Angelica decides. I mean as long as she doesn’t decide to get on a plane and never look back.”

"Wait, what do you mean Gretta?"

"I told him we could try again if you agreed to try before dinner was over, but I made it clear, him joining us for dinner, trying with us, and staying in our relationship was all up to you."

"Gretta, you should be the one called Angel. Yeah, what the hell he's the father of your children we can try."

The conversation continued, but in typical Jeramiah fashion now that he had gotten what he wanted he was already lacking follow through. Instead of the interesting probing topics from mere moments ago he was now asking how far we had gone and if we were excited to have a man back in our bed. We dodged the questions and tried to politely hint they were making us uncomfortable. He reached out, patted my hand and said, "Babe, that's adorable. even with everything we've been through you can still be so shy."

Angelica scooped up the last bite of pasta then and held it out, "I'm stuffed. Finish it for me."

I quickly obeyed and waved the waiter over, "Check please." I said and he laid it on the table. Jeramiah glowed as if he realized now was the time he could remind us he was the provider, but his face fell when Angelica slid two-hundred-dollar bills into the bill and handed it back without looking at it.

"Ma'am, your bill was less than half of that," the waiter informed her.

"Gretta, did you enjoy?"

"Yeah, babe it was good."

"We're good. Have a great night kid."

Jeramiah looked like his brain had fled as he watched this, but we all left together he said he had come by cab. He was behaving now but given how much he had drunk I drove and Angelica rode up front with me. She leaned against me and began to massage my thigh.

"When we get home, I'm going to..." Angelica began, but I put a finger to her mouth.

"When we get home, we're going to take a shower and go to bed. Sorry babe," I told her and kissed her on the top of her head.

We got home and I walked Jeramiah to his bedroom, "Goodnight, husband. We can talk about the trip tomorrow. Maybe we can go see the kids. I'd love for them to meet Angelica."

"So, you're choosing to sleep with her?"

"Goodnight," I said again and went to the bathroom where Angelica was already adjusting the temperature of the water for our shower, "So, honesty is everything to me. I can't ask it if I don't give it so don't be mad about the Jeramiah thing. He's my husband and wanted a chance. I tried to convince him to either be a husband in name only for his image or divorce me, but he really wanted a chance to save at least one of our relationships and honestly, I don't know which one. I was surprised I thought for sure he'd take permission to sleep around and pretend we were married. I still left it all up to you in the end though. I told him if you ever walked away, I'd go with you. I can't leave my kids, but as long as you don't ask for that I'll always be yours. I want to know where we stand though so I gave it a deadline. I still don't know if I can even accept you being with him, but just like I did for him if you want it, I'll try. He has one week to make you want to make this work. If he has you interested enough to say I love you then we can stay as a thrapple as long as I can take it and you want. Before you give it too much thought, he offered a trip I want to take you to meet our kids."

"That's a lot of truth. Get in the shower," she said and with that we scrubbed each other in silence and went to bed. We huddled close together, me spooning her, my hand on her belly. I couldn't help but wonder what our kid would be like. Then I fell asleep dreaming of that precious face that could never be.

MEETINGS AND ENDINGS

It took three days of unease in the house, but Jeramiah got time off of work as promised and now we're on a train headed to the boarding school where my two oldest go. They are brilliant boys that luckily don't take after me or their father. They are studious with aspirations to change the world. The youngest, my baby girl, attended a school an hour away. She got a pass to come visit us so we would all be having dinner tonight.

"Johnny is the eldest and he wants to go into medicine. Andrew comes up just a year after him and he wants to go into public service. He has a few carrier paths he's considering, last I heard non-profit lawyer, judge, lower political office, senator was what he was focusing on. Sarah, sweet little Sarah, she could be our kid honestly. She's artistic and energetic and a little too unfocussed," I explained to Angelica, my head in her lap, my feet dangling into the aisle. Jeramiah was sitting across from us looking genuinely happy.

"I haven't seen the kids in almost two years," he confessed, "I love them, but work is so busy and I've kind of lost my priorities in the last few years. Even during the down time and with my annual sales quota already covered I would line up social events with the senior members of staff. I started doing it my first year thinking if I got in good with them maybe they'd refer me their client list when they retire, but nobody is due to retire for at least three years and everyone retiring before me has registered successors. I don't know why I kept doing it. I guess I just didn't know how to stop. I'm excited to see the boys, they've always been so well put together. Sometimes it's hard to believe they're my kids. Plus, this is a great step forward for us."

"Wait, Jermy, don't read more into this then there is. What exactly do you plan on telling your children?" Angelica asked, she had adopted the shorthand for his name in hopes of bridging the chasm between them in return she let him call her Angie. Saying Angel was a term of endearment from me and no one else could use it.

"The truth. The three of us are dating and we are making it work. Why?"

"I don't know how I feel about that."

"What do you want me to tell them?"

"I don't know I'm Gretta's artist friend, we're really close."

I swatted her from her lap and she looked down at me, "Be honest, babe. That includes to my kids. Do you want to be introduced as my girlfriend? We can explain the complex nature of things if you want. Either way I'm good. I get it. She's giving you a chance Jeramiah, but that doesn't make you an item and as far as whether or not it's working that's still very much up in the air."

"I don't want to give them false hope, and I don't want to be the bad guy if it doesn't work out. So, your girlfriend is fine, Gretta," Anglica said, stroking my head.

"I see so you still don't think we can make it? Could we go with my story if we also agreed that if it doesn't work out, we'll go with the married in name only thing. Even if we don't work out, we can be a family for them."

“Throw something at him,” I told Angelica who flung her shoe when she could find nothing else handy, “I just told her she can’t lie to the kids and now you want to. Do you even listen when we speak.”

“I do and I don’t think it’s the same thing. If we stay living together and present a united front, we’ll still be a family whether Angie accepts me or not.”

I had to admit I was surprised. He had listened and thought about it and had reasons to support his opinion. Maybe he really was growing, “What say you babe?”

“No. If things get awkward, I’ll still be the one who let things fall apart. I’ve been into many relationships where I was the one blamed for other people poor choices. I vowed that would never happen again. I know and the irony isn’t lost on me, but not happening, Jeremy."

“Okay. You’ve already decided, haven’t you?” Jeramiah asked with a sad defeated look overtaking his face.

“Yes, but I haven’t shut the door. You could always find a way to move me. I love Gretta and you’re a nice enough man, but being in a thrapple is hard work, it requires time management and an emotional openness that you don’t have. Plus, more importantly is our love has to be great enough to make it work but not so great as to make it collapse. Right now, we’re short everywhere. I’ve had lovers before the idea of them being ravished in front of me would make me drip. Gretta isn’t like that,” When she said that Jeramiah looked genuinely confused and I couldn’t hide the shock on my face. I was aware of how she felt. I felt it too, but to just blurt it out here and now. How was he supposed to perceive this as a chance after she told him this, “You said it yourself babe honesty right?” She looked down at me, and I meekly nodded consent, “Neither one of us can stand the idea of you making love to the other. We are not strictly opposed to having sex with you, though I certainly wouldn’t as of now, but as an abstract idea I could consider it possible. Your wife is further gone then me and I would never fall for you if I don't see longing in her eyes. You could change things but as of today I don't know if we'd even choose to stay in the state after her exhibit this weekend.

"I see, and this is how you see things too Gretta?"

"Jeramiah, I told you I care about you. I gave you two choices, and you wanted a third, so I gave it to you. Do you remember that third choice? If she leaves, I will go with her."

"What if...." Jeramiah began and the train came to a stop jerking into place. We all got up and filled out.

"Nothing is decided; we can talk about it at the hotel," Angelica said her soothing comforting tone made my heart melt all over again. Even now she was still trying to comfort him. Though he had done nothing to deserve it. All three of our children were waiting on the platform and their look was puzzled when they saw the three of us.

"Children, this is Angelica. She's my girlfriend," I said and they all just nodded slightly in confirmation they heard and understood.

Sarah stepped forward and looked at Angelica then at her father, "Did she replace dad or are you with both of them?" She asked and if she wasn't so innocent I would have been angry at the question, but she was eleven. She went to a conservative all girls boarding school for aspiring artists. Her social circle was basically the people standing here.

"We're figuring that out sweety, but either way daddy will always be your daddy and we both love you very much."

"Wow mom you traded up," Johnny said he was sixteen and so shallow it made his dad look like a philosopher.

"Johnathan she is my girlfriend and while she may be a little young for me, she is far too old for you. Control your hormones young man."

"Wow mom you never got defensive like that about dad. I was just saying you did good, not that I wanted her. I have a girlfriend; she goes to an all-girl school, and she loves to sneak out and do stuff in the park. For the record she's a ten too."

I was feeling unsure what to say to that, so I just pointed into the station. We all got into a car Johnny had rented, and we headed for the restaurant. As we walked in Jeramiah grabbed my arm, "Can you give me five minutes?" he asked sheepishly.

"Don't tell any inappropriate, no don't tell any stories babe I'll be right in," I told Angelica and the four of them walked away from us.

"I changed my mind. I want our family to stay together. I chose option one. Please Gretta, I need your support to keep me sane."

"You have it, but whether I'm in your life or not is up to Angelica. Since you want to drop trying to share our life and our bed, I can add a fourth option: if she wants to stay in your life as support and an illusion for your company we can, but we will talk about it without the kids, and you will not pressure her. I love her, understand."

He nodded and we headed inside. At the table everyone was chuckling, and Sarah was beaming at my girlfriend, "Mom you got a real winner here. She's so charming. How'd you meet?" my daughter asked, and I glared at her father.

"Well, I don't lie to you kids so for now I'm not going to answer that, sorry lovelies, but all that really matters is we're together, happy, and here to support you little monsters," I replied and she rolled her eyes, but they all three chuckled. We talked after that for hours. They were all endlessly fascinated by Angelica and unbelievably considerate. Jeramiah on the other hand drifted in and out of the conversation and was drinking at an increasingly alarming rate. His question became sharp and harsh, but I let it all slide. This was family time and if the kids weren't uncomfortable then I wouldn't deny my children their father.

That all changed when he fixed his drunken glare on Sarah, "So, my little artist, have you broken any hearts yet?"

There was an angry spite in his voice and my daughter reflexively teared up, "Daddy I don't know what you mean."

"I don't know. Did you make a man fall for you, depend on you, live to make your dreams come true and then replace him with the woman who was supposed to revitalize their sex life?"

"Um Dad...." My daughter began, but then Andrew cut her off.

"Wait a minute. So, you found a side piece on our amazing mom. Brought her home to get mom's permission. That's how this whole thing started and now that you're out in the cold you're all butt hurt and taking it out on Sarah?" Sarah's eyes went wide, as even she could follow what Andrew was saying.

"Jeramiah, about outside, no," I said with and ice-cold finality that made the whole table look at me. After a moment Jeramiah got up from the table.

"Kids, I'm in town for the week. I would love to have a meal with the four of us before I go. I was an ass today, but hopefully you know I love you all. I'll start a group chat tonight. We can set something up if you're up for it."

With that he left, he didn't even try to talk to me or Angelica.

"What was that about babe?" Angelica asked.

"We'll talk," I promised and then we went back to the gentle and easy conversation. I felt like we effortlessly bonded over the course of the dinner and I got to know more things in those few hours then I had learned in the past few years. Andrew was also dating, but unlike his older brother they were serious and taking it slow. Sarah wasn't dating, but she was pretty sure she was gay. I couldn't help but wonder if that was just because she was surrounded by nothing but girls. I didn't mention this though there was no reason to give her more to think about. Johnny had already started making inroads to his career even only being sixteen and his plans had evolved and become much more real. He wanted to open a non-profit medical facility. Eventually nationwide, with economy-based billing and Doctor donation time shares. It was massive and well thought out and I was proud. The dinner continued and I watched as the four people I loved the most grew closer and honestly, I couldn't be happier in that moment.

COMING HOME

The trip was scheduled for three days. Jeramiah had extended his stay hoping to see the kids before he left. Me and Angelica returned to the city the next morning. There was no more pretending. Us being near Jeremiah caused problems. There was no fixing this. On the train I explained everything to Angelica. How Jeramiah had wanted to back pedal too just make it look like we were a family. How I had originally left it up to her, but how I couldn't sit on the fence anymore after he told everyone what I had just told them I wasn't going to share and made my baby girl cry just for reminding him of us. Then I said something that took even me by surprise, "Let's move on after the exhibit. I know you have offers and I can work anywhere."

We were sitting across from each other so I could focus on saying everything I wanted to and Angelica was currently looking me up and down, "What if I said I wanted to move closer to Sarah. Be there for her, maybe even look into her living with us?"

"Why?" I asked.

"Like you said she could be our daughter. I see her passion and her excitement for life and knowing she's your daughter. I want to see that journey. Your boys are lovely, but like their dad they have a career path. It's a matter of time before they will have little need for us and little time for us, but Sarah, she's prepared to experience life. Wouldn't it be nice to watch and nurture that?"

"After the exhibit we can talk to her. I don't want to make her feel uncomfortable or like she's choosing sides, but I agree it would be nice to watch her grow."

In Jeramiah's absence the rest of the week flew by in quiet relaxation and my show arrived with a larger than usual crowd. Two out of three people were looking right past me and praising Angelica for the provocative pieces she had included in the show. Some of them would follow up asking how her promising protege was and the first time it was asked it stung, but her answer reminded me why she was the right partner for me, "She's my girlfriend not my protege. In fact, this is her show. I was lucky enough to get a couple slots and show her my talent. So, help me impress her guys. I'm hoping to make her swoon today, so she'll say yes when I propose tonight."

I was used to selling about half my pieces; the rest would go back into storage for a future show, but at three thirty they announced the last piece had sold. Several pieces had actually sold early in the night and traded hands before they were even picked up. Of course, both of Angelica's pieces had sold before the event had started, but this wasn't a competition and most of the people here had come specifically for her two pieces.

"So, when can we book the next show?" Judy, the owner of the gallery asked as she approached, holding out two glasses of wine.

"Sorry Judy, we're still figuring things out," I responded.

"You've supported Gretta all these years. We will do everything in our power to do another show here," Angelica added.

We enjoyed the rest of the show as traders slowly profited off of people who had waited to the end of the show and didn't want to be left out. Then we went to dinner and were eating dessert when my phone rang. It was Sarah so I put it on speaker, "Mom, dad is horrible. We are supposed to have lunch before he leaves tomorrow, and he texted me tonight. Said I remind him of you guys, and he couldn't do it. Asked me to make up an excuse so the boys wouldn't be upset and not to hate him."

"I'm so sorry baby girl. Me and your momma will always be here for you," I looked at Angelica as she spoke, surprise washed across my face, "Sorry," she mouthed.

"Sarah, darling, what do you think of my girlfriend?" I asked and now Angelica was looking at me in surprise.

"O, she makes you happy. She's beautiful, and I hear she's quite talented."

"Would you like to know her better?"

"O are you coming to visit again I could use cheering up."

"We were thinking more like moving. Maybe you could even try living with us."

"That was Angel's idea, wasn't it?"

"That's your mom's name for me. It's very precious to me. I love you kiddo, but can we find something else to call me?"

"Momma A," Sarah chuckled and the laughter echoed through the restaurant.

"If that doesn't offend your mother I don't mind," she said looking at me and I nodded in approval, "She said that's fine and yes it was, but do you want to try it?"

"Yes, I would love to live with my moms."

She hung up with that and as soon as she did Angelica looked at me with a twinge of nervous energy rolling between us.

“Honesty, always, right?” she asked.

“Always,” I responded flatly, not sure how I felt about the potential direction of this conversation.

“So, I don’t just want to see your daughter grow. When you joked, she could be our daughter and then I met her and saw it. I want her to see me as a mother. I want her to be our daughter. I’ve always wanted children, none of my partners had ever felt right. Before we went and met your kids, I was thinking about asking you to adopt, but Sarah is still so young and so sweet, and it sounds like her dad is going to leave her, because we left him. I want her to be our daughter. I didn’t lie to you earlier. I was lying to myself, but after that phone call and her calling me momma on the phone I can’t lie any more. I’m sorry. I just,” she rambled and by the end she was in tears.

“Wait sorry for what? Caring about me and my child enough to want us to be a family? I love you. Let’s give it our best. For the record I don’t mind if you want to let her call you Angel. I could see it in your eyes you didn’t want to correct her. You liked it. It’s fine I want you two to love each other.”

The next week was a blur of activity. I got divorced, Jeramiah asked me to let him say we were still together for a while at work. I didn’t care enough to argue. I closed down my studio. Donating most supplies and packing what was hard to replace. Then we packed one suitcase for the two of us and headed to the little town that housed my daughter’s school. We started looking for a house but settled on a three-bedroom townhouse instead. I started setting up our home and Angelica flew across the country to do an installation piece that would pay for six months of our living expenses.

Now settled in the new city and without anyone to spend my time with my life pulled back to a crawl. I was still trying to move forward. I'd pick out furniture during the day and have dinner with my daughter when she could, but we needed Jeramiah's consent for her to live off campus, and he was still bitter. I couldn't say I blamed him though. We had made vows, and I had broken them. The living room, kitchen, bathroom, and guest room were all complete with furniture, but I had left finishing touches and our personal space for when Angelica came home. It was less than a month but felt like more than a year.

"My god, babe it's so good to be home," she said as she came in the door and threw her arms around me.

"How do you know you've spent all of an hour here," I responded and she chuckled, in that way that was solely hers, the way that melted my body and ignited my soul at the same time.

"I meant here," she replied simply, pressing her hand firmly against my chest above my heart, "Got you something," she continued and handed me a file folder. I opened it, it was a notice from the school saying they had approved Sarah living with us.

"How? When? Is this real?" I asked and my voice kept growing louder.

"So, I have to do an installation piece for the school. To be specific we are doing an installation piece for the school. When they heard they could own the first collaboration from the hottest lesbian power couple in the art world they were happy to bend the rules. I negotiated while I was working. Wireless headsets are amazing. Finally, of course it's real. Though technically she is still a residential student and has to pay for her dorm which is assigned to her. It's kind of like the holiday pass that was issued for the dinner, only it never expires."

I hugged her then and I didn't let go for a while just held her firmly against me. The next day Sarah visited and picked out furniture. She would come to live with us when it was delivered. A week later her stuff was there and the following day she was. We had brunch to celebrate, and I had a video call with the boys. I could tell Angelica wouldn't say it, but she thought they were too old and would abandon us sooner or later. She didn't want to invite that kind of hurt in, and I wouldn't make her. Sarah for her part was still hurt; neither boy had defended her to their father. Still, they were my boys, and I needed them to know I would always be there for them. We talked for less than ten minutes before they each made excuses to hang up. Still, I was pleased I had done my part, and they knew I cared. We built a giant Phoenix rising from ash. It was metal and hollow with a system to pump oil through it and once it was filled it could be ignited. The flames would spit out of custom designed and angled ports and the whole thing would burst into flames for a few seconds before the ash below would start to glow. Cast replicas sold for over ten grand and became our first new stream of revenue. We were now firmly starting the next chapter of our life and as a family of three we couldn't be happier. I tried and some nights almost succeeded in forgetting about the lives we had left behind. Jeramiah, Johnny, and Andrew all meant a lot to me, but they felt so far beyond my reach now.

INTRODUCTIONS

The Phoenix finished, Sarah's school going well, her move completed, and she was settled into her new surroundings, Angelica started looking for other projects. It didn't take long before Angelica's connections found us the perfect opportunity. A Summer in Venice doing a series of pieces inspired by love on bridges over a canal. It would pay for quite a bit of living and Sarah was permitted to help. It would be great for establishing her as an artist. That was still a few months away though, so we settled into a routine where we spent nights and weekends with Sarah. Sometimes helping her develop as an artist but mostly doting on her as our baby girl. Days were spent in a studio space we had rented once we knew we'd have time to use it. Meals and one day a week were spent appreciating each other. Sometimes we'd go shopping, sometimes walks or dates, most of the time we just laid around the house and cuddled.

"I want to get married while we're in Venice. What ya say, babe?" Angelica asked one day while we were working on separate projects in the studio.

"If they'll come, we have to pay for my boys and Jeramiah to come. You know we've been talking again, and he seems to be doing much better. You might not want to get to know the boys, but they are my children."

"Ok, I'm glad Jeramiah's doing better."

All of the sudden we had not only a trip to plan and a massive art project to design, but a wedding to plan. Time was getting short, slowly pecking away at it after dinner as we were lying in bed wasn't going to cut it with this new event added. We worked the rest of the day, but agreed to cut studio days to twice a week until everything was ready for the trip.

The next day we started in earnest. I called the boys and Jeramiah while Angelica looked for venues. I got the boys before they left for classes, but I had to wait for Jeramiah to call me back in between meetings. All three of them had the same reaction. They thought we were already married but would happily attend. The boys usually took summer classes in prep for college, but they both happily agreed to skip them this year. Which touched me deeper than anything I could imagine. Jeramiah asked if he had a plus one which surprised me, but I was excited to hear he had moved on, so I agreed without hesitation. They all insisted on paying for their flights and stay in lieu of gifts. Next, we quickly arranged for an officiant and license. We were going to get the officiant and license here to make sure it was legally binding here. That afternoon we believed that we were wrong and simple destination weddings were simpler than people made it seem, so we decided we'd just put off going back to the studio until everything was done.

The next three weeks were a blur of phone calls and shopping. Finding dresses, we both liked and matched took three days by itself. Then we had to make travel arrangements and invite everyone. It was unconventional, but we had decided this kind of last minute, so we notified everyone with personal phone calls and made a list of who could make it and who couldn't. It was a small group of less than fifty and to save time we decided people could be free to sit where they wanted. Then the menu and then finding someone to make it. We decided to skip the bridal party. Everyone in our life mattered to us, but none of us were especially close. Sarah would walk me down the aisle and then she would stay with us. We Bought wedding favors but chose something purchased online for pickup when we got there. That took another two days as we had to pick the item and design the engraving. It was a very scenic venue, so we arranged for two photographers. One for the wedding itself and one to take staged photos for any guests that wanted one. We arranged for a bartender and a DJ. Finally, we picked out rings, both engagement and wedding. Then we decided if there were any more missing pieces, we'd figure them out on the fly. Luckily by preparing for the wedding first all preparations for the trip were done. So now we only had designing the art left and we had already made progress on that before this all started so we could go back to how things had been.

Slowly we designed a series of paintings. There were going to be six bridges so we decided early on we would make it centered around a single happy couple. The first one was them meeting in the middle of a crowd. Second, we made one where they meet by happenstance and it's raining around them while they take refuge under an awning. In the third they meet for a date candlelight atmosphere, but the only thing in focus, the only thing in their world is them. Fourth was a wedding with witnesses and a gardenscape. Fifth was them giving birth to their child and then the last was them lying beside each other in old age. The theme was to imply their journey had ended, but as to not make it too dark we made it serene seclusion in their golden years instead. Outside a shadowed circle there would be all the people their lives had touched. After consulting the client, the sixth picture was scraped. Apparently, it was still too dark to spark the romance they were looking for. So, we replaced it with the couple older now in the background and a new couple standing in front of them. The implication their child would carry their love forward. This set of sketches was accepted with joy and anticipation to see the final project. We then returned to our regular schedule though the time left was short at this point. We managed to finish enough pieces to do a gallery show when we got back, assuming we could find a gallery to work with. We had promised to do another show near Jeremiah, so we considered just shipping everything there when we got back.

The three of us flew out and days later we were joined by Johnny, Andrew, and Jeramiah along with three ladies that must be their girlfriends.

"Mom, this is Shelly, I told you about her when we had dinner," Johnny told me and I couldn't help, but scrutinize her. After all, her previous introduction had made it clear what type of girl she was. I worried if someone that adventures in her love life could even fall in love.

"Nice to meet you Shelly, I know exhibitionism is exciting, but remember it's totally different when you finally get caught," Angelica said, extending her hand to Shelly. Everybody's mouth fell open, and Shelly glared at Johnny.

"What did you say about me?"

"The truth, we hooked up at the park sometimes and you liked it."

She rolled her eyes and put distance between them.

"Mom this is Gina she is my girlfriend and we're going to change the world together," Andrew said and the short girl next to him extended her hand. She looked like she had to be a few years younger than him, and I wondered what they could have in common, but given my girlfriend was more than a decade younger than me I chose not to think about it too much. I shook her hand and then Angelica and Sarah each took their turns.

"This is Angel," Jeramiah said and my eyes became ice cold as I glared at him, "She is one of my new girlfriends, she won the lottery to come with this weekend. I hope to let you meet the others eventually."

"Yeah, he spoils us rotten, he doesn't force us to do anything and he's so busy he doesn't even want to have sex that often and he doesn't interfere with your personal life at all. As long as you're discreet you can even have a boyfriend of your own, but if you do, going on trips and stuff becomes harder. It's a really good deal," Angel said, and I was sure she wasn't supposed to say any of that. All the same Angelica quickly shook her hand then me and then Sarah. I felt kind of bad, because everyone was paired except Sarah. Sure, she was young, but she was old enough to have a date if she wanted one.

"Sarah, I'm sorry I didn't ask this before, but did you want a plus one? I'd fly someone over. Even their whole family if they can't come alone. If there's someone you want to invite. Not for the whole summer, but like the week of the wedding or something," I asked my daughter, and she looked like she was contemplating her answer.

"Can I think about it, Moms?" she asked and me and Angelica both nodded in response.

We would have dinner almost every night as a family that first week, but otherwise the two groups stayed fairly separate. Me, Angelica, and Sarah had to work every day and the boys with their escorts did touristy stuff. They'd tell us about it at dinner and Sarah was making a list of all the stuff she wanted to try to do before we left. On the first Sunday we were in Venice we were at brunch and Sarah was squirming in her seat. I could tell she wanted to say something but wasn't sure it was a good idea.

"Sarah, what is it, baby girl?" Angelica asked while I was trying to decide if I wanted to put her on the spot or let her work through it.

"Well moms, I've been thinking there is someone I want to have at the wedding, or at least here with me for a little bit, but they're not like a girlfriend or anything. I mean I'm not sure what our relationship is, but them being here would make me happy. I don't know if that's selfish or confusing or... I just don't know."

"Well, if you want them here and they want to come, that's enough. Contact them to find out if they want to come and if they need to bring their parents if they can come by themselves, we can fly them over as soon as they can leave. If their parents are coming we'll fly them out the week of the wedding. Sound good sweetheart," again Angelica answered, she really did dote on Sarah which made me so happy.

She nodded enthusiastically and went back to her meal, much more settled now. Sarah took the rest of the day off to figure out what she was going to say and to call her friend. Me and Angelica returned to painting. We would meet back up at dinner and find out how it all turned out.

A BUDDING RELATIONSHIP

My daughter was sitting alone at a table glowing when we walked in. I was glad to see we would have at least a few minutes to talk before everyone else showed up. As we approached, she popped up and walked over wrapping one arm around each of us and leaning into a group hug.

"We're dating, she's coming, by herself tomorrow."

"Wow, I thought you weren't sure how you felt," I responded.

"I wasn't. I mean I'm still not really, but I care about her and she's adorable and she looks at me like you look at Momma A. It makes my heart race. I mean I'm not sure if I love her, but I know I want to be with her. Does that make sense?"

"Sweetie, can I tell you what I hear you saying?" Angelica asked.

"Yeah, I need insight Momma A."

"You love this woman, but you're afraid that if you fall in love too young, things will turn out like they did for your mom and dad. Have you asked your mom or dad if they regret their choice? I don't know about your dad, but your mother still cherishes all those years at your father's side. Just give it some thought, kay sweetheart."

"Thanks Momma A."

With that the three of us took our seats and ordered drinks. The boys showed up without the girls in tow. Unusual, but not unheard of. They sat down and looked at Sarah.

"Well, what's the big news for family only?" Andrew asked after a moment of tense silence.

"My girlfriend will be joining us tomorrow and staying for the rest of the summer. We just started dating so be nice."

With that our night went on to your typical gossipy small talk and we all enjoyed the meal. As we were enjoying dessert the three girls came in, Johnny and Jeramiah's girlfriends were both drunk leaning on Andrew's small girlfriend. She looked helpless pinned under the much taller and larger women.

"Come tuck us in," Johnny's girlfriend slurred then gave an exaggerated wink to emphasize the innuendo.

"Whelp, that's our cue. See you tomorrow night. Happy for you kid," Johnny said and all three men got up in unison and left.

To Sarah's credit after the boys left the first thing she did was assure us that she intended to continue to work and Rachel, her now girlfriend could help as well. They had talked together about working ahead of us, laying the base coat of primer and she could come back whenever we needed help. She also insisted we keep whatever money we were going to pay her towards Rachel's trip. I couldn't help but think what a thoughtful and responsible woman she was growing up to be.

The next day we finished the first side of the first bridge. It took longer than the rest should as we had to get a feel for the circumstances we were painting under and develop the look of the couple that would be the center piece of the entire series. All the same we knocked off early so Sarah could get ready for her girlfriends' arrival. She looked beautiful in a spring dress and sandals with subtle accent make-up. She swooped her strawberry blond hair into a bun. I couldn't help but think she was trying to make herself look older. It made me wonder if maybe her girlfriend was older than her, but I couldn't make myself ask. It couldn't be as big of an age gap as me and her other mother so I wouldn't be able to say anything anyway unless it would cause legal problems.

The plane was delayed by almost an hour, and we were starving by the time we met Rachel, who I could tell just by looking at her that she was older. Not a lot, but she was well into puberty. Which, if my daughter had started, she had said nothing to me about. I thought she couldn't be older than fifteen, but she could be a mature twelve or thirteen. A small difference really for the rest of their life, but now it could be a challenge.

As I was debating how to traverse this minefield of curiosity and concern while weighing in the fact that there was almost a decade between me and my girlfriend, Angelica spoke, "My aren't you adorable. How old are you?"

"Th-thirteen, Ma'am," she responded and the innocent insecurity was disarming to the point I wanted to drop all my concerns and have faith in their love. Angelica had seen all types of relationships and interacted with all types of personalities, and I could see in her face that she wanted to know more.

"So, how long have you known our Sarah? What are your intentions with her? Have you ever dated before? Are you a..." She was shooting questions at lighting speed, but when I heard her start to formulate that last question, I had to step in.

"Angel, consider what you're saying. I'm sure we can trust Sarah to take things slow and innocent. So, let's not bring up things that have nothing to do with their relationship," I agreed it would be nice to know how experienced her girlfriend was and if we need to worry about her pressuring our daughter, I had been a mother long enough to know I would lose my shit if some adult asked my eleven-year-old daughter such an inappropriate question. We would just have to trust our daughter and be there to support her.

"Since she started school last year. To love and protect her as long as she'll let me. Yes, a boy in grade school. It was short lived and awkward. Basically, just play dates that ended and began with a hug. I get why your wife wouldn't let you ask. That's a very inappropriate question to ask, but since you cared enough to ask and I get why you want to know I'll answer. Yes, in every sense of the word and I was raised to stay that way until I consider myself married," Rachel answered, never looking away from Sarah. Sarah blushed through the whole thing.

We went to dinner where the conversation became much more casual. We ate family style, and it was just the four of us. Sarah said it would be easier introducing her to the guys if we were acquainted and, on their side, first. I assured her we were always on her side, but I understood where she was coming from so, I readily agreed. It was another week before she was ready to introduce Rachel to the rest of the family. By that time, we finished the first side of the second bridge, and the girls had primed all the panels except one. We were having lunch because it worked better with everyone's schedule. Jeramiah was as obtuse as ever; it took him half an hour to even understand they were together.

"Wait, aren't you a bit young to be experimenting?" He asked when he finally understood what was going on.

"What if she's not experimenting? I mean at her age it's more likely she's just trying to be like her mom," Andrew piled on.

Johnny just rolled his eyes and sighed about the whole situation. They had all been perfectly cordial until their dad got offended and then they wanted to claim she was just copying me. The irony made me nauseous.

"Your daughter is an intelligent, kind, caring, beautiful person who looks at me with the heat of a thousand suns. We have been together for like ever and I have no intention of ever leaving her," Rachel said and Sarah was a shade of red dark enough to make me touch her skin to make sure she wasn't in danger of a heat stroke.

"Be careful with words like that. Forever ha, me and her mom met in the nursery. Literally, the day we were born. So, this is where knowing someone forever gets you. Keep that in mind kid. If she got her type from her mom, she probably got her dating philosophy too," Jeramiah said and I heard it then, the pure disdain for me and the new life I had built. It was so thick I didn't know how I had missed it before.

"Mom was faithful to you. Even though you were closer to roommates for years. She never looked at anyone else. You brought Momma A home not mom. You told them to date. You're just mad cause they wouldn't do with you what you wanted them to. As far as me and Rachel go, she's been special to me since the week after we met and we started eating lunch together and when my roommate was being aggressive, she let me crash in her room. Sure, back then I didn't know what special meant and, in some ways, I'm still figuring it out. Unlike with you and mom though we aren't just spending our time together. We are actively getting to know each other. You're right I do want to be like my mom's brave enough to walk their own path and caring enough to support those who love me. When'd you become so mean and bitter dad. If this is the best you can manage, when we see each other, stop coming around." Sarah unloaded on her father and then she got up and left holding Rachel's hand.

"If you can't make up with your daughter don't bother coming to the wedding," I added and then me and Angelica followed her out the door.

It was two weeks before the wedding and we still hadn't heard from Jeramiah. We had seen the boys a couple of times, but the daily meet ups and pleasantries had died that day with their support for their father's harsh words. It was late afternoon, and Johnny was calling me, "Dad wants to try to make things right with Sarah and Rachel, but they wouldn't take dad's call. Can you ask them to meet him for dinner tomorrow night? He's renting a private room. I'll send you the address. He'll be there from 4p.m. until 8p.m. If she's willing to give him a chance. Mom, I love you and Sarah. I plan on coming to the wedding either way. I know I should stand up to Dad more, but it's complicated, but that doesn't mean I don't love and support you guys."

"I know son and you and your brother are welcome whether your dad comes or not," I replied not fully believing him, but wanting to give him the benefit of the doubt.

It was 10p.m. the next night when Sarah came home, holding Rachel's hand tighter than normal, "Mom, you want me to forgive Dad right?" She asked as they walked into the hotel room where I was relaxing with my feet in Angelica's lap while she massaged them.

"Yes, but only because I hope you guys can make up. If there is a reason why you don't think that's right, I don't want you to force it either. More than anything I want you and Angelica to be happy. I mean I worry about your brothers too, but they've chosen life's that will have its share of misery and things they can't walk away from. So, I can't really hope for their continued or unconditional happiness which makes it complicated you know?" I rambled at my daughter, not wanting it to sound like my love was conditional or I had abandoned my sons. I hope I conveyed the way I felt.

"Good, because he said all the right things, but the way he said them and the fact that he said everything he should've and only that. I don't know, it just felt so fake and forced. I don't mind if you let him come to the wedding, but I don't want to forgive him and I get the sense he plans to make a scene at the wedding. I think that's why he apologized."

"What do you think, Rachel?"

"I got this unclean feeling like watching a predatory salesman drain the life savings of some grandma," Rachel replied, looking at Sarah sympathetically.

"Yeah, he has that effect on people who can see sales tactics and manipulation," I replied, torn between believing them and wanting to believe the man I had grown up with was still in there somewhere. I wondered if he was ever real or just a way to sell me on a life together, "If you're both uncomfortable with the way he's being then I'll disinvite him. I'll let him know tomorrow. Do you girls want to do something before we all call it a night?"

In response they went for a walk and me and Angelica made love. We went to bed, and the girls came back some time later. We were sharing a room, so I was grateful for the alone time. I was still awake laying cuddled close to Angelica when they came back in. I wanted her to be free, but I needed her to be safe. They went to bed falling asleep almost instantly and I quickly followed.

WEDDING AND FUTURE PLANS

The next two weeks flew by and at the beginning of the second week we had finished our series of paintings. The second half was simple and quick as it was recreating what had already been done in reverse on the other side of the bridge. Rachel and Sarah both were capable enough to recreate our processes. Honestly, they probably could be doing their own projects, but they were too young and had no portfolio so working with us would be great for their future.

The wedding was here and afterwards we would go on our honeymoon, and Sarah and Rachel would head home to get ready for the new semester. The ceremony was quick, and smooth and the reception started just as well, but an hour into the reception Andrew approached Sarah, “You broke his heart I hope you're proud.”

“I broke his heart. The way you guys talk about me and mom is repulsive and after you fawned all over Momma A.”

“Have you seen her? She’s a twelve no wonder mom dumped dad for her. I’m sure it was her idea, but you could have been there for mom without crushing dad. I mean I get you’re a kid, but for fuck’s sake Sarah. Dad was just worried about you. Guys assume their girl has done stuff with other girls, but you’re going to have a hard time finding a real provider if you have a full-blown public relationship with another girl. Not to mention how bad it will be for you and the family if the school finds out. Dad is already dealing with the fallout of losing mom right after he introduced her at work. Imagene how impossible it will be to manage his image if it gets out that not only did, he lose his wife to his girlfriend, but his daughter's a carpet muncher too."

With that insult Rachel had heard enough she stepped in front of Sarah and slapped Andrew with enough force to push his head to the side, "Don't you ever talk about your sister like that again or I'll beat you until you can't stand," she said the anger and disgust thick in her voice. At that moment I couldn't help but think she would make a fine addition to our family. Then I quickly admonished myself for getting so far ahead of myself.

"Andrew, thank you for coming. I hope you had fun. It was great to see you," Angelica said, stepping in front of Rachel and extending her hand to Andrew. To a rational person this would show where we stood and signal the end of the evening. However, Andrew and Johnny had both inherited a healthy self-esteem from their father and this situation was just another chance for him to showcase his people skills.

"Angelica, you are smoking hot, but this is Mom's event too and I'm her son. She invited me here, do you really think," Andrew started and I finally reached the crowd and slapped him.

"Don't come around anymore until you're prepared to apologize to everyone. My God I can't even believe you're my son. Johnny, I warn you if you want to stir up this kind of mess then leave with him. If you make a scene later tonight there will be no chance of forgiveness for you. I get you both think I hurt your father unfairly, but I didn't look for love outside our marriage, he did. It's not my fault that we fell in love. Should I have stayed even knowing what I thought was love was nothing more than gratitude?"

Andrew was already leaving with his date and now Johnny was standing in front of us, "Neither of us feel that way mom. Dad's been bribing Andrew and threatening me. He'll pull my funding if I don't help him and originally, I did, because it was supposed to be to help you guys reconcile, but it's obvious now he's bitter and wants you to pay. Andrew is already pulling political support from Dad's network. All that goes away if Dad stops supporting him."

"Well, enjoy the party. We'll talk and figure things out when I get back from my honeymoon. He can't do anything until the end of the year anyway. I paid next year's tuition before I left."

With that he went back to his girlfriend, and I took Angelica's hand and went and sat down. Rachel and Sarah joined us moments later. We talked for another hour and then me and Angelica left for our honeymoon. We were headed to Texas. A rodeo ranch of all things and I couldn't wait. Painting sunrises and watching my girl horseback riding and line dancing in old, faded jeans sounded great. I had stayed close to town when I was with Jeramiah so I could be present as a support system for him. I hadn't regretted it, but he hadn't cherished it like I always thought he did either. So, now with Angelica I would let my adventurous spirit soar and I would take in all this life had to offer.

It was only a week, but it was a great week. We took horseback riding lessons together and paid to have someone video it and take pictures. We painted in robes together at sunrise, small canvases that could fit in our luggage. We ate a picnic in the middle of an open field. We played with livestock and gathered eggs. We even learned a little bit of rope play. Though neither of us could lasso anything to save our soul. We went line dancing twice and to a cowboy bar once. They didn't care too much for cowgirls who weren't interested in cowboys. We closed out the week by painting one of the sides of one of the barns on the ranch. It was two people in cowboy hats, Flannel shirts, cowboy boots, and faded jeans. It was very deliberate you couldn't really tell their genders as it was their backs, but there was an intimacy between them and romance in the air as the sun was just coming up and they were leaning into each other's personal space.

We returned home to find that somehow Sarah had turned our permission for her to live with us into permission for her girlfriend to cohabitate. I trusted her but told her she should have discussed it with us first and we were going to make sure her parents knew what was going on.

"Mom, her parents aren't like you guys. They're old conservative money. If you're going to tell her we're dating, she'll move back to school. They already know she's living here and don't care, but if you tell them we're dating her life is over. I'll do either one and I promise she is only living here so we can spend as much time together as possible and I can still manage all my responsibilities."

"Are you guys sharing a room?"

Her silence told me all I needed to know, "You can tell them, or she can move into the guest room."

"I would love my own space actually," Rachel chimed in from the hallway where she was waiting hoping things would work out between me and my daughter.

With that settled we started to move Rachel into the guest room. We agreed she could stay as long as neither of their grades slipped and they kept up with all other obligations and they never did anything to take advantage of their living situation. We made sure they understood obligations included her family relationship.

Then I was on to my next task. Johnny was having issues with his father. I believed he loved me and accepted me for who I was, but I was positive if I couldn't offer him a solution and soon, he would do what he had to do to continue his career path just as Andrew had done. If not so eagerly and harshly at least enough to appease his father.

It took research and determination, but eventually I came to an arrangement with the school I would teach one class twice a week and they would give Johnny a scholarship. I would also get a salary that I could save for educational expenses. Sarah oddly enough was still having everything paid for by her father; he had never even hinted he might cut her off. It made me wonder if Johnny was being honest, but as long as he was treating everyone in the family with respect, I would do this for him.

Now just as quickly as it had fallen into chaos my life had reached a new rhythm. Like this, days flowed into weeks. Then we lost track of months, seasons, and even years. Sarah was graduating, Johnny never acted up, and Andrew and Jeramiah made no attempts to make amends or interfere again.

We had done three gallery shows back in Jeramiah's hometown and he never came to one. I heard his harem had grown out of control and despite the fact he was making three times what he was while we were together and paying for one less private school he was living on credit and borrowed time. The gallery was so good to us we never did shows anywhere else. We did installations as partners when the right opportunities came along. Sarah and Rachel both interned with us for their summer breaks.

"I'm engaged. I didn't need you then, and I certainly don't need you now," I heard Sarah yelling into the phone as I came into the house. I had just come in from filling in for the art teacher at Johnny's old school. I quit when he graduated but stayed close to the faculty and helped out from time to time. Having been gone all day, I was confused and worried about what had my daughter so worked up on the eve of her graduation and less than a week from her wedding. She was marrying Rachel; she had never left our house except for family trips. We agreed she had to go on if she wasn't going to be honest and get their blessing.

"What happened, sweetheart?" I finally gathered myself enough to ask.

"Dad heard me, and Rachel are going to be interning at the gallery in between shows. He wants to reconcile and come stay with him. I think he just wants the rent and help taking care of his women. Johnny said there are almost fifty girls in and out of there. Almost a dozen he gives regular payments to; financial help they call it. Three live in the house, and he pays for everything. Johnny said Andrew said he doesn't even get to have sex every week with all that going on. Guess none of them refuse him, but between his schedule and them being talented and being unavailable. Anyway, they both say that since you left, he's lost it. He's scared to tell any of them no, and he refuses to turn away anyone who will pretend to be into him. I'd feel bad for him if he hadn't brought all of this on himself."

"I see. Are you guys still renting that little one-bedroom above the gallery?"

"Yup, she's going to take rent out of what she'd be paying us. Utilities are included; it's a great deal."

I nodded and kissed her forehead. I realized at that moment that my family was never going to be ok. Two hours later, though, the four of us sat around the table. We talked like normal, laughed like normal, and at the end went to the living room and silently enjoyed the world we had all built together. In no time, our home would be empty and our tether cut. Now was the time to see what was next for us.

SAVING THE PAST

My daughter graduated, got married, and left on her honeymoon. Me and Angelica had everything they had packed and shipped to their apartment. We then shipped a selection of art pieces to do a welcome home show for the girls when they got done with their honeymoon. Unlike previous shows, this show only had two pieces from me, two pieces from Angelica, and one piece we had done together. Everything else was done by Sarah, Rachel, or the two of them. We even avoided using pieces that we had worked on with them. It was to be an event to launch them into the art world, and I was confident it would be a success.

We had just arrived in town. Our luggage had been delivered to our hotel suite, but we hadn't been there ourselves. But Jeramiah was standing in front of us. I would be impressed he had found me if I wasn't so annoyed, I had to deal with him. I couldn't believe this man had once been the center of my world. He looked good, but fake. Unfortunately, I had known him too well for too long. I could see the pain, uncertainty, and fatigue he was holding back, and I could see the cracks in his catered perfection.

"Jeramiah, what brings you to find us on this lovely afternoon?" I asked and Angelica instinctively stepped slightly in front of me and drew in even closer to me. Not in a possessive posture, but a defensive one.

"Sarah will never forgive me, but you have no reason to stay where you're at. Are you coming back to town?"

"What do you think I'll forgive you and come home?"

"No. I mean, not exactly anyways. I don't want you to forgive me, but I've lost control of my life. If you could come back to the house while Sarah and Rachel are interning, help me, get my life back together. I don't need rent. If you help me find myself and rebuild my life, I'd even pay you."

"Just so we're on the same page you mean chase off the gold diggers you can't say no to. Help you refocus on your career and maintain your image with your firm. Sound about right."

"Just about, but somehow hopefully there are two of the three living in the house I actually like. They were my original attempt to replace you. They've been with me since you left. Hopefully you can get at least one of them to stay, but I'm afraid to ask one of them to stay. What if the only reason they want to be with me is my attention is too divided to ever do anything. Then I'll be alone."

"Let me call Sarah tonight and talk with Angelica. We can have lunch tomorrow and talk about it."

He seemed excited with that response and left me and Angelica for the night.

"Do you really want me to live with that man again?" Angelica asked, the disappointment obvious in her tone.

"Angel, never, but if we can get him to agree to favorable terms for sorting out his love life, I don't need to live there for that. The internship is only going to be six months, then they want to travel for inspiration and possibly go to college or launch their own gallery. None of that is cheap. This is just a little project I can do while I'm in town to help our daughter."

She was glowing now, and she wrapped her arms around me, raining light short kisses on my cheeks and forehead, "That's my girl. You're so brilliant and always thinking of our baby girl. I'm sorry I ever doubted you, but I know how much he still means to you."

"Not more than you, never more than you," I responded flatly, brushing my hand down her back.

That night I talked to Sarah and then drafted an agreement for Jeramiah. The next day I told him I would help him with his issues as I understood them, "Read and sign this if you agree and we can start right away," I told him after explaining the situation as I saw it.

He took it, flipped to the last page, and signed it, "Thanks," he said tossing me the contract and then I followed him in my car back to the house we once had shared. Once inside I told him I needed temporary authority over all his credit cards and bank accounts. He went and got me all his cards. I then told him I needed to speak with each of the live-in girlfriends and then I needed a group chat for me and all of his girlfriends.

I talked to the first two girlfriends he had moved into the house to replace me and Angelica. They were younger and shallower than me and Angelica, but in every way that mattered they were just like us. Free spirited and in love with each other. There was no room in their world for Jeramiah, but he almost never called on them and didn't even really pay attention to them. Which was obvious because he was unaware, they were sharing a room. The second room had been converted into some kind of office. When things changed and he was focused on fewer women they would leave on their own. Turns out they were why there were so many women in the first place. They could tell he was desperately trying to fill a hole and they knew the more distractions they gave him the less time he'd have for any of them. The third woman was different. She had joined later and wanted to make sure the girls were never forced into anything, but surprisingly she also knew this couldn't last and she wanted someone to be there when it all fell apart. Obviously, she knew about the girls and their self-destructive choices. She tried to offer them money to make a clean break and start a life together, but they were greedy and confident they could string him along forever.

It took me five hours to finish with the three live-in girls and then I logged on to the group chat, "Hi, I'm Gretta. Jeramiah was my husband. We are not together, but I care about him and the future of my family. No more money without me thinking it's needed. So, if you care about my Ex, come have dinner tomorrow, I'd love to meet you. If you care about the money, it's gone," I sent that one message. I had already removed the three girls who were in the house from the group chat. Now with my first contact with everyone out of the way I was ready to talk to Jeramiah and head home.

"The two girls you like are lovers. They share a room. I don't think you like them, or you would have noticed. You're not a dense man Jeramiah. The third live-in girl though, doesn't love you either, but if you can find your way back to you, she might love him. Either way she cares about you and is willing to stand by you. In fact, she's always known this lifestyle was going to end and stayed so you wouldn't be alone when all these girls showed their true colors. Give her a chance. Sarah gets in tonight. Do you have groceries or do you need me to leave you some money to eat?"

"What do you mean? We could just go to dinner together. You can bring Angelica. I mean you guys are living here anyways."

"You should have read the contract. Sarah's waiting. Since you don't want to answer if you don't have groceries, get your roommates to buy something. I'll be here for dinner tomorrow with you and whoever shows up."

With that I left wondering why I was doing this. My life was so happy, so settled, so why did I need to invite the chaos of this man back in. By the next night the girlfriends had gathered their stuff and left. We had already talked, and I knew they'd be moving out this week. Three girls showed up to the dinner.

"I love him, like for real, real, but I was also counting on that money he gives me every month. My rent is due tomorrow. If he can't give us money anymore, can I like, crash here babe?" The youngest of the three, a peppy blond woman who was little more than a child, asked locking eyes with Jeramiah and ignoring everyone else, but I didn't give him time to respond. His answer was obvious and wrong.

"No, you can't. No one else is allowed to move in for the next six months and he doesn't have access to money so he can't pay your rent. You can have dinner and figure things out after or I can cover this one month and you have thirty days to figure things out, but you leave now and never come back," I told her and she had her hand out before I even finished, she didn't even look back at Jeramiah after I gave her cash.

"I told them we could get at least one more pay day if we came today. Those stupid girls never listen to me, serves them right," she mumbled as she left. It made me sad to realize these were the kinds of women my husband thought replaced me, but maybe not, maybe that's why he needed so many of them.

"He saved me as long as he once me around I'll come around whenever he asks," a short dark-haired girl told me. I nodded and then I looked at the other girl at the table, his last live-in girlfriend. The one I was fairly sure I could trust with his well-being if not his heart.

"So, you both want to be here and it's not for money? There is a thousand dollars cash for anyone who wants to leave. For anyone who stays there is no financial support for six months. What do you choose?" I asked.

"I can't do that," they both said in unison. I was not surprised, but a little disappointed and unbelievably sad for my ex, but what they said next blew my mind, "If you're not going to pay our expenses anymore, we need access to our checks," they responded again in sync. I looked at Jeramiah who looked away in embarrassment.

"I forgot a couple of the girls used my bank account for their direct deposits. I pay all the bills and the extra helps pay for the other girls who don't provide as much."

"How many others?"

"None, just these two."

"So, you've known who was willing to help you this whole time?"

"I guess if I had been thinking straight, yeah. Still needed help getting rid of all the free loaders."

"Bet they could have done that too. Just marry one of them and have them chase everyone away."

"Good point. Thanks Gretta."

I sighed and handed all the bank information to the girl who lived with him, "If it was me, I would move the other girl in. You're never going to be happy with just one woman anyways and I don't think it will bother either of them. Neither of them loves you, but they'll be good for you and faithful to you. Marry one of them and let them run the house so you can't get suckered by more gold diggers. I'm done. I already transferred the fifty grand to your daughter. No, she isn't accepting your apology. Enjoy your life. Be good to your sons and protect your new family."

With that I turned and left. We enjoyed those six months, but we never saw Jeramiah again during that time, but I heard he had taken my advice and was in top form at work. Now with Sarah and Rachel leaving me and Angelica were faced with what our life looked like without a daughter to dote on.

GENERATIONAL LOVE

I wish I could say with Jeramiah's personal life settled our life became peaceful and carefree, but life rarely works that way. More often than not, we solved a problem only to find a new one rise to take its place. However, even though those problems would come, we would solve them as we had solved these, together. We did eventually reconnect with Jeramiah and Andrew both having returned to the loving and accepting people I had known when I was younger. We never became as close as we once were, but we showed up for each other. Though Sarah never fully forgave them and Rachel never spoke to them again.

I was actually really close with Misty; she was the younger woman who had stayed out of obligation and ended up giving Richard two more children, one boy and one girl. Talia, who was the older lady, had married Jeramiah and taken care of the house, but the relationship was always transactional, but reciprocal. She rarely came to social events and when she did, she stayed close to Jeramiah and really only talked to him unless he requested her to engage with someone else.

Andrew is still with his brunette firecracker trying to change the world. They had one child; a daughter named Sophia. He vowed never to have more kids after that, said he couldn't handle another girl, but he did dote on the one he had. Johnny is alone running a non-profit medical outreach center. He has a lady friend who goes to fund raisers with him, but he says he has no time to invest into a family, but I think he's afraid of what kind of family man he'd be.

Sarah and Rachel settled down in Arizona and opened a gallery. They live with us on twenty acres of land. It has three houses, two barns and two studios. Honestly it looks like a neighborhood with big yards and too much vegetation. They adopted several girls. They attend public school and work a ranch in the area in the summer. Not one of them wants to be an artist. In fact, the trio wants to open a horse-riding ranch. Not a rodeo ranch, but a low-key relaxing place to learn to ride and take in the peaceful countryside. After talking to all the children, we are leaving our estate to make that dream a reality.

We painted the horse barn with a painting of me and Angelica so we could watch over the girls after we were gone.

I am eighty now and I still paint every day and still go to sleep every night holding my Angel close to me. I have been truly blessed in this life and can only pray if there's another I can be just as lucky.

FALLING FOR MY FIANCÉE'S MOM

FIRST MEETINGS

I was nineteen and about to wash out of college. Benjamin was my knight in shining armor. He showed up and helped me study for every test, showed me how to quickly and efficiently research any topic using our archaic library. He was so helpful, so present in every moment of success I couldn't help it. I began to associate him with my success, then with my happiness, and finally with my future. It was the weekend after finals when I confessed, and asked him out. He was cold, with a hard exterior, and a distance I somehow could never close. All the same he was my savior, and I was ready to walk hand in hand into the future with this man who had made my future possible. I knew his aloof nature wouldn't allow him to make the first move, so they were always up to me. Our first date, our first sleep over, when we started part time cohabitating, and now before I officially moved in with him, I nudged him to meet each other's families. He met mine first. My mother, father, baby sister, and my nephew that had lived with us since he was six months old. He still called mom and dad his uncle and auntie, because his mom had died and he refused to give her spot in his life to anyone else. I always made sure to explain this before anyone met them, so we didn't have to have that conversation in front of Derik. He was young and self-conscious about it.

We had been there for an hour when Derik came in and tugged on my mom's arm, "Auntie April, can I cut desert tonight."

It was a small simple request and Benjamin looked at him as if he had admitted to hiding bodies in his closet. I looked at him confused, "What's wrong babe?"

"O, um nothing, just I wasn't really ready to meet extended family. Is it just your little cousin? Didn't see anyone else around."

Derik started crying and ran from the room and now Benjamin looked annoyed. It bothered me a little bit, but things automatically shifted inside of me. Instead of being bothered by his thoughtless words I was annoyed with myself, sure I had explained it poorly or picked a poor time to tell him. After all, he had selflessly come to my aide and had happily been by my side ever since.

"Sweetie, I told you he's adopted, calls them aunt and uncle out of respect for his mom. He's very sensitive about it. Can you apologize, make him feel included?" I asked, thinking maybe this was a good thing. I could see him come to the rescue, being the man, I had fallen in love with.

"Look Ta," he started and my stomach sank. This was not going to go the way I thought it would, "I have my image to think about. Plus, it will do him good. The world isn't going to sensor itself forever you know. You really should've put more effort into pointing out how complex your family is."

"R-right," I responded simply and nodded. The night progressed in carefully guarded conversation and awkward silences. After Benjamin left I talked to Derik, "Sorry buddy. He can be a lot and he's not too in tune with emotions, but he saved my life so he's pretty important to me. Can we give him one more try?"

He nodded and then my parents patted his back and sent him to go play. They just stood there with worry on their face, and I could tell they wanted to say something, but were having trouble finding the words so I waited patiently. Finally, my little sister broke the silence.

I hadn't even seen her enter the room, "Sis, are you really going to settle for that cold bully?" My dad chuckled but swallowed it down.

"Trace, go play," my mom commanded and as my sister darted from the room my mom found her voice, "He's not really your type. Is he really going to make you happy?" She wasn't wrong. He wasn't my normal type. He was assertive, aloof, or maybe cold and detached would be more accurate, he was handsome in an obvious way that no one was more sure of then him, and he was opinionated on everything, but there was another side to him. The side who had tutored me through every subject and made sure I took care of myself and gave me everything I asked for.

"Yeah, he saved me, mom and he's good to me. He might be a little obtuse when it comes to emotions, but he steps up when it matters." I gave my final verdict on the issue and prepared to leave. They hugged me and left it at that.

The next week passed in the same distant coexistence I had come to label as quiet support. Then it was time to meet his family. He told me nothing in advance, just took me to a small house and as we were about to knock on the door he said, "So my family is different."

His mom opened the door, looked me up and down, and then said, "My god you're gorgeous," she then pulled me into a deep hug. I couldn't help but breathe in her scent. It was a mix of a floral perfume and the kitchen spices she had probably been using to bake desert. When she pulled back, I instinctively looked at her. She was tall with a model's form and a pale complexation. It made her look fragile, but also ethereal. I found myself wanting to reach out and hug her again. Instead, I chuckled slightly and I could feel Benjamin staring at me.

"Told you. She's weird. Don't just grab people mom. You could at least warn them if you can't be bothered to get consent," he said and I was surprised to see his harsh, cold, detached mannerisms applied even to his own mother. I was even more surprised to see this woman that radiated with a warmth and joy that could melt the polar ice caps as his mother. I wanted to ask how they were so different, but I chuckled slightly and then my voice ran away on its own like it wasn't even connected to my brain.

"No, no, it was nice. Don't make her feel bad," I interrupted, blushing and averting my gaze from his mother.

"Whatever, mom, this is my girlfriend. She thought it was time we met our families. Good news, hers was a train wreck so you probably won't embarrass me too badly. Where's Jewels you made sure she stayed home today right," he said with his trademark disinterest and pushed past her to the couch.

"Yes, she's here. She'll be down later."

"Figures she'd wait until the last minute to show herself."

"Ta, right?" his mother asked, pretending her son wasn't being super rude. I could feel her eyes studying me and I found I couldn't look back at her.

"No, it's Tabatha. Ta is just a nickname."

"Figures. Benjamin could never put in more effort than needed," she said and I felt confused by the statement, "So, what do you even see in my son?"

The bluntness caught me off guard, and she took my hand and led me into the house, "He's my hero," I responded matter of factly. She looked at me with something between confusion and surprise.

"Mom, too much, don't you have a dinner you're making," his curt tone made me feel uneasy, but I dropped her hand and walked over to Benjamin and sat down. She practically fled the room, and we sat in silence after that for what felt like forever. A small girl who couldn't be more than eleven entered the room at some point. I was scrolling on my phone trying to pretend the atmosphere wasn't awkward, so I didn't see exactly when, but she patted my hand to get my attention.

"You're brother's special friend, right?" She asked shyly.

"Yes, I'm Tabatha and you are?" I asked, not confident Banjamin had used her full name or even a name she liked.

"Juliann, it's lovely to meet you," she said, doing a curtsy that I found absolutely adorable. I chuckled slightly and an image of his mother flashed in my mind. Benjamin looked up from his phone, and I looked over at him embarrassed.

"My you have such an adorable family," I praised honestly.

"Yeah, they're great," he responded and went back to his phone.

Dinner was shortly after that and somehow the conversation flowed easily, and Benjamin felt like the outsider. He kept alternating between looking at the clock and his phone like he had more important things to do and was only waiting for permission to go. We finished our food and finally his mom spoke to him. For the first time since she had left us on the couch, "If you have things to do, I can get her home. Don't force yourself, dear."

He glanced at me and when I didn't object, he hopped up, kissed my cheek, and was pulling the door shut before he even had his coat on. After that the atmosphere became even more relaxed and if I had to describe it, I would say it felt like coming home. Not like when I go back to my childhood home with my parents, but that sense of comfortable finality when you get to your end destination and it's everything it's supposed to be. We talked for more than five hours about everything and nothing. It amazed me how warm and effortless it all felt. Eventually though I gave Juliann a reluctant hug and prepared to leave with her mom. The reluctance came from not wanting to leave and I know it, but they have their life, and I have school and Benjamin. Again, I'm surprised that these two open, happy and optimistic people are his family, but I get into his mom's car, and she drives me home.

In front of my dorm, I grab her hand again and look at her and I'm appalled at myself for letting my body and mind run unchecked, but in her presence, I can't control them, and I don't know why, "What's your name?" is the first question I ask and now I'm praising myself for not asking any of the more sensitive and inappropriate questions running through my mind.

"You dear can call me Maddy," she says and I blush, that's obviously not just a random nickname used by everyone, or just a convenient shortening of her name either, it's familiar and casual. I feel the feverish heat of my blush return but I hold my gaze.

"Maddy, thank you for welcoming me into your home. I had a lovely time. I genuinely hope we can do it again sometime."

"Sure, but next time tell that wet blanket of a boyfriend if he doesn't want to have fun, he can just skip it," she replied beaming with joy, giggling slightly and patting the back of my hand. I don't know why or even really when, but at some point, we exchanged contact info and the next morning I was staring at a message inviting me to dinner next weekend, "BBQ, Friday night. I know it sounds harsh, but for real if Benjamin doesn't want to come leave him at home and trust me on this he doesn't want to come. Juliann took the night off from all her social commitments to see you again. No pressure."

I didn't feel pressure, I felt pleasure. Her consideration and enthusiasm were infectious. I responded, "I'll bring dessert." Then I got into my week.

ROUTINE AND FUTURE PLANS

The week dragged and the time with Benjamin had shifted. We were more distant and for someone who always seemed to be on another planet that's saying something. He still did whatever I suggested might be good, but I stopped suggesting so much. I thought maybe his mom was right, maybe I had been pushing him into things he didn't want to do and maybe that's why this distance had grown. That weekend I showed up at Maddy's alone. I had planned on bringing it up to Benjamin, but I was sure he would just agree as soon as I brought it up and after last week, I had no confidence he wanted to be here so I never mentioned it when I realized I wouldn't know how to convince him not to come once I told him, so I figured I'd tell him tomorrow. We were having brunch so I figured it would be fine.

The BBQ was just the three of us, but it felt like they had scooped up the universe and bottled it for me. It started with the meal, homemade fruit salad, potato salad, and deviled eggs sat alongside two whole racks of marinated smoked and perfectly prepared ribs and on the other side of the ribs a platter of meat, boneless pork chops, burgers and a steak.

"We didn't know what you liked and we wanted to make sure you enjoyed the meal," Maddy confessed as we all sat down on the same side of the picnic table.

"Thank you," I said and then we ate in near silence. Afterwards we talked casually and then Juliann begged me to swim. But I didn't have a suit.

"I knew Juliann would want to swim so I asked Benjamin what size you were and picked up a couple options. You don't have to," she said and I smiled at her.

Ten minutes later I was in a tasteful black one-piece swimsuit splashing Juliann in the pool. Maddy was sitting on the edge of the pool sipping wine and splashing with her legs. I waited for her to put the glass down and then I dragged her into the pool. The three of us played for hours and then Juliann looked at me, "Um, could I stay with you tonight?" she asked, her eyes getting large in anticipation.

"Juliann, I'm sure Tabatha has her own life. Don't be rude or she won't want to come back."

I smiled and then I thought about it and grabbed my phone from the edge of the pool, "Your sister wants to come to brunch tomorrow. Thoughts," I texted Benjamin and then waited for his response. It took him less than a minute to respond.

"Well, she'll pout if you don't let her, but can you bring her. Sure, you noticed but mom's a lot," his response said and I gasped as I read it. A lot, what was that supposed to mean? She was stunning, positive, friendly, smart, and a great conversationalist. Honestly, I was in awe every time I was in her presence.

"Sure, but I'm having brunch with your brother tomorrow. We can hang out and then I'll bring you home tomorrow," I said and Maddy looked surprised, but behind it was another emotion I couldn't identify. We all sunbathed and made small talk after that and before long it was time for us to leave. I gave Maddy a hug and she pulled me in tight. We were still in our bathing suits so I couldn't help but feel the warmth and curves of her body as she pressed into me. My breath caught in my throat, and I told myself it was from surprise.

Me and Juliann stayed up until two in the morning that night, slept for four hours and then had muffins and juice in the quad before I showed her around the campus and we went to meet her brother. We arrived at the patio cafe and Benjamin was already there, "Huh," he simply said glaring at his sister. I felt instantly uneasy and Juliann took a step back and positioned herself behind me, "Wow she took to you fast," he added after I set Juliann down and ordered for both of us. He tried to sound lite hearted, but I could tell the whole situation made him uncomfortable. Luckily though Juliann was more than comfortable just having my attention even if I had to split it between her and her brother. We didn't talk about anything serious, but by the end me and Benjamin had made plans to meet up tomorrow night. We were going to meet up that night, but Juliann said since I had let her stay over, she wanted to return the favor. I was going to refuse, but then Benjamin said, "Sure sis whatever."

I was stunned by how this little girl was more vested in our week-old relationship then Benjamin was in our relationship after we had been together longer than a year. Juliann and I left Benjamin and went shopping, then to the arcade, and finally we each bought Maddy something. I bought a pair of earrings and Juliann bought her a little crystal figure. We bought dinner and I took her home.

"Ha, my girls are here," Maddy said and she wrapped one arm around each of us. She hugged us firmly and I breathed in her scent. Then my mouth ran away all on its own again.

"Better be careful, your son might get jealous if you try to claim his girlfriend," I said, chuckling into the nape of her neck.

"I'm sure even my foolish boy would react to having such a catch snatched away," Maddy replied, chuckling into my hair.

"Who cares? Mommy deserves you more," Juliann replied and I swallowed hard as all the sudden this didn't feel like a joke. Maddy must've had the same thought as she released us and took the bags of food.

"Anyways, let's eat and Juliann don't be such a troublemaker."

As we were eating Juliann kept asking questions about me and Benjamin. How long we had been together, Why I loved him, what we liked to do together. Simple basic stuff like that and I giggled happily as I answered every one of them. Then all the sudden she looked at me and took a deep breath, "Have you guys, ummm, had sex yet," she asked and I looked at Maddy. I didn't feel the need to hide this information from anyone, but Juliann was a child. I wasn't going to just discuss adult matters.

"I'd prefer you not go into details, but she's well educated and very mature for her age and she really cares about you. If you want to answer I don't mind."

"No, we haven't," I said and then took a deep breath, "I don't want to make a mistake again so I'm not doing it again until I'm married," I said and I puffed out my chest in pride of my conviction.

"I see," Maddy surprisingly answered first and she was smiling. My heart skipped a beat, and I swallowed like a meatball was lodged in my throat.

"Mom can Tabatha stay the night," she asked her mom who was still staring at me. I was blushing a dark crimson at this point.

Maddy shook her head and looked at Juliann, "What sweaty?"

Juliann rolled her eyes and I giggled, "Can she stay?" Juliann asked. This time locking eyes with her mother and talking slowly.

"She can stay whenever she wants," Maddy said, smiling at me.

"Sure Juliann."

"Can the three of us sleep in the same bed? Like a slumber party," she asked and now me and Maddy were staring at each other unsure of what to say.

"If that's what you want and your mom doesn't mind, but we can't do this all the time," I told Juliann when I couldn't stand the weight of the silence anymore.

"That's fine baby girl, but you have to sleep in the middle," Maddy chimed in. I was relieved and disappointed in equal measure. I didn't know if I could handle laying too close to her. I was beginning to understand I was attracted to her, but I was with her son, and he had saved me when I needed it. I was disappointed because even with the reality of the situation pressing down on me there was a part of me, and it was larger than I wanted to admit, that wanted to brush against her as we slept. Her skin was soft and warm; I knew that from her hugs and to feel that as I slumbered could only make me rest easier or so I told myself. We munched and talked and then took turns getting ready for bed and then we all climbed into Maddy's bed. I slept soundly that night and over the course of the next months this became my routine. Juliann would stay with me one night I would stay with her and Maddy one night. I would have Benjamin over twice a week and I would focus on studying the rest of the time.

I became really relaxed and super comfortable with all three of them during this period of time and all the sudden I had a thought. I was aware I wasn't sure if I loved Benjamin the way a wife should love her husband, but I wanted to be part of his family. So, I saved and I planned and as mid-terms came to an end I proposed. It was a beautiful event with a band and wine.

His answer, “Yeah, that probably makes sense,” that was it, but I would be part of his family now and I couldn’t be happier. The answer barely even settled on my ears before I was dragging him to tell his family.

REVELATIONS

We were at Maddy's house. I was beaming, my arms wrapped around Benjamin's.

"O, Tabatha and you have Benjamin with you. What's up?" She asked, clearly unconvertible with her sons' presence on her porch.

"Ta decided we should marry. She wanted to tell you. She's being a lot, mom you talk to her," Benjamin said, pushing past Maddy who looked like someone had just punched her square in her stomach.

"Maddy, we'll be family from now on. Isn't that great!" I said beaming with joy, even as I hated myself for using Benjamin to stay close to his family.

"Yes dear," Maddy replied in that distracted tone parents use when their children interrupt their dinner party to show you a picture they drew and wanting to know if it looks nice. I took a sharp breath and forced my smile to hold firm.

"What's wrong, Maddy?" I couldn't help but ask.

"It's nothing, but can you wait to tell Juliann? She's going to be heartbroken," she said looking past me and I could see a tear in her eye.

I didn't understand and I was already heartbroken, but I could tell she was in no mental state to discuss this, so I went to find Benjamin. Juliann was at a friend's so the three of us went and had a celebratory dinner. It felt more like a funeral, and I couldn't figure out why. We went our separate ways from the restaurant, and I returned to my week. It crawled by as all I wanted to do was talk to Maddy and figure out what had happened. Finally, it was Friday night. I hadn't talked to Juliann or Maddy really all week. Just confirmed she was still coming over. I showed up in a sky-blue summer dress and sandals. I took the time to do my hair and make-up and I knocked. Juliann answered the door a minute later.

"We can just stay here. Use the pool and stuff. Momma had a business trip and she'll be gone until next week sometime."

"I see. Sure."

"Hey, Tabby," she began tentatively.

"What's up sweetie," I coaxed her with a soft reassuring tone.

"Why is mommy sad? She keeps saying it's not fair and it's too much. I think we're moving."

My heart dropped and I hated myself for what I thought next, "If Maddy and Juliann are leaving me why am I even marrying Benjamin," I admonished myself immediately, "He's my hero, my savior, isn't that enough of a reason," but I knew my answer, and it only made myself loathing grow. No, it wasn't. I didn't want to marry Benjamin; I wanted to marry his family.

"I don't know Juliann, but if you promise to keep it a secret, I can tell you when it started and maybe you can tell me what's up with you. Maddy and....." I began and then I heard the door push shut.

"Trip got canceled," Maddy said at the front door, "What were you talking to my daughter about?" Maddy asked and there was a cold detached tone I had never heard in Maddy's voice before. It sounded like her son only harder and more final.

"Maddy, Juliann was telling me you've been different lately and we were trying to figure out why."

"So, you were just going to tell her. Without me even here. Fine, we can tell her now. Juliann, she's marrying Benjamin. Now Tabatha, she knows, you can go. I'll see you next month. O and call me Mother from now on," she said, taking a step forward and pushing the door open behind her. Juliann was openly crying.

"Ma..." I started, but her hard glare let me know none of this was up for debate. So, I bowed slightly and left.

She wasn't wrong. Telling Maddy was a horrible and selfish thing to do, but I honestly assumed Maddy had exaggerated. I wanted Juliann to tell me why this marriage was such a bad thing, but I couldn't shake the need to go back to the way the three of us had been.

"Maddy, all I wanted was to be part of your family. Please tell me what's wrong," I texted and then headed back to the dorms to wait. I basically stopped seeing Benjamin. We weren't broken up, but we never did anything together either. In fact, all I did for the next two weeks was go to class and stare at that message. She had read it. She had done that much while I was still in my car in front of her house, but she had said nothing. Juliann also remained quiet and me, I felt like I had just been dumped for the first time. Sometimes I would cry and sometimes I would just sit in the shower and let the cold-water wash over me.

Friday night, I stood staring at the bed where me and Juliann should be squireling under the blankets to discuss teenage gossip. You know pop celebrities, cutest people in her class, who got what and what it meant for their social standings. I giggled as I remembered how truly perceptive, she was. Then a knock came on my door.

When I opened it, Juliann stood there with an obviously forced smile. I was overjoyed to see her even if she looked less than thrilled to be there.

"T-Tabby, why are you marrying Benji?" she asked and I was caught off guard by the question and by the brazen use of the nickname. Benjamin visibly flinched whenever you called him anything besides Benjamin.

I thought about it for a moment. Then I said, "I wanted to be part of your family, but I guess that's not going to work out," then I paused again. Thinking to myself that can't possibly be the only reason, but I already knew the truth. That's it, but I'm not ready to admit to his sister that I was using him just to stay close to his family. So, I take a deep breath, "When I first met your brother I was in a dark place. I considered leaving school. Maybe even worse, but he saved me. He tutored me through every single class and got me back on track."

I felt better about that answer, even if it felt hollow.

"I see, so you think my brother is a hero? He's a follower. Helped one of his buddies steal test papers. He didn't actually take them, and he didn't look at them. He got probation and community service. He got a lot of hours, but my brother is smart and has a good eye for people. So, he found someone who was smart but lost. Someone floundering in a system that ignores individual needs in favor of mass efficiency. Then he sunk all his hours into that one project. I should've told you sooner, but I liked having you around and you made mom so happy. If you love him, I'll listen to momma, but if you love us then I'll stay and we can go talk to momma tomorrow. You should know the reason me and mom don't spend much time with him isn't because we don't love him, but this stuff happens all the time. You'll get caught up in it and sometimes it's really messy. Second and maybe you've noticed, but you can't really tell how he feels because he always just agrees and lastly is hurt feelings. He'll always agree with whoever is right in front of him. If you have plans and someone asks for help, he'll do it. Every time no matter how important the plans are or how frivolous the favor is. Finally, we just stopped asking him for things. If you marry him, you'll become broken down by that lifestyle. I know you would still make time for us, but me and mom won't be dragged back into that life."

I understood now and I couldn't form words. I wrapped my arm around Juliann and led her inside. As we cuddled into my bed, she hugged me and said, "Do you love me and momma the same way?" The simplistic innocence of the question made me gasp.

"Juli, I love you very much, but not like I love Maddy," I answered, unable to find the resolve to hide my feelings or lie to Juliann anymore.

she giggled and covered her head with the blanket, "Thought so, that's what I told her."

I glared at her in silence for what felt like forever. Eventually I kissed her forehead and rolled over and went to sleep. I woke the next morning to my phone ringing and Juliann sitting against the wall in the fetal position.

"I'm sorry. I'm really, really sorry. So, very sorry," she kept repeating as I picked up the phone and saw Maddy's name on the caller ID, I got a sinking feeling about what Juliann was sorry for.

"Maddy, I didn't know," I managed to get out before her angry voice pushed in on me through the phone.

“Tabatha, you have my daughter. Send her downstairs in five minutes. Don’t come with her. I don’t want to see you,” she commanded and hung up. My heart broke at those words, but I looked at Juliann.

“Get dressed. This will probably be goodbye. I’ll always love you and cherish our time together,” I said and Juliann was openly crying now. She shook her head no and I was at a loss. She had never disobeyed me or her mother before let alone both.

“Just tell her I’m refusing. She has to come up and get me,” she demanded and I sighed deeply and texted Maddy.

“I know you don’t want to talk to me, but Juliann is refusing to get dressed let alone go downstairs. She says you have to come get her. I can carry her downstairs, but I can’t get her dressed. I can leave the room if you’ll come get her,” I sent it and stared at the screen.

“Fine,” she texted back almost instantly.

ENDING AND BEGINNING

I was in a small nook where people would go to read, waiting for Maddy to calm down Juliann and to leave my life for good. I had decided, Benjamin wasn't who I thought he was and I wasn't even going to get his family, so I was done. I would be done with Benjamin and Maddy was clearly done with me. My phone vibrated and I nearly dropped it.

A text, from Maddy, "Can you come back?"

I walked back quickly, took a deep breath and pushed the door open. There she was as beautiful as the day I met her, but she also looked worn and defeated somehow and then I saw the defiant Juliann still sitting near the wall in the fetal position.

"She says 'I don't understand. We need to talk, but I won't get dragged back into Benjamin's drama. Not even for you."

"I'm not marrying Benjamin, but I'm a horrible person, Maddy. I love you," I said and by the end my voice was so weak I couldn't even be sure I was producing sound.

"We're family. It's only natural to love each other. I love you too dear," Maddy responded and I couldn't tell if she didn't get it or if she was giving me away out. Either way after last night I needed to confront this and see where we stood.

“Maddy, not like that,” I whispered.

“So, like I love you then,” she said tentatively, extending her hand to mine and intertwining our figures like it was their natural state, “I’ve been so horrible to you. Trying to respect your choices and my own boundaries, but God Tabatha, I’ve missed you.”

I looked at her then, my desire crashing like waves against my heart, but I held firm, “Maddy, I want to be with you, but I can’t tonight. I have to talk to Benjamin first. Can we have dinner tomorrow?” I asked, afraid she would accept this step back as hesitation or something and this whole thing could fall apart before we ever had a chance to figure it out.

“What if he fights for you?”

“I’ll tell him gratitude isn’t love.”

She nodded happily at that.

“Awesome, moms, I knew you guys could work it out,” Juliann said now standing beside Maddy and beaming with joy and pride at the outcome of her tantrum. The word moms rested in my ears, and I blushed at the thought. I wasn’t much older than Juliann, but somehow it felt only natural that she would call me that.

“What would you guys like to have for dinner?” I asked not wanting to let go of them just yet.

“I want you guys to have your first date, so I’ll just stay here,” Juliann responded first.

“No date, little miss. Not until I talk to Benjamin. You coming or not?” I asked and Juliann nodded her head with determination.

“That sounds lovely,” Maddy answered, but she seemed to be weighing if it was really ok for us to be doing this. I nodded once and took her hand.

We were sitting waiting for our food. Juliann was scrolling through my phone trying to find something to entertain herself, “So, Maddy, can I ask you something?”

“Sure, what do you want to know?”

“How long have you been gay?”

“What makes you think I’m gay?” She asked and I gestured vaguely at my boobs.

She giggled then locked eyes with me, “Those are nice, but I love you. Never been attracted to a woman before. Not sure you can even call that bisexual, but I guess to answer your question the answer would be. Somewhere around the time I went shopping for your swimsuit. When I pictured you wearing each one of them that’s when I knew the care that was building wasn’t maternal at all. How about you? Was I the first woman you’ve ever been attracted to, or have you been bi for a while?”

“I’ve noticed women were attractive before but never been interested in them romantically. As far as you go, I don’t know honestly. I knew when I saw your face after I told you I was marrying Benjamin. I actually thought to myself if I lost you what was the point in marrying him. I was going to marry him, but the relationship on my mind was you and your daughter.”

“Can you stop saying marry and Benjamin in the same sentence. It makes me angry even now.”

“You’re cute even when you’re angry.”

“Can you sleep over?” Juliann asked all of a sudden, sitting my phone down and looking at me with pleading eyes. Luckily as I fidgeted the food arrived, so I sat the question aside and we ate then made small talk.

We had been sitting there for about an hour when Maddy looked at me and her eyes softened, “No pressure, but she’ll be there. It’ll be like old times,”

I nodded and the three of us went to their house. It was not like old times. Maddy fell asleep first or at least it looked that way and I lay there watching her, wishing I could be holding her. The ache all that much worse now that I knew we both wanted it. Juliann was grinning a knowing smile laying in between the two of us. She was just staring up at the ceiling clearly proud of herself for bringing me and her mom together and if I’m being honest, I was proud of her too, but more so I was grateful. There was no doubt in my mind without Juliann’s help we would not have made it this far.

Two hours later Maddy’s eyes fluttered open, “Ugh, you're still awake,” she said as our eyes locked. She slid out of bed and waved her hand for me to follow. She made tea and we sat on the couch, “So, tomorrow you tell Benjamin. Then what?” She asked as she pulled her legs up under herself and pushed herself into the far-left end of the couch.

“I’d like to try and be together. Juliann feels fine with it.”

“You know when you’re my age I’ll be retiring. I’m likely to be dead before you retire,” she said and my heart ached at her second statement. The idea of her not being here was almost unthinkable.

“Yes, and it crushes me to think about. However, the fact that I will most likely lose you someday hardly seems like a good reason to never have you. So, I hope that’s not what you’re suggesting,” I responded and she looked pleased with that answer.

“Nope, just making sure you thought about it.”

Not sure when, but at some point, as we talked, we drifted together and started leaning into one another. We found sleep eventually in that intimate embrace. I woke, my head in her lap. Her hand resting on my cheek and her laying back against the arm of the couch, a single drop of drool escaping from her mouth which hung open. I got up, made coffee, and wrote a note, “Got to go, see you tonight, Love Tabby.”

With that I slid out of their place and went back to my dorm. I texted Benjamin as I walked, “Do you have time to talk, today?” As I sent it, I swallowed, realizing for the first time I had promised a concrete timeline without any idea what Benjamin was doing today. Then I realized I rarely knew what Benjamin was doing and I scoffed at how truly terrible and unfair I was being to Benjamin.

“Just getting coffee with a friend. I can meet you in the quad in twenty,” his text came back instantly.

“Where at? I can just meet you,” I texted back, anxious to get this over with.

“She says she’s uncomfortable with you being here, but I’m just wrapping up,” he texted back and I was confused. Why would his friends be uncomfortable with me? So, I asked.

“Why would she be uncomfortable with me there?”

“Because you’re my fiancée and we’re on a date. She thinks you’ll be mad. I told her "I always give you what you want, surely you won’t be petty about me granting one request for a friend,” the text popped up and my eyes bulged in shock and disgust.

“Not at all, but I really need to see you. Can you please tell me where you are?” I responded and I meant it. I wasn’t at all upset. In fact, I was relieved. If he was cheating just because someone asked him then I didn’t have to feel guilty and yet I did. At least a little.

He sent me a pin, and it was close. Five minutes later I was standing staring at my fiancée eating a croissant and chatting with a tiny brunette and laughing at myself for not realizing how deep his people pleasing went and how truly indifferent to it all I was. I took a deep breath, walked over, and sat down, "Sorry to interrupt," I said looking at the brunette.

"It's fine. He said it was an emergency and you weren't upset," she said and her calm composure seemed to be sincere, like she also didn't think this was inappropriate, just aware most people would care.

"Right," I responded with a curt tone from nerves. Benjamin must have thought it was something else as he turned his focus to me as if warning me not to make a scene, "So, Benjamin, thing is I'm in love with someone else," I said and sighed deeply.

"I know," he replied flatly.

"Excuse me?" I asked, genuinely confused. I had known for less than a month.

"I assumed mother turned you down and that's why you wished to marry me."

"How long have you known?" I was shocked and ashamed.

"The day I introduced you two it was obvious how you felt for each other. Juliann noticed too."

"Well, me and Maddy didn't," I responded a little hurt he hadn't told me.

"I see so you guys just figured it out and she is willing to be with you?" He asked, but it was more like stating the obvious state of things.

"Yes, but I told her I wanted to explain things and end things with you first."

"I see, has mother told you about her rules regarding me?"

"We've talked about it, but no rules per say."

"Holidays and major life events only. If I miss an event, then I can't schedule anything for the next six months and I have to get Juliann to forgive me. Sometimes we go years without seeing each other."

"Yeah, that sounds fair. For the record, if I had loved you this would not be ok."

"Yes, I'm aware, that's why you were perfect to be my wife. The relationship you valued wasn't me. Enjoy. Mother is truly a great woman. You know she's the one who taught me that others should come first. Anyway, thank you for telling me. I'm going to return to Bridgette's date now."

With that he returned his attention to the brunette, and I walked away feeling nothing at all.

STARTING OUR FUTURE

The ease with which I had broken up with Benjamin still weighed on me, but the excitement of finally being able to be with Maddy outweighed my apprehension. I went to class, but I couldn't concentrate and then I packed a bag and headed for Maddy's place. I knocked and Maddy answered wearing a seductive black dress.

"Juliann is staying at a friend's house. Is that ok?" She asked, looking genuinely nervous that my interest in her might be contingent on the presence of her daughter.

"Sounds lovely, but I can't promise anything," I responded and she hugged me tightly.

As she led me to the dining room I couldn't help but feel under dressed, she was truly stunning in her skintight black dress. Meanwhile I was wearing an alumni t-shirt and sweet pants. Thinking we would just grab food and lounge like normal. Maddy noticed my stare and chuckled slightly.

"Like it, Sweetness?" She asked looking back at me and I blushed and looked away, but I answered shyly.

"You're lovely. I'm truly lucky."

The dinner was not like the ones we had shared in the past though it still housed that effortless closeness that I had come to associate with our relationship. The conversation was more serious and pointed, mostly about what we wanted, from life, from each other, and from a relationship. By the end of the night, I was more convinced than ever that this was the woman I would grow old with. I sighed thinking of the heartbreak that would inevitably bring, but I beamed at all the memories we would make between now and then. After the dinner I took her hand, led her to the patio, and sat behind her on the lounge.

"Maddy, would you want to live together?" I asked, surprising myself with the brazen suggestion.

"I don't know Juliann really likes those sleep overs," she replied giggling lightly before leaning firmer against me, looking up and kissing me. It was our first kiss, and my body was on fire with desire, but I pulled away.

"Maddy, I'm serious. I want to start my life with you and Juliann. I'm certain I want to be with you, and I don't want to miss any of the time we have. If you still have doubts, I won't push, but please give it some thought," I explained and she kissed me again more forcefully this time and as she slid her tongue into my mouth her hand slid into mine and I felt a key pressed to my palm and I instinctively intensified my kiss.

When we broke apart for breath she locked eyes with me, "We can work out the details later love, but you've always had a place here."

A single tear drop fell down my cheek and I hugged her from behind. We laid in that lounge watching the night sky until we found slumber.

We woke the next morning to Juliann screaming, "Moms, you're going to catch a cold sleeping outside like this," She rolled her eyes turned away and then said, "Well at least you're dressed," me and

Maddy both blushed a deep crimson and admonished Juliann with our eyes, but she was headed back inside, "I assume things went well I'll make breakfast," she said and I could hear the smirk in her tone. She was clearly quite pleased with how things had turned out and I felt like I should correct her, but I couldn't figure out what for. She had made our family possible, and I had never been happier. So, I resigned myself to watching her proud march of triumph. I nibbled on Maddy's ear to make sure she was awake and she swatted me playful with her hand.

Maddy went and changed, and I sat to visit with Juliann, "So, mom, are you going to live here full time?" she asked as I sat down. She placed a cup of coffee in front of me as she smiled at me expectantly.

"Possibly, would that be ok," I answered, not quite sure exactly what we'll figure it out later meant.

"Of course. You make mom so happy and you're so nice, but we can still do slumber parties on the weekend right?" I chuckled knowing it wouldn't be long before she wouldn't want to be tied to her parental figures in even vague ways let alone weekly sleep overs. I nodded my head. As long as she wanted even if they changed a little, I would make sure I took time for her. Maddy reappeared in yoga pants and a black sports bra. The three of us ate breakfast. Juliann carefully observed and me and Maddy playfully bantered back and forth effortlessly adjusting to our new roles in each other's lives. After we all got dressed, I brought a couple outfits and let Maddy pick what I wore. We spent the day shopping. Not that we needed anything and we only bought a few little things that Juliann liked, but walking the stores made Juliann happy and spending time together made me and Maddy ecstatic.

As Juliann darted in front of us Maddy leaned against my shoulder, "Tabby, if you still want to live with us at the end of term you can move into my room during break. We can figure out bills and things later, but Juli is already very attached to you so please be sure, love."

Her protest was to protect Juliann, but I could hear the hint of uncertainty in her voice. Not for her own feelings, Maddy was too cautious for that if she were unsure, she would have never let things go this far. This was more a fear that I had been swept up in the moment and that at any moment I would become disillusioned by reality. I had never been more sure of anything in my life though so I simply hugged her tightly and kissed her forehead.

Break was over a month away and while we agreed I wouldn't move in until break I was spending most nights there anyways and there was a suitcase eternally camping at the foot of our bed. Juliann would wake us up every morning before she left for school, I'd go to class, and Maddy to work. It was a basic routine that we fell into as if it had always been our life. This weekend would be different. Juliann was starting vacation earlier than I did and she had plans with her father. So, before she left, she was spending next week at my place helping me pack. For the weekend Maddy came with us during the day and took a load of boxes back to her place at night. I didn't have that much, but there was as much getting distracted and reminiscing as there was packing. During the week was the big help, we were going to clean the apartment. Of course this meant I'd actually be moving in a little early, but Juliann really wanted to help and me and Maddy were solid, so she was happy to speed things up. The week passed in a blur, and I said goodbye to the few floor mates I actually knew. The first week Juliann was gone, me and Maddy settled my life slowly into her space. We trimmed some of her stuff and packed away some of mine keeping what was needed and most valued by each. We had open and honest communication about what mattered and why and by the end of the week our two worlds formed a home. The second week was just me trying to get through finals and turning in term papers. Then finally I was on break and Maddy had taken vacation to surprise me. We had been intimate, but that week was like a damn splitting wide open. We made love multiple times a day exploring every inch of each other and searching for the edge of our endurance. Most nights we would eat delivery and never wore more than robes. The following week she went back to work, and I took up a part time job myself. It was during this week toward the end of the week I came home from a shift in the bookstore where I was working and Maddy was sitting on the sofa sipping wine.

"Before Juliann gets home I want to figure everything out," she started and I chuckled to myself for being nervous. It felt like a very different conversation. We agreed to tell Juliann she could call me mom and we decided we were engaged, nobody really proposed, but we were both assuming we were headed that way and Juliann was already calling me mom, so it only made sense. We decided we'd go get rings this weekend before she got home. Then we discussed the living arrangement. Which we both put off for far too long. Obviously, we should have agreed how living together was going to work before we started living together. We agreed I would help pay for utilities and food during the summer and during the school year I would hand over the part of my grant that was allocated for lodging and half of the food portion. It probably didn't cover even a quarter of the expenses, but it's what the school allotted, and she was determined I should not work during classes.

That weekend we got a gorgeous set of engagement rings. Both the same style with three stones one for her, me, and Juliann. Hers was a ruby in the middle with an emerald on the right and a diamond on the left. Mine had the ruby and emerald switched. We took photos and after waiting for Juliann to arrive home and sharing the news with our daughter we posted the photos.

Benjamin called fifteen minutes after I posted it, “You couldn’t just be happy in quiet. You had to embarrass me,” he said in a sharp condescending tone I had never heard him use before. He hung up and I just stood there in shocked silence. Maddy pointed out reputation was the only thing he ever had an opinion on. I sadly had to agree with that.

We fell into a happy routine after that though. Maddy and I drifted off every night holding each other. The three of us would have breakfast together then we’d split up to do what we needed to do. Then we’d come back together for dinner. Not always just the three of us Juliann loved to bring over friends and brag about us. I would muse at how long that phase could last.

FINALLY, A FAMILY

Are routine stretched on for years in much the same way. There would be small breaks for holidays and our sleep over nights became the three of us crashing on the large sofas in the living room and then monthly road trips with two beds in one room, but for the most part nothing really changed until I graduated. All my job opportunities were out of state, but Maddy had five years before she could retire. This was almost as complicated as how we had met and there was no simple answer. Even in five years it would be an early retirement buy out, and she would have to go back to work unless my career had taken off by then. We hadn't discussed it, because I was looking at three local companies, but they had no slots for new hires with no experience right now.

It was honestly putting strain on our relationship, and we were spending night after night looking for an answer and passing out. We would still sit everything else aside and enjoy our weekends with Juliann, but during the week even our dinners were filled with stressful conversation that was impossible to hide from Juliann.

Then one Saturday I woke to my phone ringing. I answered without even looking at the caller id, "Hello."

"I'm sorry for the way I spoke to you last time mom," it was Benjamin and he was calling me mom. What the hell was going on. I was fully awake then.

"What's up Benjamin? Aren't you supposed to schedule visits through Maddy?" I asked, afraid he was trying to circumvent the house rules.

"This has nothing to do with that. Juliann came to see me. Told me our two moms are in trouble. Told me to fix it. So, got you an internship. No pay, but it gets your foot in the door and keeps you in the industry. You interested?"

"Sure, but how?"

"Easy I told them you were a better fit for it. Me being out of state isn't a big deal. Maybe I can even get a paid internship this way. Anyways, tell my other mom I do love her, and I hope this shows it."

He hung up then and I couldn't help it, I jabbed Maddy and she shot up glaring at me, "Benjamin called," I told her and her glare hardened waiting for me to explain how this was good news worth waking her for, "He found me an unpaid internship locally. Puts me on the short list for the company and builds my work history. It will be tough, but I can get something part-time. We have a way forward finally. God I'm so glad you didn't just let me take something for now, but Maddy, we're you really going to try to make us do long distance?"

"I don't know. Honestly, I had a few different ideas I was working on, but before I would let you give up on your career, yes, we would have made long distance work short term," she said softly and leaned over and kissed me with passion I hadn't felt in weeks, not that it had died we had just both been so tired trying to find an answer, "That's kind of surprising though. Benjamin's not usually so thoughtful," she said when she finally released me.

"Yeah, about that, Juliann went to see him. Not sure exactly what she said, but when he called, he apologized and called me mom," I explained looking at her for any sign of her opinion on the matter.

After a few moments she said, "Guess we should let her order dinner tonight and this weekend we can take a special trip of her choice."

With that she rolled out of bed and climbed into the shower. I got up, got dressed and she came back into the room, her hair wrapped in a towel and water still gliding down her naked exposed flesh, "Things will be tight, but as long as we are careful and it doesn't last too long, we'll be fine."

With that hurdle conquered, the three of us started to plan our wedding. Benjamin was invited but given no critical role. Maddy still couldn't trust he'd show up. My family was invited but sadly had chosen not to support our relationship. Even so we moved toward the day with unwavering commitment and certainty.

With me still being an unpaid intern, we obviously had to be careful with our spending, so we went for a small intimate affair in our backyard. Less than fifty people gathered in a casual seating arrangement and watched as the three of us officially became a family. Surprisingly Benjamin not only showed up, but he stayed in town for the next three days to watch Juliann while me and Maddy went on our short but romantic honeymoon paid for by the guests. We already had a house full of things and with no registry someone had organized everyone to make this happen.

That was when I realized I hadn't just found the woman of my dreams, or built a good family, no I had stumbled into an amazing life populated with people who truly cared. Whatever would come in the future couldn't outweigh the joy of this moment.

ACCEPTING THE PAST

SUPPORT WITHOUT BOUNDARIES

It was a Tuesday, and like most weekday nights I was on Emily's couch complaining about how my boyfriend blew off our evening plans yet again. She huffed and plopped down next to me.

"Well, that just means it's girls' night," she giggled, wrapping her arms around me and squeezing. She had been this way as long as I had known her. Overly affectionate, overly attentive, overly positive and honestly, I loved her for it. There was no doubt in my mind her personality and willingness to accept me so completely weren't just the reason we were so close, but the reason we had been able to stay friends for so long at all.

It's not that there weren't other reasons we were friends, but I had been through hard times, and I feared I took way too many of them out on poor Emily. If it wasn't for that radiant personality of hers, she would have surely cut contact with me long ago.

"Yes, and I love our time together, but Spirit it would be nice if every night wasn't girls' night. Makes me wonder why I put in the effort to be in a relationship just to promise not to sleep with anyone else and have mediocre sex once a month," I said using her childhood nickname to offset my complaint. I had made up some lame excuse when we were kids that honestly, I couldn't even remember now, but it was because her spirit was what I saw and what I loved about her, but for some reason I could never tell her that.

“Mediocre, um, Imp?” she asked, replying with my nickname from the same time period. Which she had bestowed upon me saying if she was a spirit then I was an Imp always getting into trouble that somehow made life more enjoyable and worth wild.

“Well, you know I rounded up,” I replied and we both laughed rolling toward the center of the couch and against each other.

“So, for real, you’re such a cutie if things are such a mess, then why not call it a day?” She asked and the bluntness of that caused my chest to ache a bit. She wasn’t wrong, things weren’t great with Brent, and I had no particularly strong feelings for him, but besides being a workaholic, he was a good man, and we were slowly building a decent life together. I sighed heavily, took a deep breath and tried to organize my thoughts.

“He’s stable and you know.... I want to settle down and stuff I guess,” I said after my delayed response and careful consideration that was the best I could come up with which made me sad all over again.

“Well, that’s honest at least I guess,” she said and after so long together I knew she had wanted to make a joke and I admired the fact she had avoided the temptation.

“What if you invest years and he’s like every other man?” She asked and I couldn’t quite piece together what she was trying to say.

“Meaning?” Was all I could think to respond with. I was truly confused by this latest inquiry. What were all men like? I knew she had an unfavorable opinion of men overall. So honestly it could have been anything. She thought they prioritized their own self-interests and took advantage of the woman in their life. She thought they were greedy and fecal and most important prone to cheating. She thought no man could or rather would refuse a woman he was attracted to if he thought he could get away with it. That was my guess as to what she meant, but I needed to be sure.

“I could introduce him to a friend. She’s...” She started and trailed off, which I knew could only be bad.

“Who’s the Imp know,” I teased assuming she was playing, but her response made my stomach knot.

“Her name is Selia and I wouldn’t do anything, just introduce them. She’s always very available,” she explained.

“I remember. I believe she wanted to be available for you. How was that?” I teased, desperate to lighten the mode.

“I stopped dating men to get away from people who would sleep with anyone in the room. We stayed friends though,” she explained flatly, seemingly intent on pushing this subject to its end.

“Not needed, but I don’t control who Brent meets or what he does,” I finally said, releasing a sigh and rolling my eyes. I couldn’t help but feel our typical girls’ night was coming off the rails, but as quickly as it had derailed, she put it right again.

“Well, whateves, I’m here for you and it will sort itself out. Now romantic comedy or comedic romance?” She teased knowing my taste would allow for nothing else with the way things had been going with Brent, but she had caught me off guard, so I decided to return the favor.

“Let’s watch one of those raunchy girl love girl shows I know you watch on days when my dates actually show up.”

She looked at me, her eyes wide and her mouth a gap, “You, um, you won’t like them. It’s just romance and sex. No men, no comedy, and no light hearted approach to the subject. Babe, I love you and I know you want to support me as your best friend, but me getting turned on and you feeling awkward is not going to bring us closer."

She was always so honest and so blunt, but I couldn't let this go. I needed something different, "Fine, is there a middle ground. I need something different. Please Spirit find that perfect answer to make me feel better," I pleaded, playfully tugging on her arm and pretending to pout. She got up and pulled a dvd off of her shelf and put it in the player. Three hours later and I was laying in her lap crying. The movie was a low budget indie film that looked like the dvd's had been burned on someone's home system in the nineties, but the story was moving. It was about two women who fell in love, but circumstances kept them apart. One of them got cancer and confessed to the other on her death bed.

They had been in love, they had walked through life side by side, but never together. I cried not because of the tragic ending but because I knew out of cowardice that's not what I had been seeking. I envied that bravery. I couldn't tell Emily that, so I allowed her to assume it was for the tragic ending. Though she looked a little nervous by my reaction.

"You ok, Imp? You usually don't take fictional drama so hard," she asked, and I meekly nodded, but I made no move, and she let me stay there until I drifted off to sleep ever my rock.

PEOPLE DON'T CHANGE

I woke to find Emily sleeping, her head pressed against the back of the couch, hand resting on my cheek. I slowly slid off the couch and made us breakfast before I woke her. She left soon after for work and I was left waiting and wondering if Brent really was worth the sacrifice and compromise.

That very morning Brent texted me as if answering all my questions, "Hey babe sorry I've been distant lately swamped and not doing great balancing. You free? We can do lunch."

"At Emily's, you can pick me up," I responded, and this began a week of undaunted pursuit and affection by Brent. We ate lunch together three times, had dinner together six of the seven nights, had terrible rushed sex twice, and we even went and saw a movie I picked. On the eighth day he had a business dinner with a new client. He apologized and told me he tried to move it or something, but it was a big client, and he couldn't pass on the chance, but he'd make it up to me that weekend.

After the meeting, things changed. He took more face-to-face meetings with this one client then he did the rest of his client list, and he had already signed a six-month deal. He needed to be nice, but the hand holding didn't really make sense.

Meanwhile I was back on Emily's couch. The first night she was radiant as ever. She hugged me close and squeezed me hard, "So good to see you, babe," she said as she lifted me off of the ground and shook me slightly. Placing me back down, she smiled at me, but I thought I saw a tear in her eye.

"Well, he's back to the same old habits. If he's not careful this new client is going to work him to death," I complained. The night progressed with the same effortless cheer and silent comfort I had come to associate with Emily. The next week slowly changed though. At first it was small, we talked more and the movies started later. Then the conversation became constant even during the movie and passing out on the couch together. Then on Friday she stopped the movie halfway through.

"We started this one too late. I'm beat. I've never seen it so instead of falling asleep during it, let's crash out in my bed and we'll finish it with breakfast," she suggested and I agreed with a simple nod. The next night she did the same, but on Sunday night I was on the couch over complaining about a man that would never change so I had no conversation to start, but Emily sat further away from me then she had in years biting her lip and looking at me with the intensity of a predator who had just found the only prey in a thousand miles.

"Giselle, we'll be friends even if I mess up right?" She asked, the question terrified me, but I nodded meekly anyways, "Like even if I mess up really bad?" This time I had to think, what could she have done that had her concern about our relationship, but eventually I gave a stiffer more deliberate nod, "Thank God, um, I think Brent is cheating on you. The new client is Selia. I'm a horrible friend. I put him in a room with that predator, and I didn't even tell her he was involved. I just told her he was great with money and finding opportunities. Then I said I thought they could have a lot of fun together. I even gave her my best seductive wink."

"Well, I told you I wouldn't interfere so how do you figure you did wrong?" I asked genuinely confused. She had asked me before she did it and I knew if I had said no, she would have listened. More importantly I had avoided saying no. I mean that was the right response if I really trusted him without evidence. Maybe some part of me needed to know what he'd do if given a chance. To make my best friend feel better I decided to be honest that's what we had always done, "I think deep down I wanted you to test him. If you're right and he's failed, then we're done."

She smiled at this and I sighed. We each leaned into the center of the couch naturally coming to rest against each other. We giggled slightly, "Then what now, or do you want me to surprise you?" She asked and I couldn't help but muse that she really had become far more impish than me.

"What do you have in mind?" I questioned in curiosity.

"O' want to follow them?" She suggested shooting straight up, I plopped over as she did landing in her lap staring up at her excited face glowing in the lamp light.

"We are not stealthy enough for that."

"How about a sting?"

"You watch too many crime dramas, dope," I replied, swatting her playfully from her lap.

"You could... No never mind that's totally not you," she started then looked half embarrassed, half ashamed and I really wanted to know what was so bad she couldn't even bring it up. Then it clicked and I smacked her again.

"I don't even like sleeping with him. Wouldn't having sex with someone else just be punishment for me?" I asked, blushing and rolling to face away from her as I heard the words I was saying.

"Wait, it always feels like that?" She asked, seeming to have completely forgotten the original subject, "I thought it was weird you would settle for an ok guy that was a lousy lover, but you've never had a good lover?" She asked and the subject was getting a bit too intense for me.

"What, you have?" I teased swatting her leg and praying she'd let it go with a huff like she usually did when I retorted.

"Once, she was a horrible person, but she made my whole body weak."

Now I sat straight up, "Really, that good umm. Like see stars take a vow kind of good?" I asked, trying hard to pretend I was just being curious, but positive the interest and excitement were written all over me.

"Yup, but she was when I learned men didn't monopolize being selfish pigs, but at least the sex was earth moving. So, I'm on a mission to find a faithful woman I love who can make me feel half as good as she did. No luck so far. All my prospects are straight or involved. So, let's focus on you, doll," she explained and she now looked sad and defeated.

As her best friend I felt the urge to cheer her up, so I said the first thing that popped into my head, "Straight and married you could still get any girl with any sense. Spirit, you are the most amazing person I have ever known. Your love, passion, and acceptance are intoxicating."

"Yet......" She began, looked into my eyes, and clapped her hands, "Why didn't I think of this before, but we could have a girls' night. That will tell us whether he's cheating, probably," she was back to her usually radiant self, and I was once more confused and intrigued.

“What?”

“We can schedule a girl’s night out. Me, you, Selia, and a couple others. We ask regular questions. She loves to share her conquests. Good or bad she’ll want to talk.”

Her logic was flawless, but I couldn’t help but feel bad for Selia. Even so I let her set it up.

CONFESSIONS AND HISTORY

The week seemed to drag forever and mine and Emily's routine had become depressingly standard. Not that I didn't love spending time with my bestie, but my boyfriend had started to feel like a cover story more than a real person. We would talk every day. He would complain about the unreasonable demands of his new client while bragging how big it was for his career. He would barely even let me speak before he'd be gone again. I was so depressed that me and Emily would barely even talk, she'd just stroke my hair, and I'd fall asleep in her lap. She'd wake me when she got tired and she'd hold me while I slept. I thought 'I'll be fine once I know,' but the limbo of it all was driving me crazy. In typical Emily fashion she didn't make light, or criticize, or try to force her opinions onto me.

That weekend got shifted from girls' night to brunch as we thought the noisy crowd of a club would be harder to hear what we wanted to hear. It ended up being Selia, Tabatha (the girl who had made Emily weak all over), Gretchen (some stripper Emily had met while she was rebounding from some relationship), and then us. Emily said if all the girls were lose it would make it easier for them to tell stories about being slutty. She had way more experience and much better interpersonal skills then me so I trusted her on this completely.

It was a little awkward for me as these girls were all Emily's friends or exes, I was meeting them all for the first time. When we got there, they were all sitting around chatting already.

"O, yeah you were totally right. He had no hesitation dropping five figures for a trip. We had sex once the whole time and I didn't even spend most of the week with him. Great deal for me. He still sends me gifts and asks me to drop by again," some brunette with tattoos said then downed her drink in one gulp. She gestured for the waitress to bring another while some blond tart in a red spaghetti strap top and overly tan skin picked up the topic.

"That's nothing. I was dating his brother, and the moron gave me a car so I could keep coming around. All because I left the bathroom door cracked when I showered. I never slept with either of them," she said and all three girls were laughing now. It was obvious they were well acquitted.

"Hey ladies, been awhile," Emily greeted them, stepping slightly in front of me and taking a defensive posture.

"So, that's her," the blond said and tattoos elbowed her, "Sorry what I meant was, long time M."

The last girl to speak was a girl with jet black hair and a cold distant look in her eyes. She had a small frame and an innocent look. The kind that makes you instantly want to protect them. She was also the only one in the group I recognized. Selia looked me up and down as if deciding whether or not to let me join the table, "So your Brent's old lady. Sorry he really is bad, but if you take the lead and put in the work, he can get the job done. Plus, Emily introduced us, so I assumed she wanted us to sleep together for some reason, but since you're her... Well, I guess that makes sense."

"Her, who?" I asked, but I was looking at Emily.

"My very best friend. Don't worry about it. You got what you wanted to know, let's just have a good meal," she replied nervously in a way I had never seen. Like one wrong breath could implode the world.

"Nope you dragged us all out here to meet her for a reason. Time you explain to her. I mean come on you broke up with Selia before you guys even went out," Tattoos said and everyone was now staring at Emily.

"Fine, but can we sit down and get drinks first," Emily insisted which was weird because she doesn't even drink, "But for the record, regardless of what you all believe I'm not with any of you because you're as slutty as the men I used to date."

She sat, ordered two beers, and then asked me if I wanted anything. I tried to order a coke, but Selia said, "Nah, you're def gonna want booze, luv," with that in mind I ordered a glass of wine. Emily downed the first beer then looked at all the girls at the table except me.

"I hate you all," she said and they smiled wickedly, "They are talking about the fact they all think I broke up with them because I'm in love with you," she said and now she was looking at angry glares, "I'm sorry your lovely girls, but even if I didn't love her, we wouldn't have worked."

With that last line I found my hand drawn to hers, "Wait, what are you saying Emily? You love me, like love, love? Like sexual partners and stuff kind of love?"

"Yeah, and I've been a coward about it. It's kind of hard to tell your straight best friend that you love her. Especially when you relish every moment you spend together, but so many of those moments could be stepping over the line if you realized I find you attractive. I have never done anything with the thought of getting physically closer to you, just so you know, but yes, I would like to be physically closer with you, because I love you. I will continue to love you in whatever context makes you happy and lets us stay in each other's life," she said and with every word my hand tightened on hers.

I swallowed hard and then looked at Selia, "So, did she ask you to seduce Brent?"

"First no she didn't, but she knows what I'm going to do when introduced to someone. I'm the most promiscuous one here," she replied quite proudly, "Second no one had to seduce Brent. Also, I wasn't the only one. He even had me have a three way with him. Best sex we had. He was done in less than a minute, but the woman was a vendor's daughter. He had basically pimped her out to land the contract and I got to enjoy her the whole night. Brent never found the energy to go again. Not trying to hurt you.... Ok, maybe I want you to hurt a little. I mean Gretchen was honestly ready to turn over a new leaf and our girl wouldn't even try to make it work. She said a leopard can't change her spots, but we all know she chose you and that's the real reason none of her relationships worked. She's been in love with you for a really long time luv," Selia explained.

"Is this true?" I asked Emily looking in her eyes. My shock must have looked like panic as she averted her gaze before she answered.

"No," she said plainly, glaring at every other girl at the table in turn, "I'm only saying this because you deserve to hear it and you'll listen. I'm tired of telling these idiots anything. Even if I hadn't loved you, those relationships wouldn't have magically become a good fit. Mike just wanted someone to lose his virginity to. Jacob just wanted someone he could take home to his mom while he messed around with cocktail waitresses and strippers," she was explaining when Tattoos cut in.

“Yeah, that’s when we met,” she said and that’s when I was finally able to organize the names with faces. Gretchen was Tattoos so that left the blond to be the infamous Tabatha who had melted Emily completely.

I decided I didn’t need to hear about all the guys she had dated. I knew there had been a lot of them and most had stopped before they got physical, “I’m more interested in you three. Why didn’t any of you work out? What couldn’t you give my bestie?”

They all glared at me at this question and said in unison, “You.”

I flinched at the response but couldn’t help but give a soft pleased chuckle to which Emily squeezed my hand slightly.

“That’s not true. Gretchen cheated on our anniversary and Tabitha cheated the same day we slept together the first time. Selia was the best she told me when she asked me out, she didn’t believe in being faithful, but she said she’d always be honest, and she could love me, but I didn’t want to share my love.”

“Doesn’t that make you a hypocrite?” Gretchen asked, “I even offered to stop sleeping with other people if you would stop canceling on me to be with her. You slapped me and left that night. You didn’t talk to me until after you broke up with Tabitha.”

Emily was squeezing my hand tightly now as if she was afraid, I’d slip away.

“Emily?” I said my voice was quivering. She was my best friend, but to think she had been treating her partner with such indifference because of me.

“I offered to be with only you and I asked you to show me the same respect. Before you say anything Giselle it is not the same as Brent. I told them before we started dating, I would love them romantically. I would try to let go of my feelings for you, but you would always be my top priority. It might not be fair, and it is definitely a double standard, but it was also honest and upfront. That is why Selia and I are closer than I am with the other two, because they couldn't appreciate that. I didn't toy with them or lead them on. I know you can't love me back, but I hope we can stay close and I need you to believe I'm not like that," she was desperately rambling trying to help me make peace with what she had done to these women.

"Emily, I don't know how I feel about any of this, but I'm still your best friend and as long as you weren't nice to me just to get close to me, I think we'll be fine."

With that we finished lunch and we left. Back at Emily's we crashed back onto the couch and our same routine. I was surprised at the ease in which we fell back into our relationship. I even fell asleep in her lap again which was quickly becoming the only way I could get to sleep.

REALIZATION

It was more than a month since our brunch and I had learned the truth about Selia and Brent as well as the feelings Emily had for me. I hadn't officially broken up with Brent, but even when he had time, I would give reasons to avoid him and then go about my life with Emily. We were living as best friends and roommates. Even if her feelings ran deeper then I liked to admit.

However, that suddenly changed one night, "Gieselle love," Emily said, pushing me off of her shoulder to sit upright.

"Sup, babe," I replied without a thought. Though if I had been pushed to be honest, I had no idea how or when our nicknames had transformed into pet names.

"That and this. I can't. I've been giving you time to decide what you want to do, but the closeness and the pet names. With you knowing everything it feels like I'm being teased and tested all the time. We'll always be friends, but this has got to change. Boundaries or definitions, I don't know but something. I still enjoy being with you but sense you called me sweetie while handing me that towel the Monday after brunch, there's been this tension and anxiety building from uncertainty. I wanted to deal, but I haven't dated anyone since Tabitha. I swore I wouldn't date anyone again until I was sure they'd be enough to help me move on to make me forget. So, the pet names and increased intimacy it's too much," she dumped on me looking at me as if studying an alien.

"I had no idea, Emily. I'll be heading home then," I said, getting up and preparing to leave.

"Don't be so dramatic. I didn't say leave. I said boundaries. Like no leaning, holding, or petting. No hanging out while either of us has to be naked. Stuff like that. I mean I wish I could just fix this with you not knowing or me never having heard your sweet, sweet voice calling me sweetheart, like you were begging me to kiss the pain away. However, both of those things did happen. I don't want to lose you so please help me learn to live in this life," she was pleading now, but I was putting my shoes on.

"Maybe I was," I mumbled and she asked me to repeat myself, "Nothing, babe. Don't worry I'm not saying we're done. Just give me a couple days to figure out how we make it work," I replied and headed out the door, but I couldn't figure out how to make it work and I was ashamed of the distance that haunted us now.

I went home and, on the way, I texted Brent. I didn't want to be with him, but I couldn't be alone with my thoughts. There was no conversation, no explanation, no apologies. We just fell back into our same soul crushing routine, but I had already decided we wouldn't have sex. He was getting that other places and I didn't enjoy it. He came over most nights, and we went on dates on the weekends. I no longer thought about marrying him, but I still figured this would be my foreseeable future. Until one day me and Brent were on our date it had been three months since I had seen Emily and we hadn't talked in over two months, but on that night, she stood in front of me hands in her pocket face down and voice weak.

"Gieselle, how have you been," she said and then saw my hand in Brent's and stepped back. I winced at the pain I was sure she felt and even more at the fact that I hadn't been able to figure out how to fix things between us, “I see you figured things out. Good for you. Hope you’re happy luv,” she said though her voice lacked any of her characteristic support and warmth. It sounded hollow and warn and I ached for my involvement in extinguishing her light.

“Well, we’re late for dinner. We’ll have to catch up some time. I really do miss you, Spirit,” I said and she took another step back at the playful nickname I knew I no longer had the right to use, but trying to convey how much I genuinely still wanted her in my life.

“Sure, Imp. reach out I’m always here luv.”

That simply we parted ways once more. At dinner Brent was even more distant than usual and when desert and coffee was brought out, he questioned me about Emily, “Giselle, I’m glad you’ve come to value our date nights, but you went from dragging her along and making me feel like the third wheel to a conversation that sounded like a funeral notice. What happened?”

“I was in a rush Brent that’s all!” I said far sharper than I meant, and Brent glared at me. I could’ve admitted everything, or I could’ve let it go, but my mind was still on Emily and how everything was wrong between us now, so I blurted out what was on the top of my mind, “Look I don’t question you about your ‘friends’ so maybe butt out!”

With that our dinner was over. Brent went back to his place that night which he almost never did. Without him by my side I could not wrestle Emily from my mind. With sleep being ever allusive I settled down at my desk and pulled out my laptop and began to journal.

I wrote about the pain of losing Emily and the confusion of realizing we couldn’t stay as we had been. I wrote about the admiration I had for her little friend group who had always lived true to themselves. I wrote about things I had planned on doing with Emily that would probably now never happen. It was at this time the sun was rising, and I realized I had never mentioned Brent or a feeling of betrayal. So, I thought about what that meant and where my heart really was. Then I returned to journaling only this time I wrote about feelings I didn't want to admit I had and of fears that I had admitted them too late. Then I closed the laptop having organized all my thoughts and I wondered why I couldn't have done that three months ago when I promised Emily I would. I was a coward, but I would change, because I had to change or lose everything I ever cared about. First, I texted Brent, "You were right. We're done," That was it. Then I got dressed, bought muffins and headed for Emily's.

FRIENDS ALWAYS

I was standing outside of Emily's town house brushing my pristine skirt like there were crumbs that wouldn't come off. Finally, I gathered my courage and went up to the door and knocked. I waited patiently, I knew her well and if I wasn't there, she would be settling down eating something terribly unhealthy out of the microwave and watching something that past for romantic drama but was eighty percent sultry sex scenes between two women. When she didn't come out, I knocked louder. Those shows could get pretty loud and she could get caught up in them. I began to feel uneasy and decided to break down and call her. I hadn't wanted to because I was afraid everything would leak out when I heard her voice and this conversation, more than any conversation I've ever had before I wanted to have in person.

It rang only once, "Gieselle, twice in a week. I feel special. Feeling guilty. Just kidding luv. Look in the future you should message first though ok. Consider it a new boundary, ok. I'm on a date. I've promised to give this a real shot. I am moving on so we can be friends, but there will be ground rules. I hope you're happy for me and psyched about our renewed friendship, but message first, set a plan, execute the plan. Fair? Anyways, shoot me a message. We'll find time to meet up. I got to go luv."

With that she hung up. I never even got to say hi. I swallowed hard and messaged, "Can you call when you get done with the date."

She messaged back ten minutes later, "I can call tomorrow after she goes home," with a little winky face and devil emoji. My stomach curdled and my heart raced, but I could do nothing about it today, so I went home. I showered and then dropped to my bed telling myself, "Tomorrow I'll confess and everything will be fine," tomorrow came and so did the phone call. My voice hitched and my heart shattered. I had kept her waiting for so long that she had moved on and I worried her heart had followed. I had no right to interrupt that happiness and if I fractured our friendship further, she could disappear from my life forever.

"Sup, G?" Emily asked as I answered the phone late the next morning with a forced casualness, I had never heard her use and honestly it made me chuckle for a second before I regained my composure.

"So, is that our new thing, M?" I teased pleased with the ease we slid back into lighthearted banter, "I wanted to tell you..." I began, but then completely lost my voice.

"Tell me what?" Emily asked after I drifted off for a while.

"Right, umm, I'm sorry for the distance. I just didn't know how to go back and the idea of setting ground rules for the one thing in my life that was genuine and easy hurt, but I get it and I don't want to lose you. So, if you still are willing to be my friend let's talk about what you need," I offered and a tear fell down my cheek. I stifled the sobs I could feel. They would come, I was sure of it, but I could get through this call first. I had chickened out again, but at least she would still be in my life. I could cope with whatever she needed if I could hold on to this one reality.

"Sure, luv. Personal space. Arranged meetings. You can drop by or I can, but if we're not there no follow up calls. I can't feel like your everything. No risqué moments. Hugs are fine if their brief, shakes, and momentary touches too. More than anything if something feels like too much you need to respect that. Understand it's not me pushing you away or devaluing our friendship. Just like I know our time apart wasn't you condemning my lifestyle it was processing. Finally, we can't exclude partners anymore. We are both going to date. If we want to be part of each other's life, then it should be the whole life. Lastly the give and take can't be one sided. What do you need?"

I sat in silence for a moment, the truth running through my mind. *You all of you all of the time.* I had let that time pass and this was our reality now, so I settled on a half-truth, unable to deny it completely, "Just to hang out again."

"Great me and my new girl are doing casual pjs and movie day. Why don't you bring yourself over round lunch and we'll watch some rom coms."

"Sounds good," I replied and then continued in my head. *I can't wait to see you,* my darling.

The morning crawled by, but I eventually showered, got dressed in lazy loungewear, and picked up finger sandwiches before heading to Emily's. True to her word her girlfriend, a drop dead gorgeous, mocha skinned goddess, was sitting in her oversized armchair already watching something. Emily was making popcorn and putting together a cheese platter. I noticed there was no real food instantly.

"Emily, is your girl on a diet? There is no solid food here," I shouted to the kitchen.

"Well, I didn't want to compete with the sandwiches my bestie would be bringing to apologize," she replied casually as she walked in with the finished cheese tray in hand, "This is Monica. My girlfriend. She wanted to order pizza, but I told her to save that for dinner you would be bringing lunch. Don't worry she knows all about our history and she's cool with us. She did point out one more thing though, if you sleep over, it's the couch, luv. Sorry," she said and she sounded genuinely apologetic like she herself had never considered how far her rules would reach.

Emily settled on the end of the couch closest to Monica and I took a position on the other end. The distance felt immeasurable, but I forced myself to make pleasant conversation and focus on the movie. The sign on was still on the screen when Monica finally spoke, "Just a reminder of the rules. Personal space, that means the middle cushion is off limits. These boundaries are important. Let's enjoy," she said, smiling like she hadn't just smashed my world to pieces.

I stayed the whole day. We laughed, had fun and talked with a casual ease I hadn't ever experienced with anyone else. There was no doubt this relationship, even like this, was the best thing I had in my life and yet the pain and restlessness of it all tore at me. I didn't sleep over. Made up a lie about having an appointment in the morning. I could tell from her strained smile she didn't believe me, but I could endure the torment to be near her. It was the least I could do. She had done it for years, maybe longer, but I couldn't lay on the couch and watch the two of them disappear into her room together. Even if I could make myself believe they were doing nothing that had been my spot until I surrendered it.

This was our new routine three days a week and all-day Saturday or Sunday we would hang out. Sometimes Monica would be there, but often it would be just the two of us like old times, but even then, the taboo subjects and the invisible lines were suffocating. Still, I endured I had to, I owed us that much.

UNDERSTANDING RELATIONSHIPS

Slowly our routine gave way. Not deliberately and not all at once, but slowly I found it harder to commit to more plans and Emily noticed but didn't push. I couldn't help but wonder if her overly friendly nature had kept us friends through the hard times would her forced distance mean we were doomed. If so, she deserved freedom from all the trouble I had caused her.

At the same time, I became painfully aware of the hole her physical touch had left in my heart and my mind. On days when I couldn't bring myself to face her radiance I would go to clubs. Looking for someone that reminded me of her. They could look like her, or talk like her, even a sparkle in their eye that reminded me vaguely of her spirit I had fallen in love with way back when we first met. I had never admitted it until I journaled about those nights, but I didn't just love Emily I had always loved Emily. I would find these women and dance rubbing everywhere I wanted to rub on her, but I refused to cheat. I would not cross that line. So, the song would end, we'd part, and the shadows would push back in on my mind.

It became almost impossible to hold a conversation with Emily anymore. She asked me what was wrong once and I told her I was sad because I had to go on a long business trip. Even though we were just getting used to our new rhythm. I don't think she believed me, but she let it go. Since we started hanging out again, she always let it go. She was never pushy or blunt, never called bull shit. It was another thing that made me feel sad. Not because she did it, but because I had made it where she felt she had to. I had fled when she told me what she needed and now she feared any more resistance would shatter our now fragile relationship.

With loads of free time now that I had excused myself from Emily's life, I began to expand my night spots. I would now go to bars and drink until I couldn't stand and let some beautiful lady take me home. Where I would then dismiss myself and get sick in the bathroom. That always ended the night. On the rare occasion I didn't get sick I would fake it, but while they were taking care of me and I was too drunk to see clearly, I could pretend I was with her. I had been doing this for a month when I stumbled across a strip club on the way to the bar and I longed to see Emily's skin right after a shower glistening in the moonlight as she got ready for bed, but that would never happened again so in my desperation I decided a proxy should be fine.

I texted her as I often did, "Miss hanging out. Sorry been crazy. Hope you and the misses are well," I added a blowing a kiss and angel emoji and sent it. Then I went into the club. It was the first time seeing a naked woman outside of myself and Emily. I watched for three hours, got two private dances and a dozen lap dances and I felt nothing. I was preparing to leave when I saw some women I recognized gathered around two younger stripers and tossing large bills shouting loudly.

It was Emily's friends, so I went over to see them. I thought maybe they could give me insight to how Emily was doing, "What's up ladies?" I asked with as much excitement as I could muster.

“Umm. No offense dear, but what are you doing here? Did your new boyfriend drag you here, cause that’s gross. Even Brent wouldn’t do that,” Selia asked, not hiding her annoyance, but I was anxious and lonely and had been spiraling for over a month now.

“No, just drowning my sorrows,” I replied, my lack of energy and enthusiasm seeping out of me.

“In a strip club? You're straight,” Selia continued to badger me, and I was in no condition to withstand probing, so I folded instantly.

“Was, now I just desperately look for anyone who reminds me of the one I let get away,” I confessed and it felt great, even if it wasn’t the person I needed to confess to.

“Wait, what does that mean? Didn’t you blow Emily off to start a new relationship? That’s the story we heard,” Selia was leaning forward now the other two girls had turned their back on us much more interested in the entertainment.

“No, I gave her space to be with her girlfriend. I couldn't watch them together with all the rules. It just feels so forced and I don’t want to force her. If she needs to be free of me then that’s the least, I can do after taking too long to realize how I feel. It hurts, but maybe with time and enough booze I can forget. Even if I end up like you pervs,” I said chuckling slightly then sighing at the absurdity of it all.

“So, you love her? Like real love? You’re sure?” Selia asked and the other two girls were looking at her shaking their heads no, “Her new girlfriend is one of Brent's failed conquests. She’s staying there while she gets her life figured out in exchange for being a buffer between you two while you adjust to the new rules. You know she would have accepted you dropping the terms of endearment too, but she couldn’t have both and it still makes her swoon when you say sweetheart. She didn’t think she could hold back if she let you stay so close, but she will only ever love you. Just thought you should know.

If you don't see me again this is why. We all promised to be quiet and stay out of it, but you guys are chronically on the wrong page. So, I did my part. Make it work or let it fall apart. I'm getting a private dance bye," she said following a stripper she had clearly been waiting for back to the private area. I left and wondered if what Selia said could possibly be true. Then I thought back to all the time I forced myself to stay around them. I couldn't find one hug, peck on the cheek, not even a brushing of the hair. Then it dawned on me; the couch was a three-seater and yet she had never even sat with us. At the time I had assumed she was giving us our space, but we were supposed to avoid the middle of the couch, a reminder she had to issue more times than either of us would admit, but still she left it empty. Surely their relationship couldn't be that serious. I decided on the spot to drop by Emily's and they both were home.

"Come in for a drink," Monica said when she answered the door. Emily was showering, which made me nervous and jealous. If Selia was telling the truth I would think there would be reservations of coming out of the shower while Monica was just laying around the house. Twenty minutes later Emily came out fully dressed in pjs and I chuckled.

"Well, aren't you adorable," I said and Monica glared over her cup as if to warn me to not push, but pushing is exactly what I had come for today.

ACCEPTING FEELINGS

We talked and drank that night and I watched as they carefully orbited each other. Their boundaries maintained more rigidly than our own, "Hey can I crash here tonight? I'm a little lightheaded from the drinks," I lied, but I needed to push this to the end. Emily looked at Monica for approval which stung and then nodded yes. Sure enough, when they went to bed they went separately. No pretext of intimacy let alone physical signs of it. I decided that night I would confront Emily and tell her how I felt. I left the next morning after breakfast and began to plan.

Two days later I arrived at the park outside of Emily's neighborhood and I texted her, "In the park, need to talk, please!"

It took fifteen minutes and Monica texted back, "This is against the rules. Please respect our boundaries."

Our boundaries she had said and I was furious. I texted back without thinking and regretted it immediately, "I know everything. I need to see her. I promise I'll keep boundaries just ask her to meet me. I don't want to hurt her, I swear."

I waited another twenty minutes, and Emily appeared at the entrance to the small park, "What do you want? I really don't miss this selfish, demanding side of you," she said and that hurt, but I needed her even if she was upset now, I had to believe she'd forgive me.

"I know I'm late, but...." I began and raised a small velvet ring box in my left hand, "I've always loved you. I was scared and confused, but I've sorted it all out. If you still love me, I want to be by your side forever. If not, I'll still come by whenever you let me as a friend. Please if you can still love me let's be together, but even if you can't please never cut me out, I'll die," I said and I dropped to my knees crying holding the ring box in trembling hands.

"I could never cut you out. I get you want to go back, but this isn't the way back. It's the way into a world you're not built for. I've looked into your eyes for so very long and I've looked into the eyes of a woman when she hungers for another woman, and you have never had that look let alone that look aimed at me. Come over for dinner and be nice to Monica. She's a friend and she's helping. We won't mention this," she said and walked back towards her house. I followed her feeling broken inside. Not because she said no though that certainly didn't feel good, but because I had left her so certain I couldn't feel anything real for her.

I followed her to the house, but I wasn't done yet. As I walked, I hacked out a quick text message to Selia, "Need help to win Em, come to her place tonight with girls and wine."

I tucked my phone away and followed Emily back to her place. We made small talk and enjoyed the food and while Monica was clearing the plates a loud knock echoed through the house. Emily and Monica looked at each other, and I went and opened the door, "Selia, girls, come in," I said and showed them in, "She doesn't know I asked you to come," I whispered as Selia walked by.

"Brought wine, felt like catching up," Selia said meekly.

“You don’t do drop byes. What’s up?” Emily asked, taking the wine.

“Well after bumping into your girl at the club trying to shake you off her brain I just had to know if you guys finally kissed and made up.”

Wow she had told the facts I wanted her to but somehow picked the worst possible phrasing ever. Emily looked truly surprised by what she heard, “Wait, what club?”

“Dixie Line, it was Taby’s birthday, and we wanted to get some private dances. Your girl was there crying about how she needed to connect with someone that reminded her of the...” She was explaining when I cut her off.

“Ok, Selia, I only wanted you to tell her I was there. She doesn’t need to know everything,” I screamed before I realized what I had just admitted.

“So, you were invited by Imp. God you really are as mischievous as ever. Let them tell their story then I’ll decide your punishment,” she said with a playful flirtatious smirk I hadn’t seen in a long time.

I nodded and Selia continued, “Any way as I was saying she was trying to connect with someone that reminded her of the love of her life that she had let get away from her. We told her about you and Monica. We just want you two to be happy. She said she love loves you and I for one believe her.”

“Wine stays, you three out. Monica, would you be a dear and take them to dinner to thank them for the interference,” Emily asked and I was a little confused. I had heard she was straight and not her girlfriend, but this seemed to go beyond casually helping out.

“Sure boss, but don’t let her sweet talk your guard while I’m gone.”

With that the four of them left and I was alone with Emily. My curiosity overwhelmed me instantly, "Boss?" I asked and Emily looked away.

"Yeah, I thought you said you knew everything?"

"I was told she was one of Brent's exes."

"I see, so they told you half-truths. Selia may have you beat Imp," she said but she was grinning and chuckling.

"Look, I'm going to be honest with you, and I need you to be honest with me. Just for today, ok?" I asked, but I was really pleading for her to meet me halfway.

"Sure, until Monica gets back, I'll answer whatever you want, but you stay on your end of the couch. No matter what we say."

I nodded and wasted no time, "Why'd you change things? If you were sure we wouldn't end up together, why introduce me to them, you had to know what they would do. I mean one of them, maybe they'd do what you wanted, but those three together."

"Some part of me needed things to change. I hope that makes sense. I said it was the names, but it's been building for years. It gets harder to be casual every day. The lighthearted banter feels forced and heavy. I loved our friendship, and I prayed it would survive, but I know I couldn't survive the touch and intimacy of the woman I loved without reaching for more. I'm greedy. I would have took and took until I took too much and I destroyed us, so I needed boundaries, but I didn't know how to bring them up. I thought when you heard how I felt you'd pull back, but you didn't, you leaned into me and it scared me. I thought I could take you and you might let me and maybe that was close enough to love. I hated myself for that and I've been punishing myself since then."

"Why don't you believe me when I say I love you?"

"Because, if you loved me how did you break my heart so many times and never know?" she replied tears were spilling down her face and my heart was breaking.

"Same way I broke mine without noticing," I replied, tears were spilling down my face now as well, "I closed my eyes to the things I didn't want to see. You were my best friend, and I needed you in that role. When I heard you were gay my heart fluttered and I told myself it was surprise, but the truth is I've loved you for as long as I can remember. You know I journaled when I was having problems with Brent. For weeks I wrote my feelings, my fears, and my dreams. One day I read over it, and I hadn't mentioned Brent once. In fact, I hadn't mentioned a single love interest. There was only you and that's when I realized I loved you not as my friend, but as my everything. It made sense right away when I thought about it. You were the only person I wasn't related to I ever said I loved you to without being prompted or trying to shut down an argument. Guess I got off topic, but my point is ignorance. I refused to face what was right in front of me for fear of losing what was right beside me. I can't apologize enough."

She put out her arms for a hug and my chest tightened, "I can't," I replied and she beamed with a smile. I knew for all her calling me Imp she was just as inclined to mischief and that had been a test. If I had hugged her then I wouldn't have been capable of keeping a simple promise and I didn't know where that would leave us, but I knew most of her didn't want that. We talked easily until Monica got home. I explained how I had already loved her when I named her spirit and she told me she fell for me when I had invited her to my junior prom despite her family demanding she take a respectable suitor. She also clarified Monica had been tricked by Brent, but when they met, she had hired her as a personal assistant.

When Monica came in Emily beamed and pulled my head into her lap, "You did good. We're going to be fine babe," she said and leaned over me and kissed me. Monica sighed deeply.

DREAMS REALIZED

The dam broke that night and we fell into each other. Monica left as we started making out on the couch and when we moved to the bedroom she still hadn't returned. She taught me how to make a woman's body melt, and I showered her with my love and enthusiasm. With her guidance we both finished multiple times despite my inexperience. She was the Emily I knew again. Whatever I thought I could say and all of my feelings were validated with a single embrace of her arm. When we finished and the sun was rising outside, we slept in the exact same positions we had when we were friends.

When we rose in the morning Monica was in the kitchen cooking eggs and bacon with orange juice.

"I took the liberty of pushing all your meetings for the day. You broke your word. You said she was in the past; it wasn't going to be an issue. Your father is not going to be happy," she sounded different today and more importantly I realized that at some point during our fractured relationship she had taken over for her father in charge of the family business. Monica made a lot more sense now, but Emily had fought her father for years on taking over so why had she given in.

"I don't really understand the problem? When'd you take over for your dad? Thought you were never doing that. You needed more freedom," I was confused and afraid I had messed things up already

"Don't worry, babe, I went back, because with the new rules I didn't need to be on call for you. We had boundaries. I had never refused; dad wouldn't give me the company as long as I was prioritizing you over the company. If he takes it back, I'll go back to freelancing, but she won't be a problem, Monica. She'll support my dream. Right, babe?"

"I'll do what I can, but I can't do much and I'm thoughtless and kind of selfish," I admitted sheepishly.

That night she told me her dream was to run a company in a way that would make her grandfather proud. She had gotten into business, because of his influence and she was hoping to make her dad proud as well, but her dad was complicated.

"I haven't missed a single meeting, and the business is flourishing. What's the problem?" I heard Emily shouting into the phone two days later when I came in.

Monica was sitting on the couch, "You did this," she said as I entered the room and I sighed heavily, because some part of me knew she was right.

I was debating what to say when Emily's voice cut through the room again, "Fine we'll be there," she screamed and then I heard the phone strike the wall. I rushed to Emily's side, but before she paid me any attention, she looked at Monica, "Are you mine or his?" She asked in a demanding voice.

"I was brought on by your father. My loyalty belongs to me though. If you have a good plan, I owe him nothing. Does that answer suffice or are you firing me?"

"If I tell you what I plan, will you promise not to take it back to him?"

"I'm curious. You're good, so ok," she replied.

Then Emily finally looked at me, "Things got messy, babe. Can you make food while I talk to Monica? Then we'll all talk over dinner."

I didn't answer. I didn't need to. I went into the kitchen and began to prepare food for three. When the food was done, we ate. The conversation was all business. Monica had agreed to stay with us. She had nothing to lose her position was to keep Emily in line, failing to do that her job with the company would come to an end either way. In short, if we couldn't keep control of her father's company, she would take the out clause and use the buyout to start her own company. Either way I would be included from now on. If I'm being honest the insistences in my inclusion weren't needed, but it felt amazing.

It was lunch the next day in Emily's office. Me and Monica were sitting in chairs to the side of the office. Emily was moving through paperwork with speed and efficiency I had rarely seen her use. Someone knocked tentatively on the door then opened it.

"Your father is in conference room three. He is requesting you there. He has several board members and a lawyer with him," she said with a sheepish tone that was barely audible.

The three of us went to meet him and to see if this was our company or our end. We entered, sat in silence, not even a greeting and then her father spoke, "So you're the distraction that has derailed a legacy. You know what legacy means, right? Immortality," he said bluntly and coldly, "Well until some ignorant selfish brat decides she can piss it all away. This building was here since the birth of the city, and it will be here when this city crumbles into dust and is cataloged into the history books. That is what true legacy looks like, and it will not be undermined by your kind," he said, his tone getting sharper with every syllable. As he spoke it finally clicked for me. He didn't have a problem with me, but the fact that Emily hadn't found a man. I looked at Emily, had she agreed to find a man in order to get the company. She looked away from me, and I was certain that was exactly what had happened.

"Look, father, nothing really has to change. You told me I just needed a child with our last name. I can adopt or something, you can have an heir, it's not that big of a deal."

"Seventy percent of our clients are conservative. Old family money and old family values. Do you really believe this is the same as what we discussed?"

"Things are different now, father, can't you accept that?"

"I do and I love you, but this is business. Here's your check. I know your heart; I won't try to sway you. End of the week I'll turn things over to someone for now. You're brilliant, you'll do well, but not here. I will adopt someone and make them the heir. You are free. Let's have dinner sometime," he said and his words were absolute and he didn't wait for a response. He stood and left followed by the men who had sat beside him. It was over.

We never discussed the settlement or her feelings on the termination. Instead, we turned our attention to our future. She had made a living making deals putting up and coming entrepreneurs with like-minded venture capitalists and she had no intention of changing now. What would change was our approach and our demographic. We would help smaller companies find gap funding mostly for short falls. Focusing on roi instead of acquisition metrics.

I was proud of her growth. I knew neither her day job she had before nor her role with her family company had made her happy and that was all I had ever wanted. We spent the next week cuddling late, filling in dream boards to figure out exactly what we wanted, and making calls to get our first office and clients ready at the same time. Everything was set and it was the Friday night after the last of the paperwork had been signed. Our offices still weren't ready, so we were in a locally owned restaurant in a private room. We had just brought financing in to keep a whole neighborhood going while they rebranded. It was a risk. If they could turn things around, they would secure futures for the whole neighborhood. If not, our investors would buy out their business for next to nothing and own the neighborhood.

The investors were betting on them coming up short, so they had given them favorable terms on the loan to secure equally favorable terms if things went their way. We had warned them of the risk, but they really had no choice and their rebranding was a good strategy. It was a very clean scenic shopping district with B&Bs and a park. Perfect for weekend getaways. We helped with the plan and the implementation. We connected them to several travel agencies and even advertised bus trips. Adjusted pricing models for tourist mind set and at the end it was a huge success. We did thousands of deals after, but none ever touched us like that first one. After they had paid everything back and built up two years of business expenses for their joint contracts, they gifted us a house. It's where we still live eighty percent of the year.

Two years later we were celebrating our one hundredth deal when Emily proposed. After that our life was a whirlwind deals and wedding prep consumed our every moment and eight-teen months later we walked down the aisle. It was a small ceremony everyone who loved us was there, but we kept the business separate. Monica officiated and her dad gave her away. We took time off for our honeymoon but got dragged back for what Emily called a once in a lifetime opportunity.

For the first time in our long relationship, I was upset with my wife's business acumen. When we got back into town though we were greeted at the airport by a social worker and a newborn baby. It was a private adoption request from someone who had seen us in the news. She said she wished she had moms like us and wanted to give her baby her best future. We happily signed the papers and named the baby MiRai Kibou which was Japanese for future hope and to us she was. After that we worked less delegated more and doted on our precious daughter. When I look back, I can’t think of a life lived better.

MY HUSBAND'S MISTRESS IS MY GODDESS

DISCOVERIES

I had been working overtime lately and instead of being upset or asking me to try to get out of it like he used to, my husband seemed almost glad. I tried to tell myself I was overthinking he had just adjusted to the fact that sometimes my job needed me to go above and beyond. We always went on a vacation when things settled down so maybe he was just looking forward to that. One day the system crashed and we would all be free until it was back up. I got dinner from his favorite restaurant and headed home. I no sooner opened the door, and I knew all my worst fears were real. My husband was having an affair, and he wasn't even being cautious or reserved about it. The food slipped from my grip as I entered my house, their enthusiastic screams echoing through my home. I wanted to turn and flee, to run far away and never look back, but I needed to see, to know.

I snuck up the stairs and slowly pushed open the door. There on our bed was my husband behind a woman. She had skin that looked like coffee with too much cream in it and breasts large enough they swayed with every thrust of my husband's passion. She was toned and glistened with sweat, but her face was what really caught my attention. She was moaning and her eyes were shut but, in her expression, there was a softness, a vulnerability, something akin to longing and loss. I wanted to know more, and I found myself standing there transfixed, not watching them have sex, and not gathering courage for a confrontation, but studying her face and body.

She was fucking my husband. Objectively I should be furious, I should hate her, maybe even want revenge, but I was captivated. Her face in between moans would show glimpses of her raw emotions and none of them said love or attraction. There was no desire or deception. I would see despair, self-loathing, a current of warmth that looked like it wanted to embrace the world until it felt better, and dread. I backed out slowly, went downstairs, picked up the food, and went out to the car. I picked up my phone and texted Brian, my husband, "Systems down. Picked up food. Home in twenty."

Fifteen minutes later he walked the beautiful woman to the door and leaned in for a kiss, she stepped back, shook her head no and walked to her car. I was parked down the street filming the whole thing. Not for divorce, though that was coming, for research. I needed to know who this captivating woman was and why she was spending evenings with my husband. As soon as she left, I pulled up in front of the house.

"Hey, it slid off the seat, but I think it's still edible," I said, holding up the messed-up bag of take out and delivering the prepared excuse I had come up with. He took it with what appeared to be a forced smile, but I could have just been projecting. After all, if I was making love to her and he had interrupted I would have to fake the smile that followed. I should have been embraced or trying to deny these thoughts, but he had broken his vows and betrayed my trust so I could see no reason to force my feelings aside. The system was down for three days, but I didn't tell Brian that. I left every morning like I was going to work. First, I hired a private eye to figure out who the woman was. He probably thought I wanted proof for the divorce, but I had no intention of getting this entrancing beauty caught up in my divorce. Next, I started the divorce proceedings. Then I spent the rest of my time seeing how entwined these two had become, but what I found surpassed all my expectations. The beautiful goddess that had entranced my heart was not the only woman my husband was bringing into our marital bed. The first night was a blond, the second a girl with jet black hair in waves, on the third my wild goddess finally reappeared. Still looking somehow reluctant to be there, but obviously excited by his touch. I had a name now it was Misha and she was his secretary. She had been promoted a month ago and before that she had been on the verge of being fired. Paperwork errors that cost the company millions were blamed on her. No evidence, but stories of convenience often win in the corporate world.

He had shielded her, then elevated her, then manipulated her into being his plaything. I was disgusted by this man I thought I loved just days before. Now I knew I had felt settled in a life filled with illusions and now that the light was on and the props revealed I could never go back.

On the fourth day I went back to work. I was working even more overtime now, but I had the private eye taking photos of every woman my husband brought home and gathering evidence of what they were doing. I told him not to watch him with Misha but get pictures of her going in and out. He seemed confused but followed my orders. Meanwhile I also had him figuring out Misha's schedule. I know it was a little creepy, but I wanted to meet Misha and hopefully before she learned who I was. I'm sure he thought it was some kind of confrontation I was trying to put together, or I wanted to trick her into helping me ruin him, but I didn't need her help to ruin him and if I wanted to confront her, I would have to take sabbatical from work or rent a lecture hall for all the women who had appeared in his life.

"So, from what I can tell the parade of women are one time. He picks them up through dating apps or bars sometimes. When he doesn't have someone and you'll be gone he brings Misha in. She doesn't seem to have much say in it though she does make him wear a condom. She knows about the other women," Jermey, the private eye explained to me. We were sitting at a table at a small cafe near my work on my lunch break, "She takes lunch by the fountain near there building. If you still want to confront her that's the best spot."

I nodded. I had explained several times I just wanted to meet, but like all the other men in my life he never listened when I spoke. After lunch I talked to my boss, and we agreed I didn't have to come back after lunch tomorrow, but I had to make up the hours tonight. I did data entry and all information needed to be caught up by the end of each quarter so their quarterly reports would be accurate.

I texted Brian and he quickly replied with fake sympathy, "That's rough babe, but I'll be strong."

I could imagine him tripping over himself figuring out what he would do with all that extra free time. I could only hope he had a girl lined up and I had not forced Misha into a longer than usual night with him. I finished at one and decided there was a little hotel a block away. I would crash out there for a few hours instead of driving home. My nervousness wouldn't settle down as I prepared to meet the girl of my dreams.

LOVE AND OBLIGATIONS

I approached Misha at the fountain and sat down next to her. I thought I saw shock for the briefest moment, but it was gone in an instant, so I told myself I imagined it and I moved on to introductions, "Hi, I'm..." I began, but Misha cut me off.

"I know who you are. You're Brian's wife. What brings you here today ma'am?"

"How do you know Brian?" I asked, flustered, but trying to cover.

"I think you know. I'm Brian's secretary. Are you finally ready to confront me? I don't regret it so you know, and you can't slut shame me. I get why you're upset though. I have a hospitalized mother and a baby daughter. Brian offered me away to keep us all safe and taken care of. There was nothing more to it for me. In fact, I'm gay," She explained and that last confession pushed the air from my body.

"R-really?" I stammered the question, and she looked back at me with confusion, "What's your type?" I asked before I could stop myself.

"You wouldn't believe me. I promise I'm in love with someone who is unavailable and it's not your husband. I've known about your investigation for a while now. I'll stay out of your way, and I'll accept my consequences. Whatever they are."

“Do you know I have a video of Brian with every woman he’s slept with for over a month?” again, that look of confusion held her face and she waited patiently for me to continue, “Except you that is. There are some pictures certainly, but I have no intention of getting you involved in my divorce. I didn’t even intend to tell you who I was until we were friends, but o well. I took this afternoon off. Would you care to play hooky with me? I do want to get to know you better.”

“Why? I’m your husband’s mistress,” she inquired, not pulling away, but looking visibly unsettled by my interest.

“I saw you guys fucking and honestly I want to take you on a date,” I said, my honesty catching both of us off guard.

“So, you want to see me naked again?” Misha asked bluntly and I blushed at the accusation. I had to admit she wasn’t wrong, but I needed her to know there was far more to it than that, “It was your face, I mean your body is lovely, but it was your face that entranced me. I could see so much there just waiting for someone who wanted to see it and I do want to see it all.”

“God, you're like your husband. I told you I’m in love.”

“Yes, but my research shows you love being at my house and I know firsthand you got truly turned on when you were with my husband. So, I’m hoping maybe I’m the girl you love and if not, we can still be friends and if you can’t be with her.... Well, I just might love you enough to overlook the fact you don’t love me back. Unlike my husband though, I'm not going to propose anything beyond getting to know each other. I’ll tell you upfront unless I learn something I don’t like. I'd be open to hearing anything you’d propose, but that is for you to decide. So, what do you say?”

“Sure, let’s catch a movie and hang out.”

"Both of our lives are complicated right now," she said as we were waiting for the waiter to bring our wine. We had watched a movie, went for drinks and now we were at a restaurant preparing to have dinner. Her phone buzzed and she picked it up shaking it without reading it and began speaking again, "If you settle your divorce and I free myself from your pig of a husband and land on my feet it would be nice to get to know each other," then she read the text out loud.

"I know you wanted some time, so I gave you your half day, but my date backed out, and you know how I get when I miss a release. Be here in an hour. I took new pictures. I know how that gets you in the mood," her face blushed a deep crimson and I could tell she wanted to be transparent, so she didn't bother reading the text in advance. Now she regretted how open she had been.

"What kind of pictures does he use to get you in the mood?" I asked again my mouth seemed to be moving on its own. She seemed to have that effect on me.

"You, sleeping usually. Though he has taken some of you in the shower, changing, and stuff like that."

I wanted to be offended; I wanted to be angry. The violation of my personal space and the intrusiveness of it all. I should feel violated or creeped out at the very least, but I was flattered and a little turned on. Sure, I was disappointed she had slept with my husband, but knowing I was the catalyst that made her able to do that was flattering in a way I can't fully express in words.

I picked up my phone and typed, "Work wrapped early see you soon," I ended it with an emoji blowing a kiss. Less than a minute later her phone buzzed again, and she hesitated for a moment. Who could blame her after her accidental reveal.

“Forget it. Your girlfriend's on her way home. If she was as passionate with me as you get when I tell you about her, I wouldn’t even need you. Tomorrow, I guess. Maybe you can...” she was reading and then trailed off.

“Look I’m kind of obsessed with you so maybe we shouldn’t hang out,” she admitted and I snatched her phone.

“Wear her underwear or something. I know how you like to be close to her. God you’re a freak,” I read.

“So, it is me you love then?” I questioned daring her to own this simple truth. She nodded meekly and I smiled with intense satisfaction, because after one afternoon with her I was quite sure I loved her too.

We talked for a while. The baby daughter she mentioned was a niece left by her junkie sister. Her mom had Alzheimer’s and required around the clock care which my husband was paying for. She had a neighbor that was basically coparenting the baby girl. She was a stay-at-home mother raising three children already and Misha gave her money to help out. Brian was also providing that, so it wasn’t hard to tell why she felt the need to keep her word to him.

“I don’t want the woman I love sleeping with my dick of a husband. If I can keep you from having to, will you stay away from him personally?” I asked her with an almost desperate pleading tone I couldn’t keep out of my voice.

“I’d go as far as saying if you could make that work, I would be grateful. I mean not grateful enough to rush into a relationship with you, but honestly, I’ve wondered what curling up on the couch with you on a cold winter night under the same lap blanket would be like for a while now. We get through all this. I think we definitely could see if what we think is there is real.”

I typed quickly, “Traffic sucks. Totally stressed, be a doll and run me a bath.” I could play with him like this as much as I wanted and he would always have to cancel whatever plans he had even if he stopped believing me, because if I showed up his life was over. I would be leaving regardless, but he didn’t know that, and I had to keep it that way until I figured out a way to make sure Misha landed on her feet.

After that text we turned to more lighthearted subjects. What kind of movies, music, and books we liked. Our favorite restaurants and dream vacations. Eventually my phone buzzed, “Not sure what happened. If you need something I’m here. Baths ran; I'm laying down.”

We talked for another hour then went our separate ways.

FIRST STEPS

I called in to work the next day. I had over two months of pto at work and I needed to get this all sorted out. I went to talk to the lawyer they were starting to think I was backing out. I wanted them to do a forensic audit and see what I could get if I gutted him. I needed to make sure I could take care of Misha while she figured things out. I wouldn't be rich, but it would be seven figures so I would be able to take care of things for a while.

I texted Misha as I was leaving the lawyers office, "Want to see you. I think I have an answer. Can we have lunch?"

She sent back an animated emoji given a thumbs up and I made a reservation. It was a romantic spot that was basically deserted during the lunch hour. I had preordered and timed everything. It was her lunch hour after all and I knew she wouldn't risk upsetting Brian until she was convinced, I had a plan, and her family would be taken care of.

I picked her up in an uber and we went to the restaurant that was less than five minutes away. Like I said lunch hour, so location had been key. The food was on the table already when we walked in, but it was still steaming.

"I wanted to have a conversation, so I went ahead and ordered based on what you told me last time. It might not be what you're in the mood for and I promise I will not make this a habit, but I wanted to respect your time," I said wanting to explain myself. Fearing another comparison to my husband.

"I get it, you love me and want to take care of me. So, what did you want to discuss?" She was so casual about it all that it sent a shiver down my spine.

"I talked to my lawyer. If we invest cautiously and live modestly both of our houses could function for close to five years without accounting for any money, we each might earn. If we combined expenses, we could add another two years. That's with the most conservative settlement. No strings attached I'll support you as long as you don't manipulate me or betray me. What do you say? Will you trust me to be better than him?" I asked and I hated saying it, but honestly, I didn't know how else to say it.

"I think I'm starting to trust you more than I should," she admitted. She leaned into me and I let her. She hugged me quickly and sincerely, "I can't wait to see where things between us go. I had better head back to work. I can't betray him until you win, but I'm on your side. If I had known, you would like me back I would have approached you ages ago," she said and then clamped her hands over her mouth as if she could somehow scope her words back into her mouth. I looked at her funny and she quickly relented, "You picked him up from his interview when he got promoted. Took him out to celebrate or that's what he told everyone at the office. I saw you then and I was done. I mean I had been gay since I was in high school, but I could feel the shift. I didn't want a woman anymore I wanted to be closer to you. It's how I ended up on your husband's radar and eventually blackmailed into his bed. He didn't give me money at first. He had photos of me watching you. He was going to tell you and hr. Back then I could have dealt with hr. I was all alone with no bills, but the idea of you knowing how I was looking at you and you actively avoiding me. I couldn't take it and like the coward I am I gave in to his demands which became more and more outlandish. I disgust myself."

"We're going to get through this, and I don't blame you, I'm not disgusted, or anything by you. I'm enchanted and fascinated. I can't wait to get to know more about you and be closer with you," I told her, reaching out and patting the back of her hand, "let me drive you back now. Do you know if it is you or another girl tonight and do you want to have dinner?"

"No idea, but if he doesn't drag me to your place, I would love to have dinner, but don't you have overtime?"

"He's enjoying this time so much he hasn't bothered paying attention quarter end was yesterday. He should start to question all the hours, but he doesn't care."

"Sorry," she responded as we got into the uber. I leaned against her without thinking and she let me with a smile on her face.

"You know I could just keep you to myself and let him foot the bill for everything until he figures it out," I said half joking as I realized he hadn't touched me in months and if I kept him from Misha there was no real reason to disrupt are mutual lie and deception, "Not forever, but if you wanted instead of risking things with the courts we can make sure everything is taken care of before I leave him. You could tell him your baby needs more of your time, and you want to spend more time with them. Then offer to be his maid instead of secretary. I bet he'll move you in happily. Thinking he'll get more time with you."

"Wouldn't that make it harder to prevent him from stealing moments with me. I want to be done with him as soon as possible, but I need to be sure my family is taken care of. I trust you to decide what we should do," she gave me her opinion as she stroked her hand absentmindedly threw my hair. I was touched by her faith and her honesty.

We had dinner that night and every night that week. I had only had to cancel his moves twice and on the second time he had called me a liar. I sent stock photos I had taken in traffic jams and tore into him, "Honest faithful people have trust, deceptive manipulators have doubt. Are you keeping something from me that you would doubt me when I've always been honest with you," He lost his will to argue then and he didn't reach out to me again that night. I stayed at Misha's and finally met her daughter. She was a ball of joy, and she slept soundly between us and in the morning, I played with her while we waited for Misha to wake.

When she finally woke up, I smiled brightly and touched the side of her face, "I would love to spend my free time with you. For this weekend can we pretend there are no other concerns and just enjoy each other?"

"As long as you can get time away from him that doesn't result in my presence being demanded, I'm all yours," she responded, trying to play it down, but I could see the joy on her face.

I shot a text, "Retail therapy you really hurt my feelings last night. Meet me for brunch, you can make it up to me. I'll send you a pin."

I sent a google pin for a little diner he had been promising to take me to and set my phone aside. Then I asked Misha, "Want to take Tabby to the park? I think she'd love the baby swing and it's a great place to talk."

She nodded and we got dressed to start our weekend together.

A WAY FORWARD

The weekend was great by the middle of the first day he had given up texting me, but I got an update from the pi. He had gone to a strip club that was known to higher escorts. I thought how the mighty had fallen but gave it no more thought. Sunday after I had dinner and rocked little Tabatha to sleep, I reluctantly headed home, "I think we can't do this for long. It aches having to leave, but I will make sure you are all protected in anything I do," I said and gave her a quick kiss on the cheek. We still hadn't been physical, but we had been more intimate than me and my husband had ever been.

When I arrived, the house was empty, and I texted the pi, "He hasn't left the club and attached hotel all weekend."

Then I texted my husband to see what he would say. His first response was predictable, "Ran out babe, be back soon I've missed you."

"I've been home since 10a.m. so where was this errand to?" I responded and now he responded with anger and hurt.

"You stopped texting yesterday. You blew off our brunch, so I was upset, got drunk and rented a hotel room. I was embraced and didn't want to tell you," he said, trying to sound apologetic, but failing miserably.

"That's fine I know I've been neglecting you lately and I did let this weekend fall apart. Can you forgive me?" I typed back and then my phone rang. I answered it without a thought.

"Babe, thanks for appreciating the effort I put into our relationship. Let's go shopping together next weekend. We can get a hotel room and make a mini vacation out of it. Couples message the whole works."

"Sure, sounds nice. Will you be home tonight or are you going to work from the hotel in the morning?"

"The rooms already paid for so if you don't care probably just crash out here. I'm pretty tired to be driving."

"Ok, love you."

With that I hung up before he could respond. I didn't need to hear him say it; I didn't want to hear him say it. With that I called Misha, "He's at a whore house. Can I stay over?"

"Of course, Tabby misses you already."

With that I was back out the door and at her place in no time. We went right to bed, but it felt like home. The next morning, I stayed at the apartment with Tabby and gave Misha a kiss, not a peck like we always had in the past, but a full passionate kiss packed with desperation and longing. I couldn't hold my desire for this woman at bay any longer. That day as Tabby napped I made a plan, and I contacted my lawyer. I moved assets to Misha's name. She was my husband's mistress so his legal options would be minimal and any of them would ruin his reputation. It included a half a million-dollar trust for Tabby and a two hundred-thousand-dollar medical savings for her mother. I personally would get far less this way, but Misha could see my firm resolve in protecting her.

I shot Brian a text around 1p.m., “Another day of overtime. Can probably get out for a late dinner if you want to meet up at 8 o’clock.”

Ten minutes later, “Days been crushing think I’m going to grab food on way home and crash out.”

Twenty minutes later Misha called, “What did you do? He’s losing his mind talking about how you’ve ruined him and you must be having an affair, being swindled by a conman.”

“Misha, sweetie, he’s not really wrong. He’s ruined and I am having an affair, but don’t worry I don’t think you’re conning me and I’m only making good on his promises. I’ll show you all the details when you get back. Love you have a good day at work.”

“I’ll trust you. I love you,” she said and I could tell it was a conscious choice to place her trust in me, and it hadn’t been easy. I would be sure to be worth that trust.

She came home a little early and as she came in the door, she smiled at me holding Tabby and reclining on the couch, “God you two really make days like this feel worth it.”

“Well, you only have to make it until the end of the week. This weekend you should start looking for another job. Consider working from home or part time. For now, come look at this,” I said, pulling a lap-top from the end table to rest on the couch beside me.

“Here give me her and bring up what you want me to see,” Misha requested, extending her arms. I handed her Tabby and brought up the banking tabs I had set up earlier. Her eyes bulged and her mouth dropped for a moment, “How did you set these up? That takes a lot of personal information.”

“Brian is lazy. All the details he used to take care of you guys in the past were with our banker. So, I just authorized the accounts, and he set them up right away. I checked with my lawyer, and I used an email attached to my husband that I have access to, so the odds of him pressing the issue is less than one percent and even if he does the transfers were initiated by him for his mistress, he has no case. Now you guys are taken care of as well as he would have been able to do himself."

"I see so this is why he's freaking out."

"Probably it's almost a million dollars. I'm sure he's noticed it, but it will take him a while to put the pieces together and by the time he does, we will have moved on. This weekend I'm serving him the divorce papers."

"Great, so what do you want to do for dinner?"

With that we settled in as a happy family enjoying each other's company. I couldn't help myself and at the end of the night I stayed over. I was hopelessly addicted to being part of this family.

The next morning, I waited until Brian would be at work and went home with Tabby in tow. Suddenly my phone buzzed and I answered it.

"Hey babe, don't go home," Misha said the second I picked up.

"What?" I replied pulling over. I was only three blocks from my house.

"Brian didn't come in today. Took a personal day."

"Thanks for the warning, I'll take Tabby to the sitter and go see what's up."

I took Tabby to her neighbor who was all too happy to receive the bundle of joy. I then made my way back toward my house. I went inside and found Brian in our room looking for incriminating evidence or something. Clothes were tossed about, and the bedding was laying on the floor. It honestly looked like a home invasion.

"What is going on here?" I asked and he turned to look at me. His eyes were red like he had been crying until just recently and his face was contorted in anger.

"I know," he said and I looked at him in utter confusion, "You stole from our joint accounts. You're having an affair. You betrayed me."

"Honey, you sound unhinged," I replied in mock sympathy. I hoped he heard it for what it was a taunt.

"Unhinged then what did you do with my money?"

"I think you mean our money, babe. How much is missing?"

"Almost a million. Are you saying you know nothing about it?"

"No, should I call the bank and get to the bottom of it?"

"N-no. I'll look into it. Maybe I'm over-thinking it. Clerical error perhaps or an investment I forgot about."

He was back pedaling quickly. Obviously realizing if I looked into this money, I'd see what he had been doing with our money.

"Well, I came home to gather some valuables that are just collecting dust. I'm sending them to a charity auction for abused and exploited women," I told him smiling brightly. Letting the subject switch like I trusted him to get to the bottom of things and keep me informed.

We then spent the rest of the day packing up over a million dollars' worth of jewelry and antiques and preparing them for the auction company to pick up. The proceeds of course all would go to my girlfriend that he had been exploiting. So, it wasn't a complete lie.

SETTLING ACCOUNTS

I had decided to take the rest of the week off. I had tons of PTO and I always met deadlines. We had just gotten past our busy season for now, so the company was happy to let me use some of it. My boss even joked, "Thought you were saving for an early retirement," I chuckled in response and hung up. I was just making Tabby a bottle when Misha called.

"Hey, Babe, what's up?"

"Brian tracked the money. Said I had forty-eight hours to return it or he's going to the police."

"Do you even know his banking information? Did he text it to you or anything?"

"No."

"Good, then just tell him the truth. You thought it was a gift from him and you've already used it. If he insists you took it, tell him he can take you to court, but you didn't do anything. He may cut ties with you; he may even fire you, but we can get by without that money he's not going to risk exposing the affair over this. Not when he'll lose everything he has left if he does."

"I see. You really thought this out. Remind me not to piss you off."

“After you tell him that you should tell him you're taking a half day while he figures things out.”

“Sounds good babe I’ll be home for lunch if all goes well if not, I’ll shoot you a text.”

It was a little after eleven when the door opened and Misha walked in.

“He said we're done and not to ever come near him or his money again. Starting next week, he’s transferring me to the office pool of secretaries. He’s giving me the rest of the week off. He arranged for me to use PTO days. So, we both have the week off,” Misha explained as she walked over to me and Tabby and handed me a bag, “Got food. What do you have left to do before the divorce?”

“Pack my clothes. I’ll pack tomorrow; you keep Tabby. I’ll have the papers delivered in the afternoon. No reason to wait until this weekend if you don’t have to see him again.”

With that she wrapped me in her arms and hugged me. We enjoyed our day together and that night we laid Tabby in her crib and as we were pulling into each other, Misha kissing my neck, my phone rang. Brian was calling. I hesitated as I lost myself in Misha’s warm embrace, but I answered. I couldn’t bring myself to stop Misha though, so I simply held it to the ear away from her.

“What’s up Brian? Super swamped babe.”

“Wouldn’t we normally be on vacation now? Busy season has been over for like a week,” Brian said, making no attempt to hide the obvious accusation.

“Babe, I don’t know what you’re saying. Do you really think if being at home with you was an option I’d pick something else?”

“Not something, someone,” he responded flatly. Apparently, he was done playing coy and beating around the bush.

“Do you want me to blow off work and come home so we can talk about your recent trust issues? We signed a big new client with a lot of data that had never been archived. So, we need to take care of all of that while training new staff and keeping up on our regular work. I’m sorry our trip got pushed back, but honestly you hadn’t even mentioned it, so I wasn’t even sure you wanted to go this year.”

I was struggling between not being able to moan despite Misha only getting more intense and my desire to just be done with Brian. I couldn’t grasp a clear thought in my mind.

“No, your work matters to you. We’re still doing a trip this weekend right?” He asked and Misha chuckled at his absurd question, “What was that?” he asked as Misha’s laughter echoed through the phone.

“Some of the younger workers have started to lose focus. I better go get them back on task. See you,” I said and I hung up. I didn’t want things to blow up, but I couldn’t get myself to say I love you to someone else in front of Misha.

The next day I packed and the papers were served to his office ten minutes after I left in the moving truck. Everything went into storage and then I went back to Misha’s place. We left Tabby with the neighbor that helped out, and we went to dinner to celebrate my freedom. We made love for the first time that night. It was passionate and desperate. Full of all the love and longing we had felt. For me it was a new and intense feeling that left every inch of my body feeling claimed. We slept in the same space that night. Literally and figuratively. I lay on top of her, my head cushioned in her ample breasts, one leg stretched in between hers and the other hanging of her side and my arms hugged around her as if letting go would mean being dragged to the bowls of hell. We were so emotionally in sync even our breath rose and fell together.

The next morning as I was preparing for lunch my lawyer called. Brian had reached out twice. Once to demand to know where I was and what was really going on and the second after the evidence that we had was presented to him he just wanted this over and for it all to go away.

He left me the house, my car, half of all cash, and all our joint retirement. There would be no further payments, and anything not specifically mentioned in asset division would go to whoever possessed it. The settlement had been even better than I expected. His desire to make it all go away really had worked out well for us. Which is why I had waited and gathered plenty of evidence.

Misha became a stay-at-home mom to Tabby, but we stayed close to her neighbor who was still the only person allowed to watch little Tabatha. I proposed and she said yes. We moved into the home I had shared with Brian.

We were on a date one night when we heard Brian's voice behind us, "What the literal Fuck," he shouted and we both laughed.

"What's wrong Brian?" I sneered at him as I turned to face him. Misha turned a moment later squeezing my ass as she did.

"You know how I felt about her when we were together. Why are you so surprised?" Misha asked, leaning forward kissing my exposed neck.

"How long?" he asked and we smirked at him.

"I walked in on you two having sex. It was love at first sight. Took me a while to track her down, but before the divorce. All those nights I'd be on my way home but never made it home, were because I was with her and couldn't bear to let you touch her. I'm sure you understand, right? I mean look at her, fuck who would want to share her. I guess you don't know what it's like to not have to share her though as she was never that into you," I taunted my ex.

Misha took my hand and led me away. Brian had collapsed to the ground. Understanding only now what his ego and libido had cost him. Me, Misha, little Tabatha, and eventually Dominica made a happy family that is still just as happy as we were the day we came home together.

IN LOVE WITH MY MENTOR

BECOMING CLOSE

I was nineteen. I had graduated and taken some time off to see Europe. It was the start of my new job. I had been hired through family connections, so I was slightly nervous that people would know, and I would be pushed out of the crowd. I had social anxiety anyways, so being in a position I hadn't really earned with girls who were better than me by all metrics only multiplied those feelings of inadequacy. Without fail I stepped out of the elevator and a woman in her early to mid-twenties approached me. Her four-inch heels clacked her superiority against the floor as she approached. Her silk blouse flowed loosely over her body, but even with the carefully casual fit there was no hiding the stunning figure underneath. Likewise, her skirt was a free-flowing design. She clearly didn't want to be appreciated for her body, but even still as she walked you could get a sense of her form as her clothes swayed against the hard lines of her body and there was no denying those lines were stunning. She walked right up to me and hugged me firmly.

"Welcome. You know how many people are too ashamed to use connections to get opportunities and end up with nothing. It's funny they want a job where half the job is networking, but they don't want to network to get the job. Funny fact, it didn't matter who your connection was. Anyone who networks to get the job, gets a trial run at least. It amazes me, too proud to use connections, but they shamelessly want to sleep with anyone that might be able to get them a five percent raise. Isn't that just insane?" She asked and I just stared.

"I was afraid I'd be judged for using a favor. I was so nervous, but when you put it that way, thanks," I stumbled my response, and she beamed back at me.

"Absolutely, and with that small town charm the clients are going to love to work with you. Bring in six of your own investments in the first ninety days and have a list of leads. They don't have to go anywhere but there have to be notes and leg work behind them. You're adorable though so if you're willing to tease a little, flirt when needed, you'll be done with probation in less than a month. I can mentor you if you want. Come with me to my office we'll talk about it," she excitedly explained to me and then wrapped her arms around mine and pulled me down the hallway. Girls were giggling and pointing, and I was squirming in discomfort and then we were in her office.

That was how I met Kacey. At the time I thought, "This company really goes above and beyond for its new hires, so friendly."

A week later we had another new hire, and I learned how wrong I was. This was a woman who had been in the business of making deals for over a decade. She brought a list of more than fifty leads with her and over a million in investments just waiting for her to select a project. Kacey didn't even introduce herself and on the third day when I had a chance to take a meeting with her Kacey grabbed my arm and leaned against my shoulder to whisper in my ear.

"Don't go. She'll get you fired. I hope you can have faith in me," she said and then glared into my eyes until I responded.

"Of course," I responded as cheerfully as I could though I felt a little uneasy with the invasion of my private space. I took solace in the fact she was always like that and pushed the thought from my mind.

I sent a response back to Celine, the new hire, "Can't make it thanks for thinking of me though," put down my phone and looked at my blank appointment sheet for the day. Not going to lie I was having doubts about whether or not I was doing the right thing letting Kacey guide me. Not only did I have no appointments for today, but I hadn't even started any deals in fact I had only had two meetings since starting. I mostly watched Kacey and pitched ideas.

We were coming back from lunch the next day. Kacey huffed and leaned against me, "I overate, we don't have any appointments, let's go get massages and relax," she suggested and I sighed heavily.

"Some of us still have to worry about our probation period, Kacey. Are you even taking being my mentor serious?" I asked the hurt and betrayal I was feeling leaked into every syllable

"Yup and today's lesson, deals are easier to make when you're relaxed. Come with me I promise you'll get through this. In fact, I'll bet two grand against a dinner that by the end of the week you'll have your first deal and by the end of the month you will have finished all six. If you listen to my mentorship. If I'm wrong, you'll have two grand in your pocket and two months to figure out how to fix it."

"Deal," I said before I could really think about what I was agreeing to. As we were headed for the door, I saw a girl crying in the corner holding her knees and staring at her phone. Again, without thinking I walked to the girl and asked, "What's wrong?"

"She said it was just to prove I would do what it takes. She said it was just once. She said I'd be top five by end of the week. Now she wants me to do it again. She's threatening me. Ethics violation she says. It was her idea, but she has video. Of me like that, my husband. God, we need this job. But I don't want to be a whore," she rambled and sobbed, and at that last comment my throat went dry, and my eyes went wide. The fury I felt in that moment. I took her phone and read the open text message.

"Since you were such a good sport yesterday and had so much fun, I have three more clients dying to meet you. Two of them will sign contracts with you directly. Isn't that great news. I showed them this," the text read and there was a video attached. I didn't open it; I didn't need to.

"I see. I'm sorry," I said and handed her the phone back. That was the moment Kacey became my best friend and savior. That girl disappeared the next day and me and Kacey only became closer. Not surprisingly her recognition of personal space only diminished.

She would prop against me as we ate lunch, and she would put her feet in my lap after stressful meetings, "Rub them for thirty seconds," she'd plead and after meekly protesting I'd comply. She'd hug me when we greeted each other and she'd hold my arm and pull me along on the way to meetings. Before I knew it, I had been there a month and had brought in nine clients with four more on the line and my probation was over. Kacey had arranged it so we could share office space. Everyone knew she was my mentor, so it was a natural fit. As I was getting settled Kacey playful leaned against her desk and was watching me move around, "Tonight, I'll bring you home and make you a meal. I don't cook that often so be grateful," She commanded and I looked at her confused, "Did you forget our bet already. Think you would be this forgetful if I owed you two grand?" She questioned pushing off the desk and grabbing me in a firm hug around my waist as I walked by. She lifted me in the air for the briefest moment before putting me back down, "Come on it's a celebration."

"Yeah, but this is your win. Should you really be cooking?"

"It'll be fine."

That night she cooked. Her house was perfectly put together, and she wore an apron and a dress that looked right out of an old sitcom. We ate on the couch. It was salad and chicken wraps. Afterwards she brought out a bottle of wine and a fruit tray. She handed out a strawberry as she set the tray down and refused to let me take it with my hand, so I sighed and took it into my mouth as I bit down and the sweetness hit my tongue. I couldn't help, but smile.

"See, they're in perfect season. I just had to see the moment you tasted your first bite," she said playfully giggling and I felt a warmth in my chest and the smallest flutter in my heart. We talked. drank, and nibbled on the fruit. Before I knew it the second bottle of wine was gone as was the night. Now in the early morning hours I prepared to make my way home, "You know I have a guest room. You're free to crash if you want."

"Sure," I agreed, already mostly asleep. She led me to her guest room and dropped me into the bed. I fell asleep still hanging out of the bed. When I woke, I was wearing silk pajamas and Kacey was lying next to me in boxers and a bra. She had her arm laying on my stomach, "Kacey, what are you doing in bed with me?"

She slowly stirred awake and then blushed for a second before her usual cool in charge persona took over, "You were having trouble sleeping in your street clothes last night. You rolled out of bed, so I lent you some pajamas and put you back in bed. You asked me to talk until you went back to bed. Guess I fell asleep first," she explained and while I didn't remember anything she said I did remember hazelly glaring at her and the warmth that coursed through my body.

I was eating breakfast, she had cooked again, when she started talking, "You know I've been thinking of getting a roommate. Any interest?" She casually asked. I had to be honest I was more than casually curious, but her constant presence in my personal space I feared was more than I could take. I was a simple woman with simple relationships. I had never known someone like Kacey before let alone been friends with someone like her. In my life people had roles and boundaries. I had friends my whole life, but they were call you on their day off grab brunch kind of friends. Maybe bring you soup for dinner when you're not feeling well. They absolutely were never hold your hands or give you hugs kind of friends. That being said I couldn't say I disliked being seen and cared for like this. So, after only a moment of hesitation I nodded.

"What do you have in mind?" I asked and with that one simple question me and Kacey became roommates.

IN THE PAST

Me and Kacey had been living together for six months when she brought home a woman for dinner. We had not come home together; she had gone to have drinks with this woman instead. She still hugged me when she came in, and she cooked for all three of us. She didn't treat me differently, but we weren't quite as close, as her attention was being shared with this mystery guest. She had introduced her, but I was in my head and had missed the name and was too embarrassed to admit I didn't know it, but more importantly, she never defined her relationship. I mean she never defined ours to anyone either, but I found this maddening.

"Come on girl TeeSai Nailed this risotto, try it," Kacey said, extending a fork with cheese risotto on it to my mouth. I turned with a blank look on my face and took it into my mouth. It was creamy and truly delicious, the perfect risotto, but then my mind finally processed what she said. This mystery guest had cooked. Kacey always cooked our meals unless we went out. She wouldn't let me touch anything in the kitchen. In that moment I felt like I was not only being replaced, but she was giving this person more access to her than she had ever given me, and I felt a crushing weight in my chest, and I could feel tears burning in my eyes.

“Sorry, Kacey, you and your friend have fun. I don't feel well. I’m headed to bed,” I said in a rushed, breaking voice and then darted from the room.

Ten minutes later Kacey pushed open my door and walked over carrying a saucer with red velvet cake and cherries, “TeeSai said I should bring you soup,” she said giggling, “I couldn’t help, but notice you seem upset, not sick. You don’t have to, but I like to think we’re pretty close. So, you can tell me what’s bothering you,” she said, handing me the cake.

Kacey was always so open and honest with me. She had no boundaries and our relationship itself was a little unclear, but she never hid anything. Never sugar coated or past blame. Never really even bad-mouthed people even when it would improve her standing. Honestly all that honesty and compassion made me want to be open and honest with her too, even if I didn’t know what that honesty meant.

“C-can I?” I asked weakly tentatively starting a conversation.

“Of course,” She simply replied, a sly tempting smirk playing at her lips. I wasn’t great at reading social cues and was terrified as to what this one meant. Did it mean she was only humoring me or did it mean she cherished me as much as I had come to cherish her. As I was debating the words hidden in her smirk and nibbling on the cake she had made this morning, she climbed into the bed behind me and wrapped her arms around me, “You know I got you,” she whispered and what it all meant no longer mattered my mental damn broke and my words flowed like a tsunami I would never be able to control.

“Do you know I’ve never had a close friend? I’ve had friends, people I would certainly say cared about me on a more than surface level, but with my social anxiety and my clueless nature.... Well, someone close, I kind of thought was impossible. Even my parents told me I was too high maintenance and I’ve never wanted to push that on to someone else," I began and somewhere along the way my tears had started to fall, and I could feel Kacey's grip on me only tighten, "You though, you never made me feel that way and I mean you can be a bit much for me to process sometimes, but it's like great for me I think. It makes me never doubt we're close, and it makes me feel warm and seen and cared for. I consider you my best friend and I've noticed you don't care for labels and I'm not trying to push, but it's important to me you know you're great to me, and I value our friendship so much, but today when you brought home that girl. You showed her attention similar to how you show me attention and you even let her cook in your kitchen. Your special space that you don't even like me to go into let alone use and well.... I mean, you know I guess I... Shit I got jealous ok. I know it sounds weird and creepy. If you want me to move out, I'll figure it out, but I can't help it. No one has ever been as kind and caring to me as you have. You're so open and you make me feel seen so... I'm not saying you can't have more than one friend, I'm just saying it affected me. I wish it hadn't, but there you go," I rambled and stammered and tried to defend myself until I was out of breath, my mouth was dry, and my head felt light. I began to sway and that's when I noticed Kacey had never even loosened her grip in fact, I could now feel her pressed against my back.

"It's not that I don't like labels, but I grew up in a weird environment where labels weren't used, and I never learned to define roles or understand what feelings meant. It makes me great at connecting with people, but terrible at building long lasting stable relationships. Before you I've only had one long term friend in my life. She was my best friend, but only because she was my only friend. We would pick each other up when the world got too much and remind each other the world doesn't work for everyone the way our father saw the world. That person is TeeSai and she's here tonight to be introduced to my best friend, so she knows I finally have someone who has my back. She's been worried about me since she got married and started a family, but I guess that's an elder sister's job. As for the kitchen, she cooks whenever she comes over. She taught me and everything in that kitchen belonged to her so not much I can say about it. Lastly, I do all the cooking because I like to see your face when you bite into my food not to hurt your feelings. I didn't know I had expressed that poorly. Now I would like for you to meet my sister. Do you still not feel up to it?"

Now I was feeling a whole new wave of emotions at the top of the list was embarrassment for not even asking who our guest was. Even so I gathered my inner strength and followed her from the room. She wrapped herself around my arm as we entered the living room where Teesai was eating her own piece of cake, "Let me start again," Kacey said beaming with pride, "This is my best friend, Carey. Carey, this is my overprotective mildly narcissistic sister. Be careful she has less of a sense of personal space then I do and she just loves little cuties like you."

"Why'd you start over? Was that supposed to be better? Narcissistic? No sense of personal space? So, is that what makes your girlfriend feel better, trash talking your loving devoted sister?" She said and now I felt bad.

"Have you ever met a cutie you liked that you weren't positive loved you back?"

"I can't help it, I'm popular."

"See my point," Kacey responded and the two sisters laughed, but Kacey didn't release my arm. After she settled down, she dragged me over to the couch. She pushed me into the seat at the far end and settled in between me and her sister.

"How much did Kacey tell you about our childhood?" TeeSai asked in a serious tone the second I settled into my seat.

"Almost nothing. Just that you were raised without labels and she blamed her up bringing for her lack of awareness for personal boundaries," I replied with what stuck in my mind about our previous conversation.

"That's one way to put it. Our father was a sexual predator. He took women in who had nowhere to go. He'd string them out on opioids and aphrodisiacs and enjoy them until they got pregnant. His wife would raise the kids while the mothers would be turned into junkie whores. We don't know who our moms are. He didn't like labels because it clarified what he was doing. As some of the girls got older, we realized it was a cycle he had no intention of breaking. Three of our sisters became pregnant before we were rescued. One of his women had been picked up in a prostitution sting and gave up the whole family. Most of the women and all the men over ten got locked up. The rest of us were put into the foster system where only me and my sister managed to stay together. We lost track of everyone else. She never trusted anyone but me with anything beyond surface level. She would make a new friend every week and she would lose a friend every ten days or so. Either she was clingy, or shallow, or whatever cruel word they would choose to describe not in the same emotional space as normal friends. In less than a year she stopped introducing friends. She'd still met people, and they still hung out, but she stopped calling them friends. She stopped expecting them to show up and she shut herself off. Then she told me her girlfriend had moved into her place and after talking I realized in typical Kacey fashion, she had meant it literally as a friend who was a girl. So, I just had to meet this amazing woman that had broken my sister back open to the reality that the whole world doesn't suck, just most of it, you know?"

"That's terrible," I responded with a glazed over look on my face, desperately trying to process the story and find the right words to support my friend as she had always done for me. Kacey had wrapped her arm around my shoulders and pulled me into her.

“I know you. You can’t think of the right thing to say and it’s killing you. You don’t need to say anything. You never make me feel judged and you show up every day, you're perfect,” she told me and then leaned in and gave me a quick peck on the cheek, “I love you for being my best friend.”

Her sister got up and hugged us both in one embrace, “I can see she’s in good hands. We’ll hang again, but I’ll be leaving this hot mess to you from now on.”

With that she stood, grabbed her jacket, and left. We sat on the one end of the couch. Kacey’s arm pulled me into her, in total silence for what felt like forever, “Want another piece of cake before we call it a night?” She asked.

“Kacey, you want to bunk with me tonight?” I asked. I hadn’t thought and I totally dismissed her question. I was being selfish and needy, but I couldn’t stop myself.

“Sure. That sounds like fun,” Kacey responded and we got up, took turns showering and climbed into bed together. We slept, not embracing each other but nestled in the same space of the bed. Almost as if we would entangle if we weren’t both making a conscious effort not to. As though there was some invisible line we were not prepared to cross. Looking back that’s probably exactly what it was. Either way that was the night me and Kacey started sharing a bed.

PLANS FOR SPACE NOT USED

We had been sharing a bed for over a month now and work had been going great. We were eating dinner, leftovers TeeSai had sent over, some kind of pasta casserole, "This is good. I mean I love your cooking, but you can tell your sister taught you. Similar, you know?" I wanted to let her know I wasn't threatened by her sister anymore, but I felt guilty for the compliment, so I tried to rationalize, backpedal if only a little.

"Um, yeah," Kacey responded, but it was obvious her attention wasn't on the conversation I had awkwardly tried to start.

"What's up, Case?" I asked, we had finally become close enough that I didn't feel the need to tip toe around. I could tell she was preoccupied by something and wanted to help.

"You know we could make more money at work if we had a home office," she said, but something about the way she said it made me think that wasn't really what she wanted to talk about, but I went along with her train of thought.

"So, you want to set up an office nook in the living room?"

"No, that would be terrible for when we have company. I was thinking we could turn one of the bedrooms into an office. I mean we basically only use the one anymore, right?" She asked and I couldn't help but giggle.

"I happen to be happy with how much I make. Do you need more money for something? Why don't we turn it into an entertainment room instead? Or do you love your job that much?" I asked her teasingly.

"A pool table and a poker table?" She responded and I chuckled as she grabbed my hand across the dining table. We held hands while we finished eating with our free hands.

The next morning, I woke to banging in Kacey's bedroom and found two men in my living room drinking coffee.

"Sorry," the older man said, "Bed must have been in there forever. It's being a bitch to tear apart. She just started wailing on it all of a sudden."

I walked to the door to Kacey's room. I could hear her banging and screaming at the bed, "You have to go. You've been here forever, and I found you a new home. Look at it as retirement. Come on, I need this. Go away," she screamed and fell backwards. Her usual cool and collected image was gone. She was wearing sweat pants and an oversized sweater and for the first time I wanted to know what exactly that carefully concealed body looked like. I mean I had seen it once when we slept together, but even now we changed separately and she wore bagging pjs to bed. I told myself it was a passing curiosity because of how adorable she looked fighting with the bed. I sighed and went in to help her.

"Case, why don't you let me give it a try?" I asked and she turned red and stood up.

“Yes, do, I’ll go make breakfast,” she replied, brushing the dust from her before she left the room. I hadn’t seen so I have no idea what she had been trying to do or why it had been so difficult, but I simply lifted up on the side rail, and it popped free. As though it was waiting for me specifically. I laid it aside and removed the other one before calling the two men to take it away. I went to the living room and sat on the couch.

I watched Kacey busy in the kitchen and smiling radiantly as always and I smiled reflexively. I couldn’t help but think it would be nice if these days could last forever, but then I started to think about these days not lasting forever and I couldn’t help but get sad. Kacey instantly dropped what she was doing and came over, “What’s got you down all the sudden? You seemed so happy a minute ago,” she was already wrapping me in that warm and comforting embrace, and I wrapped my arms back around her and squeezed her back, perhaps for the first time in our relationship. She squeezed tighter and I sighed audibly.

“I need this, never let me go ok,” I said without thinking. I instantly turned red and looked away. Kacey chuckled slightly and gave me another firm squeeze.

“What was that?” She asked teasingly.

“Can we always be like this, or will we end up like you and your sister when you get married?” I asked, putting a fine point on my anxiety. It was an ability I only seemed to have when it came to Kacey. With the clarity and courage, she gave me I always found a way forward.

“So, that’s what you meant?” she said clearly asking for clarification. I nodded meekly, unable to give voice to more, “Well I don’t think I’ll get married, but if one of us does we’ll probably have to go back to separate beds. Though I’d be willing to ask either of our wives,” she said and once more chuckled, but I wasn’t laughing. She didn't say spouse, significant other, or husband, she had said wife. That is when I could no longer lie to myself, I loved this woman, and I wanted to be that theoretical wife.

"Breakfast will get ruined, go finish it. I'm going to shower. I have some errands this morning. Are you going to keep clearing your room? We can work on combining furniture this afternoon," I said, pushing her off me and darting for the bathroom. I was afraid she could hear my heart racing or sense the change in the air, and I was afraid if I stayed, I would say something I couldn't play off or take back. I rushed through getting ready and came back to find my plate being placed on the table.

"Want some juice," she asked, her tone somehow colder and more distant than normal.

"Sure, what's wrong? You seem off," I said inquisitively.

"Nothing. I ate why you were getting ready. I'm headed back to see what I'm tossing and what we're combining. Have fun, sorry I've been so clingy," she said and then speed walked out of the room. I could tell that the last bit had slipped out and she was regretting it.

I ate quickly and called TeeSai as I was pulling on my shoes, "I know you're busy, family and stuff, but can you meet it's urgent, for Kacey?" I begged into the phone before she could even greet me.

"Sure, five minutes, coffee shop on Pine," she replied and hung up.

"Be back. We'll move furniture and order dinner," I shouted to Kacey and left. I got to the coffee shop in three minutes and TeeSai was already there.

"So, did she confess or something," she giggled as I sat down.

"I wish," I blurted out and then blushed in response to my own honesty, "I realized I'm in love with her. When she moves close my breath catches, when she shows attention to others, I get jealous and when I picture my future whether it's ninety days or ninety years she's by my side, but I could have accepted all of that as friendship. Until she casually mentioned us getting our own beds if we got married. It makes sense right? I mean what are we doing even sharing a bed in the first place? I'm the one who brought up marriage anyways so why would I be so upset that she went there? Yet, I am angry, hurt, and insecure. She went there; she gave it thought. A world where I wasn't the one next to her. That's when I knew. I love her and I want the person that occupies the center of her world to be me," I said, proud of my composure which quickly fell apart.

"Wow sis, welcome to the family. So, you know you're like, a lot, right?" TeeSai said and I giggled, "Anyways, what did my sister say to you? Did she say when I get married my husband and I will need our own bed or did she say something more like when one of us get married we'll probably have to sleep in separate beds? Bet it's the second. I know she's thought about you moving on a lot, but she's decided to give it a try and let you in while not holding back or changing who she is. For some reason she is positive you have and always will accept her. She loves you for that. We've never spoken about what kind of love, but I know she has no intention of letting another occupy your spot."

"Thank you TeeSai. One more question and then I'll let you get back to your family. If I tell her how I feel and it doesn't match the love she feels, do you think it will ruin our relationship?"

"No. I mean maybe if she's adamant she doesn't want it, and you push or coerce her into being something she's not or doing something she doesn't want to then maybe over time, but the confession itself no. Even if she feels the same though she may not return your feelings now. For what it's worth I think it's right to tell her."

With that I left and so did TeeSai. I got home and Kacey was sitting on the couch with her computer in front of her and a notebook on the seat next to her. I looked at the notebook first, it was a list of furniture, and each piece was marked either move or pitch. I picked it up and plopped down and looked at the computer then I looked at Kacey. The computer had a listing for a Futon on it. She met my gaze instantly.

"I think maybe I put you on the spot so I was thinking I could get something like this for when you need space to put in the game room. Otherwise, if you changed your mind, I could get a new bed. I don't want to make things awkward. I know I get clingy and I'm an emotional train wreck, but I like being your friend so tell me when I'm too much ok, don't put distance between us, ok?" She said looking at me like I had just told her we would never see each other again. My heart ached and I wanted to tell her everything, but my tongue was numb. I swallowed hard, took a deep breath, and closed the computer. She looked at me, and I dropped my eyes to the floor. I knew her insecurities were in response to my abnormal behavior this morning. I would have normally invited her on my errand, and I had just showered less than twelve hours ago. I had basically said I needed space, but only because I couldn't express my love.

"No, we're good. I am going through something. You know how my anxiety gets. Even when it's a good thing my head spins it until I'm convinced the world will swallow me whole."

With that we worked the rest of the day and in time for a late dinner Kacey's bedroom had been completely dismantled and the guys from that morning were loading the stuff we had taken downstairs. Now me and my roommate were officially sharing a bed and bedroom, and I couldn't be happier, but behind that I wondered if it was wrong of me to let her disassemble her life without telling her how I felt. As I was wondering that, she picked me up by the waist and swung me around then sat me back down and took big bouncing steps around me.

"Let's go to our room," she said and then grabbed my arm.

EMBRACING OUR FUTURE

It had been two weeks since I realized how I felt and I still hadn't found the courage to breach the subject. It was summer and our ac was broken so I was laying in our bed with a fan pointed at me in just my panties. Kacey was out and I was thinking when I was going to tell her about my feelings. This was a terrible habit I had developed recently, but it was a cycle I couldn't seem to break. I would promise myself I'd tell her I'd spend all my time alone, just to throw everything out the window at the last minute when my nerves failed me. I was zoned out when I felt a hand on my leg. It was cool and it's touch soft, but it was too high and creeping higher. I shoot up at the intrusive presence and locked eyes with Kacey.

She giggled and her hand stopped sliding higher, "Sorry I couldn't help myself. You look good enough to eat."

My legs spread slightly at her sarcastic comment before I gained my composure and snapped my legs shut, "I, I lo, I was, um, trying to stay cool sorry."

"Sorry for what? I'd usually have to pay for a show like this," she said and giggled once more.

"Stop teasing or I'll think you mean it," I said turning away again blushing and again beyond my control my legs pulled apart, but this time I didn't fight my natural impulses. Her eyes darted to my panties for the briefest moment and my blush deepened, but I didn't draw my legs back together, "Seriously you're going to take responsibility if you keep playing with my emotions." Finally, I drew my legs closed and rolled away from her, but she reached out and grabbed me in a hug. It was nothing we hadn't done a hundred times by now, but now I was all but naked and my heart was swimming in feelings I couldn't voice. At that moment I moaned and rolled into her, "I love you. If you don't feel the same way, can you let me put a shirt on if you're going to roll around with me like this?"

She released me and my heart sank. She was laughing, not her low teasing giggling or her throaty chuckle of amusement, but a full-bodied uncontrolled laugh, "Sorry, so if I feel the same way? You'll stay like this with me till dinner?"

I blushed but nodded my head. She lowered her head to my stomach and licked my navel, "I love you too," she said as her laughter finally died down. She rained kisses all over me for what felt like forever. Finally, I couldn't take it anymore and I pulled her to my face and kissed her deeply and passionately. Still somewhere in the back of my brain my anxiety was trying to find a negative spin. Maybe she was just using me for my body. Maybe she didn't mean that kind of love. Maybe I was rushing things. If things didn't work out, what kind of relationship would we have left. Was it too late to pretend the whole thing had been a joke? Above all though I had promised I would have faith in what Kacey told me, and I would be open and express my true feelings.

"You know I'll probably screw this up," I confessed to Kacey.

"If you do, I'll be there to help you fix it," she promised and then she kissed me again. We did not make love that day though the sexual tension was like a fully compressed spring. That night though we did both sleep in nothing but panties and we slept in each other's embrace. The next day we quietly made our way to hr and filed the required paperwork for inter office romance and I prepared to be relocated. After lunch Linda from hr showed up at our office.

"So, you guys have the best numbers in the office. It would be hard to argue you are doing something inappropriate at work instead of your job. Plus, no one wants to share an office with either of you. That being said, we've decided to make an exception and let you continue to share the workspace. If it becomes an issue, we'll revisit the issue. Keep up the great work ladies," she said and quickly retreated from our office.

I found myself terribly conflicted. I was happy to get to stay in our office, but I was more than a little hurt to know nobody else wanted to share my workspace. I thought I had several good friends at work. There was a knock on the door, and I opened it without a thought. Several of the girls from around the office were standing there.

"We know how you are and we know Linda told you we don't want you in our offices. It's not that we don't like you but working in between you two would be problematic. Even before you guys were a couple, we were careful not to come in between you guys. If we block Kacey's affection even by accident she sulks for days. That was before she had company permission to cling all over you. Don't get me wrong, most of us find it endearing and find you adorable. You're like, totally perfect for each other. So, we like, support you and everything. We just didn't want to be a third wheel. Invite us to the wedding kay," the girl in front explained and the girls behind her nodded along. They all giggled at the last comment and I blushed. Kacey pulled me protectively into her chest.

"Thank you, you guys and I know you mean well, but don't tease Cory," her adamant defense of me made my chest flood with warmth and an invulnerable sense of courage swelled inside me.

"Thank you. We do make a good couple right?" I probed and all my friends chuckled. I would choose to take that as a yes.

Ironically nothing really changed. The last of our boundaries had been destroyed, but that was it. Kacey would come in and talk to me while I was showering or give me a hug while I was using the bathroom. Neither of us took space or privacy to change and sometimes, not often but sometimes, she would leave her sexy body exposed for me. We would not only hug, but kiss and on rare occasions one of us would gather courage and grope at some previously off limit part, but we didn't delve into intimacy. I yearned for her, and I could see the hunger in her eyes, but we were both so unsure of ourselves and what we were doing that neither of us could take the first step. Months went by and TeeSai came over to have dinner, but something felt different. While I was trying to figure it out, we had gone through three bottles of hard liquor, and I could barely sit. Kacey was leaning against me, kissing me more feverishly than normal and her sister had disappeared. She didn't even say goodbye. I don't think anyways, all though my memories are a little fractured of that night, the memories of us endured. I remember being consumed by passion and exploring every inch of Kacey. I remember her pushing me back on the couch and the forceful, desperate, hungry pressure of her between my legs and I remember the ecstasy of finally being completed by her. I remember weeping with joy and satisfaction.

The next morning Kacey's memories seemed worse than mine, but I suspected she was just giving me an out, "If you don't remember let me remind you," I teased her and dragged her into the bedroom where we were greeted by TeeSai.

"Sorry I'll go. Stayed last night to make sure you guys were ok. That much booze isn't normal for either of you. Have a good weekend, but one of you better call me next week," she said and fled the house.

I was so turned on that I didn't even spare her a glance. I pounced on Kacey and proceeded to do exactly what her sister suggested. I enjoyed my weekend, the whole thing, with my naked and beautiful girlfriend. The dam had shattered and we embraced each other whenever the mood struck either of us. We still had battles, but we had learned to be with each other and trust that in every sense. I like to think even today we are still happy. We still work in the same office. We still share a slightly stand-offish friend group. We still have dinner with her sister on a regular basis. We still sleep in the same bed cuddled into each other. She still openly showers me with affection in public. I still crave it and her. We still are sure tomorrow we'll wake up together. I think that's true happiness.

THE LOVE OF MY LIFE TRICKED MY HUSBAND INTO INTRODUCING US

PASSION

I had been married to Jacob for three years. He had cheated on me twice and we had a trial separation. I don't have proof, but I believe it was an excuse to have a wild month of affairs. We were back together for two months, and we were having our weekly date night. One of my ideas to keep the romance in our relationship and prevent his eyes from wandering. Our anniversary would be in a week so next week we wouldn't have a date night we'd have an anniversary celebration instead. We had finished our dinner and were discussing what events would make up our anniversary.

"You know what could be fun?" He said, wearing his best salesman grin.

"What?" I asked, already sure I'd hate the answer, but giving him my warmest smile anyway.

"We could each pick something. You know, really expose our personal interests and passion," I was touched by his idea and excited that he was going to do anything I wanted.

"Wait, is this just a trick to get me to do what you want and then you're going to come up with a reason to bail on me?" I asked, not sure I bought his story.

"How about we each guarantee no backing out and we can even do yours first," he offered and I had to admit I was pleased with his offer.

"I love you babe, that sounds great," I replied, returning my attention back to my dessert and coffee. The next week flew by in a blur and our anniversary was on a Tuesday, and he had actually taken the day off of work.

We got up and had brunch. We had agreed in advance I would pick what we did from lunch till dinner, and he would pick what we did for the rest of the night. I chose where we had brunch and he had picked a dinner spot. We went and saw a romantic drama about a nurse and a war hero, and he paid attention and made comments not complaints or sarcasm. He didn't try to make out or insist my turn was over. No, he happily took my hand and said, "That was fun. What's next, babe?" We proceeded from activity to activity in this way. His excitement grew with every activity and then seven o'clock came and he took me to a lovely candlelight table in the most expensive restaurant in town. We got surf and turf lobster and T-bone and a wine I couldn't pronounce. There also was an extravagant desert with berries and foam and more alcohol. It wasn't really my scene, but the smile that spread across Jacob's face made the whole meal easily worth it. After that we went to a hotel. Top floor suite, kind that cost five figures for one night and had to be reserved a year in advance. I could only imagine the strings he pulled and I blushed when I imagined the kind of night he had planned.

We got massages. A young woman in yoga pants and a bikini top rubbed Jacob and someone with strong and soft hands rubbed my back with the kind of attention and care I imagined took years of training and cost hundreds of dollars. After I was plied with oil and rubbed until my muscles felt like Jello, I was led to a hot tub by the woman who had been massaging me. It turned out she was short and athletic. She was wearing a one-piece swimsuit that was cut too small. As she moved around, I found myself following her curves and she chuckled slightly as she helped me sit on the edge of the hot tub and then sat on the edge of it and handed me wine. I took it and looked at her as she dipped her tan legs into the water next to me and began to sip a glass of wine herself.

“I’m Dominique," she said, swooshing her leg in the water and smiling at me with a look I recognized from when men wanted more than I was offering.

“Nice to meet you. Don’t you need to return to your duties?” I asked her, feeling more than a little uncomfortable with her attention.

“What duties?” She asked and I became even more uncomfortable with the way this conversation was going. At this time Jacob entered the room, naked.

“Dom, you introduce yourself?” He asked and now I was less confused, but I could feel my anger growing quickly.

“What is going on Jacob and who exactly is Dominque?” I asked feeling myself about at the end of my rope with this man.

“This is what I want to do for our anniversary,” he replied like he shouldn’t have to explain this.

“I need more information,” I responded and as I did Dominique stood and began stripping out of her swim suit and my mind went blank for a moment. Her body was toned and tanned and inviting. All of a sudden, I had a clear understanding of what my pig of a husband wanted for his anniversary, and I understood why he had let me go first and why he was so excited all day.

“Your husband is a dirty man. Did you know that, Kelly?” She asked me, “He’s been hitting on me for eighteen months. We talk, but we’ve never done anything,” she continued her story, dropping the suit by the tub and then sinking her entire body under the water. She rose again right in front of me with her hand on my knees, "He has all kinds of things he wants to try. He's a truly depraved and pathetic man," with that assessment of my husband she leaned in and kissed my stomach just above my navel and a jolt of electricity shot through my whole body, "Has he told you anything about his plans for tonight?" She asked moving her hands from my knees to my inner thighs and locking eyes with me. I swallowed hard and shook my head no, "Thought as much. You know I don't think much of your husband and he's really living up to the disappointing critique," she said firmly in a loud tone, and it was then I realized she hadn't addressed Jacob or even looked at him once. She kissed just above her hands on each of my legs and then looked at me again, "Don't worry I won't do anything you don't want. Can I tell you a story?" She asked and slid back out of the tub to sit beside me. At some point Jacob had climbed into the tub himself. She left her right hand on my left thigh as she waited for my answer. It took a couple seconds, but I nodded my consent.

"I've known you and your husband for a long time. In fact, my older sister was already working at Jacob's company when your useless pervert got himself hired. She got me on there as an intern two years later. I watched him play the field and I watched the way he discarded each of them and then I met you at your wedding. Someone, not your husband, but someone equally scummy was trying to pressure me into dancing with them. I told them I didn't want to I was watching you dance. You were truly lovely in your gown dancing with everybody waiting in the line. Your husband was hitting on the bartender. The man would not leave me alone and I was about to retreat from the room to get air when you came up to me and extended your hand to me and you said, 'There not wrong. You're the most gorgeous woman here by a long shot, but don't settle come dance with me,' and I did. In fact, we danced three songs and were about to dance our fourth when your creepy husband tried to cut in. He tried to take my hand and I said, 'Disgusting,' and you snickered, he got angry, and you disappeared for your honeymoon. I watched you though. When he had his affairs and you stood up for yourself when you got sick and he pretended not to know. I actually was your nurse. Face mask and scrubs. I volunteered. When he tried to sabotage my sister and take credit for her work you sent the evidence of what he did to the company. He managed to sweep it under the rug, but our company is as shitty as your husband. Anyway, he managed to get himself in a position where he could talk to me and he did and I found all his dirtiest fantasies. Including him wanting me to be here tonight. I knew I'd never get another chance like this again, so I agreed. So will you take off the rest of your clothes and let me make love to you in front of this pathetic excuse of a man?"

Finally, I gathered my courage and found my voice, "Is this something you really want to do?" I asked and she gave me a lust filled smirk, "I just don't understand if you think so little of my husband then why show up?"

"God you're gorgeous. I have never wanted to fuck someone more then I want to fuck you right now. Please surrender yourself to me?" She was pleading with me now, but she held her seat waiting for me to decide.

I peeled off the lingerie I was still wearing, tossing it on top of her bathing suit and before my panties even hit the pile, she was on top of me. We were lost in wave upon wave of ecstasy and at some point, we had moved from the hot tub to the attached bedroom I regained my senses we were embracing in the center of the large bed, and her hands were pulling me in to her as if she was convinced, we could be merged into one person. Jacob was sitting on the sofa, he was sweating and staring and when I looked at him, he began to move towards us with a hungry, desperate look. He started to climb on the bed and Dominique pressed her foot against his head, "Not yet perv. God, so impatient. For now, get one of your shirts and the room service menu. We're going to have dessert on the balcony. Then I'm going to ravish her again. You want that don't you, Kelly?" she asked, looking at me like she didn't want to wait for round two.

"Fuck yes," I said instinctively, "Get me my sweeter from my bag to babe," I added and he ran to get us our shirts. He reappeared a minute later with the shirts. He tossed them on the end of the bed and then pulled out the menu from the nightstand. She picked a bottle of champagne and some berries, chocolate, cool whip, and coffee. Then she ordered one sandwich. She made Jacob place the order and wait in the room in a robe for everything to be brought up. I sat on one of the chairs, the cold pressing against my thighs where they were exposed and Dominique sat on my lap and pressed back against me.

"It's chilly, gorgeous. I didn't get bottoms cause I'm going to sit on you, but if you want a skirt or something Jacob will bring us whatever you want."

"A skirt?" I asked and she leered at me lustfully and I knew whatever I put on she would want removed soon any ways. As I looked at her, I was certain I would give her whatever she wanted and not like I had my husband in some mad dash compromise to build a tolerable and stable life that would provide the family I always wanted, but in a way that felt satisfying just knowing I was fulfilling her wish.

"Foods here Dom," Jacob shouted from inside the room.

"Well, don't half ass it you sad little man bring the food out here. Coffee and sandwich are for you. Eat and watch from inside. Kelly wants jogging pants. I have a pair in my bag. Before you start eating go get them," she said he stepped out long enough to put the serving tray down on the small table before almost running into the apartment. He reappeared a moment later with a pair of pink jogging pants. We slowly fed each other chocolate sauce covered berries and cool whip while we sipped champagne. I picked up a piece of the chocolate bar and as I bit into it, Dominique turned around and startled me. She took some of the chocolate syrup and dumped it down my neck and then put a dollop of cool whip behind my ear then she licked from my collar bone up my neck to behind my ear and then lightly nibbled on my ear.

"Wait," I said and my voice was shaking as I wanted nothing more than to let her devour me again, "before this goes any further, I need you to answer a couple questions for me."

"For you, anything I can," she replied and my heart melted like wax on an overheating engine.

"Why does Jacob listen to you like a well-trained dog and what exactly are we doing tonight? Also why do you talk so bad about him? If you really dislike him so much, why come at all?"

"Those are all fair and good questions. We're technically having a three way. Well eventually anyways. That's what he wants for his anniversary. Specifically, he wants to fuck me doggy while I eat you out and you scream his name. However, he has to always be in control at work, so he wants to be ordered around. So, the deal is we'll have his three way. If you don't put a stop to it, he listens until we are both in the mood, and he has the stamina to do so. As far as why I talk so bad about him I thought I was pretty clear I don't care much for him. However, it sounded interesting and you are genuinely hot. I had nothing to do this weekend, and this hotel is legit amazing. Look at that view. If there is anything in this world as attractive as you writhing on top of me it's this view. If we play our cards right, we'll get to see the sunrise from here. That clear everything up for you?"

I nodded and then kissed her deeply. We made love passionately right there on the balcony and we knocked the fruit and stuff all over the place. I was learning her body now and the sweet scent of her and those throaty desperate moans had created an atmosphere that was impossible not to get lost in. When I finally regained my senses, we were back in the bedroom, but not on the bed. We were on a rug in front of a fireplace that had been lit at some point, and a blanket had been brought over. I was still breathing heavily and Dominique was glowing under the sheen of sweat.

"No more touching yourself until the three way you perv. You're going to film our next round. Then we're going to shower while you go buy us energy drinks. Anything else you want, tell him clearly Kelly," she said flatly and laid her arm possessively across me.

"Thanks, babe," I responded without thinking, but then immediately realized she always used my name. I cleared my throat and looked at her, and she had the biggest smile spread across her face.

"Damn, sexy. I thought this was just for his wish fulfillment, but if you're gonna get sentimental then I won't be able to help myself," she said, rolling into me and kissing the nape of my neck deep and hard. I could hear the pop and feel the swollen flesh that would be a hickey for the next week. She licked across the deeply reddened skin and whispered in my ear, "I hope you're ready we are going to go until he falls asleep. I'm not sharing you with that narcissistic prick."

I looked down at her nestled into my neck. I knew I should have been shocked. I should have objected. I should have pulled away and clarified I was first and foremost his wife. I didn't, I smiled at her and ran my fingers through her hair. Throughout the night she kept her word. She made him run errands, buy us food, film us making love, and even let him message our feet. While we were bathing for the fourth time that night, this time in the jacuzzi tub after a quick rinse in the shower, he fell asleep. We left him on the bed and curled up together by the fireplace. Even now I can't say why, but it never even crossed my mind to lay with him instead of her.

EVOLVING DYNAMICS

The following morning Jacob was sulking as the three of us ate breakfast in the room. All of a sudden Dominique looked at him, "Jacob, love, I'm sorry you fell asleep before your turn last night. I feel just awful, but if Kelly's up for it we could try again at your place."

I nodded consent and Jacob instantly responded, "Thanks Dom I knew you were messing with me and you wanted this to happen to."

"No, you're a pig and I'm really not sure I'll ever be able to get in the mood to fuck you, but I'll keep satisfying your wife and trying," she said and I chuckled. I wanted to support him to tell him no matter what I'd be in his corner, but I couldn't bring myself to go against how she wanted this to play out. He was my husband so at the end of all this I would still be with him, but for now I would do what she wanted. After all that had been his request for our anniversary anyways.

We checked out of the hotel after breakfast and Dominique took his credit card and then took me shopping. Lingerie, dresses, jewelry, lunch, mani pedi, dinner, and then home. We made love in the living room then we slept on my half of the bed. The next day we got up and they went to work together, and our new life began. I ran errands while they worked and then they would come home, and me and Dominique would become the perfect loving couple. She would dote on me, we would go on dates, and we would make passionate love until we passed out in each other's arms. Jacob would spectate, sometimes. After a while he wasn't allowed to watch us make love anymore. It honestly creeped me out, him looking at Dominique that way. It shouldn't have. I know she wasn't mine to be jealous of and lord knows she didn't need my protection, but still she was divine and she chose to spend her time and effort on me. Even if it was just for now it made me happy.

We had been living together for almost a month when things began to change. It was after dinner. It was the weekend, and we were drinking wine in the tub. This is the time where she would slide up next to me, kiss me and the next thing I knew it would be morning, but not that night.

"Kelly, I know you love Jacob and I will never try to ruin your relationship, but you know for me this is about more than some stupid gift for your husband and as much mind-blowing sex as I can get, right? I mean I love you. I have for a long time. You might say I don't know you, but as long as you let me stay around, we'll have all the time in the world to find out if that's true. I know you wanted to do more than curate his world. You had dreams, someday I'd like to know more about them. Maybe even help you achieve them."

"Babe you can stay as long as Jacob lets you. I love my husband, but yes, it's more than just the sex for me too."

With that a new president was set. We spent less time near Jacob. We had less sex, but our relationship wasn't less intense, but more emotional. We discussed those dreams of mine and in turn she told me hers. I hadn't wanted to settle in the city. I wanted a lot of land and small town or countryside vibes. I wanted to go back to work, but anything I could do was deemed too low brow by Jacob. Dominique in turn wanted to work from home and raise her daughters. She didn't have daughters, but she was sure she would make a good mother. I teased her and said she'd have to learn to dote less or she'd spoil them. She teased back and said all the doting is for their mother.

She took me then and I dreamed of a world where we had met first and we were living that life. We still made love five to six nights a week, but we had come to consciously set a side one day a week to deepen our bond, but sometimes we would casually come up with something we wanted to do, and we'd give up a second night. We had transitioned without me even realizing it from me and the woman my husband wanted to sleep with to a genuine couple and my husband had become more like a roommate. Sometimes I would catch his eyes when me and Dominique would be leaving for dates, and I would feel bad for a moment, but I'd remind myself it had been his idea, and he was always allowed to object. In fact, she was in the house on his invention not mine and we lived our life by rules he and Dominique discussed and agreed to. I told myself under those understandings I had nothing to feel bad about.

Dominique had been staying with us for six months and Jacob no longer even tried to approach us anymore. He would still do whatever Dominique ordered him to, but I could tell she had tired of the game and just wanted to spend time with me. We were on our weekly date night and we saw him. Almost like he was deliberately on display just for us. Jacob, with a young girl hanging on his arm. He was cheating again, but this time felt different. I was somehow relieved. I hadn't been able to give him what he wanted, but he was breaking our vows while I was still trying to make his dreams come true.

"If he kicked me out tomorrow and asked you to sleep with her, would you?" She asked, looking at Jacob's table.

"Babe, no. You were an anniversary gift to him," I chuckled, but she looked like I had just punched her in her perfectly toned stomach.

"Is that..." she began, but then she bobbed her head back up and her infectious smile was back on her face, but it looked different somehow, forced, hollow, "Let's forget that loser and go home and fuck like bunnies," she said excitedly. I was a little hurt. It was our date night. We were supposed to communicate tonight, deepen our connection, but it seemed like she had no interest in that now.

We didn't go on date nights for the next month. In fact, we did very little socializing, but we did fuck even more than we did our first week together. Though we stopped making love and I didn't know exactly why things had changed. I had some ideas based on when it happened, but more importantly I didn't know how much longer I could continue with this relationship. So, I invited her to dinner one night.

"Nah, how about you wash my back, and I make you come until you pass out," was her simple response.

"Either we have dinner and discuss what's changed or we're done," I said and her eyes grew wide. I couldn't blame her for the shock. I had even surprised myself, but all the same there was a tightness in my chest and an ache in my soul. I recognized from the old days when I was still surprised when Jacob betrayed me, but this was stronger and wouldn't let go. Maybe because it wasn't from betrayal, maybe because it felt permanent, maybe even because I cared for her more than I had him, but I didn't want to think about any of the whys. I just wanted it to stop. I held my breath as I waited for her answer.

"Jacob," she shouted, through the house in response and my legs became weak. He appeared a moment later. He really was super committed to one day getting us into bed together. Too bad for him she would never let that happen, "Go get me and Kelly dinner. Eat while you're out. When you're back after we eat, we'll give you what you've been waiting for you pathetic dog."

His eyes lit up, and he ran from the house. Meanwhile I grabbed Dominique to steady myself, “What are you doing?” I asked and she looked genuinely confused.

“What I’m just a gift for your husband. Tonight, I’m going to give it to him and then you can be done with me,” she said and I cried. I didn’t know why, but I knew my tears wouldn’t stop flowing.

“You know that’s not what I meant. I just would’ve never chosen to start dating a woman. No matter how beautiful, charming, and sweet she is,” I tried to explain in my most charming voice. I imagined it came up somewhat lacking as my eyes were still puffy with the tears still on my cheeks and a tremble in my voice.

“Date? Is that what we’re doing,” she asked and her mischievous grin had returned to her face, “You want me to stay?” She asked and I nodded submissively instantly, “Tonight, just tonight chose me,” she demanded and again I nodded consent, but this time I was firmer surer than I had been in anything in years. She took my hand and led me from the house. She gave me an address and told me to drive. I drove and she sent a text. I didn’t ask to who, I already knew who Jacob, and I didn’t ask what she had said. I had enough of an idea to know I didn’t want to know. I would face the consequences of whatever she had said tomorrow. We left the world of glitz and glam that my husband curated and we pushed through the commercial district, industrial district, and the overpopulated slums. Finally, we reached the outskirts of town and a large plot of land. There was a small but tasteful ranch style home sat deep back on the property and that was our destination.

We took a bath and then nestled in front of the fireplace on a love seat, “So, you want me to stay. You want me to look at it as though we’re dating?”

"I mean, yes and I certainly see us that way. I mean sometimes I feel like we're more of a couple then me and Jacob ever were. I get your reluctance. This only works as long as he continues to prioritize himself."

"So, if he ended it, you'd let him?" She asked and that question cut deep. Did I have the right or even the ability to prevent him from ending it? I had stopped thinking about this coming to an end some time ago and looked at it as Jacob giving me the gift of a true partner while keeping the facade of our relationship for our parents and his job. I thought about it a bit more than I gritted my teeth and committed to my answer.

"If he ends his support things will become harder, but I see myself as your girlfriend."

"So, you are dating us both or you've chosen me?" She asked and I realized this was not a casual escape to embrace as lovers, but a moment she had been building towards for a while. She wanted to know where she stood, and I couldn't blame her.

"I have chosen you. Do you want me to leave him?" I asked and my heart broke that I even had to ask, but our lives were tied together at this point. If she didn't need my freedom and he could accept our relationship, then I would rather leave more complicated matters until there was a good reason to deal with them.

"What do you want, love," she asked with a whisper soft voice, and I knew I had no choice, but to be clear and honest with her even if it hurt otherwise, I could lose her for good.

"Dominque, I want you and I want to make you happy. As long as you remain the girl I know and love I'll do everything I can to make that a reality. That being said our marriage is complicated and my parents don't believe in divorce without good reason. Sadly, there reason are only the vilest things like serious repetitive physical abuse or sleeping with someone they shouldn't. Like him sleeping with my mom or something. Finally harming our children is the first and only one guaranteed not to get you any flak from either family. That being said we don't even have children. So, divorce would cause strain..." I was rambling all my honest well-meaning reasonings, looking into her hard emerald eyes and something clicked. I fell silent and she looked at me with patience that had to be hard. I could see the hurt in her eyes, "No, I'm sorry I'm making excuses rationalizing to make my life easier, but I won't turn you into a secret. I don't know how I feel about leaving him. Our living situation is comfortable, but I chose you as my partner, as my love, please won't you choose me too."

"I chose you on your anniversary. That's why I showed up there silly," she replied simply and walked out to the kitchen she returned a moment later with sandwiches, "I honestly don't care if we stay at Jacobs for now. His place in the city is a good commute, but I do want kids and to introduce you to my family and to be able to introduce you if not as my wife at least my girlfriend or partner," she explained what she wanted as she sat back down handing me one of the sandwiches and I ate it in silent contemplation.

"Then we start by casually introducing you as my girlfriend," I said and we started to make a plan.

A PLAN BEGINS

We talked until the sun rose that night and we fell asleep on the love seat in front of the fireplace with a firm grasp on our commitment and our plan. We drove home that morning full of energy and passion despite having barely slept. We entered the house. Jacob had left already, "Went out with the boys will probably crash at Brians," the note on the counter had read.

So, we set aside talking to Jacob and we began taking pictures and then we posted them to Dominique's social media pages, "Celebrating six months with the best girl," was the simple caption for the photo bomb.

Less than five minutes later my phone buzzed, "What the hell. You guys always put me on the back burner and now you're going public?" Jacob was up which surprised me. Meant wherever he had actually gone probably didn't involve drinking.

"We'll talk when you get home. It's just low-key pictures on her private account. She wants her family to know she found someone," I texted back. I didn't hear from him again until that evening and now he was very much drunk.

"She's leaving," he shouted as he entered.

"Is that really how you want to handle this," I asked, implying he should consider my needs. I had left him to have his affairs since Dominique had moved in and we had been happy. Granted it was borrowed happiness, but it was true happiness all the same.

"She's out, you guys are done. This was the best talk we've had in months," he shouted, his voice dripping with disdain.

With little choice Dominique went to pack her belongings and loaded them into my car. The car we had been sharing since she had moved in, "Fine I'll take her home then."

I did, I took her home and I texted even as we were still driving, "Flat. I'll be late. See you tomorrow," I probably should have felt guilty, but any chance of that vanished as Dominique handed me a folder and a flash drive. I wanted to see it all before we started the next phase. More than a dozen girls since Dominique had come to stay. Hotels, their houses, his office, and one night in our bed. "So only he deserved to have his needs met," I thought to myself as I flipped through everything a second time. We got to her lovely home, and she organized a post, "Looking for clarity," she began and then she asked the internet to explain how the guy in the story had been wronged when he had cheated with over a dozen women while his wife had only slept with the one woman, he demanded her to for their anniversary. It was vague, but the pictures were clear, and she shared it with some gossips at work. Things would probably get awkward for her, but we were leaving town after things were settled with Jacob.

We had been prepared to slowly untangle our lives, let him save face and slowly slip away, but he had chosen to take everything while offering nothing so I would watch it all turn to ash before his eyes. His president had gotten married on his eighteenth birthday to a woman he had known since second grade. She was the CFO, and they were a rock. Infidelity wasn't just against the moral code at the company; it was the only reason there was a moral clause in their contracts. We had copies of his request for Dominique to join us for our anniversary and all their texts since then. It was clear he knew what we were doing and he had started it. People probably wouldn't be cheering for her truth, but the company was unlikely to punish her. Meanwhile Jacob would be lucky to keep his job. I doubted if we had overstepped for thirty seconds before the finality and cruelty of his demand echoed through my mind and I steeled my resolve.

After she had posted and shared, we turned our phones off and made love. It felt so good to be back in her embrace to be surrounded and secure in this love. It was the first time in a long time that we had made love instead of avoiding or desperately and forcefully fucking like two strangers who know they'll die when the pleasure ends. In that embrace I was sure this was what love was and it washed over me.

"I'm sorry for pulling away and assuming you'd choose him, but at dinner that's what it sounded like. Watching him with another woman and all I could hear was you gifting me to him. I was so deaf and then I treated you so cruelly," she whispered into the night. I giggled in response and rolled on my side looking at her and held her tightly in my embrace.

I woke the next morning to find she had already gone. I turned my phone on telling myself I was ready for anything, but maybe I gave myself too much credit. The phone lit up, and three messages popped up.

"You stayed with her. Really?" Jacob had texted me not long after I turned my phone off.

"Jacob managed to keep his job, but he's not happy. I'm getting a lot of weird looks," Dominique texted a couple hours after she had gone to work.

"It's your life too and you're just going to let her do whatever she wants?" Jacob texted right after Dominique had.

I was unprepared for such a lack of a spectacle. He hadn't told me what had happened, he hadn't made demands, or accusations. Through the hostility he sounded almost like he was pleading for a lifeline. I wondered if I was over thinking it or if he had managed to keep his job, but things were still bad. I quickly realized I had no information and it was driving me insane. I breathed deep and began to type, "Going through this without you, is tougher than I thought. I miss you, Love Kelly."

I sent it to Dominique and then laid back down. I should be organizing my errands for the day. Making sure we had everything ready for the week. That's what I was doing before Dominique and even while she was living with us. Now I couldn't even bring myself to go home. I slept until lunch. Then the front door woke me. As I slowly pulled myself from my deep slumber, I saw Dominique approach. Her sun kissed skin was glowing and her radiant smile made my eyes close reflexively.

"Wake up sleepy head," she whispered as she sat down on the bed next to me, "You haven't been responding to anyone's messages. I finally agreed with Jacob about something; we were both worried. I took a half day."

"I'm fine, babe. Little overwhelmed by lack of knowledge, but I'm good," I said sitting up on the bed. Despite my words my body moved on its own pulling Dominique close to me and hugging her tightly as if to make sure she was real.

"His reputation has tanked and he's been demoted. He didn't tell you right? He's trying to guilt you into making it right. I'm not telling you anything you don't already know, but he's not fighting to get you back. He's fighting for his lifestyle. With everything you've stayed through he thinks that's what you care about."

"My mom was a mistress. She was kept by a CEO in a small apartment. Sometimes we would actually have dinners with his other women, and his wife would often baby sit me while he was with my mother. That was how I learned of relationships. A mistress, with mistress friends, and whore acquaintances. I was taught my future was to have my wishes discarded and to be embarrassed and minimized. Until I met you, I bought it all. Funny truth, if he hadn't let you treat him like a bitch, I may still be afraid to leave him," I confessed and the truth of it stung me. I watched Dominique's face afraid it would have hurt her to hear our relationship had been contingent on such a shallow thing.

"Yeah, if he hadn't accepted the way I treated him, I would have left before we found out if you would have chosen me. I hate him, I had never planned to be with him. Guess we should thank him for being so desperate to taste forbidden fruit," she said and I glared at her in utter confusion. She noticed immediately, "Uh huh, so you don't know," she laughed nuzzling my neck as she did, "God you're priceless. He wasn't after me just because I'm gorgeous. If he was just looking for beauty he would have been more than happy with you. I'm gay, and have been since my pre-teens. I mean that wasn't my first time, just when I knew I was. As you can imagine since I've been gay longer than I've been having sex I've never been with a man. In fact, I've never had anything larger than a finger inside me. That is what your husband wanted," she said and she was playfully kissing and nibbling at my neck in between words and I knew this conversation was over for now.

Two hours later I took a shower alone and while Dominique was showering, I finally checked my phone. There were three messages from Jacob and twenty-seven from Dominique and a couple from various friends checking in. I texted back to my friends quickly. I'm fine, we'll talk later type stuff. Then I read Jacob's first, "Well your girlfriend is making a real mess of things. I might have stepped out from time to time, but I always came home, and I always kept it drama free. What do you have planned for dinner and how do you plan on making this up to me," he ended it with a devil and a winking emoji, "Radio silence, what's the deal," was all the second one said, "Babe, are you ok. We can talk about anything else, but I need to know you're ok. If I don't hear from you in the next hour I'm coming to find you. If you're fine, I'll be upset," was his final text sent fifty minutes ago.

"I'm fine, just woke up. I'm at my sisters. When I heard everything, I got anxious, so she offered to keep me company. Don't worry I'll be home tonight," I texted. I wasn't going home but let him stew in what he had put me through for years.

Then I read Dominique's texts. It started with a simple check in and then every ten minutes with increasing concern that I had changed my mind, hurt myself, or something she hadn't foreseen had happened. The last three were sent while she was driving toward me and even then, she never dismissed or belittled me. The last text ended with, "No matter what just be fine. When I find you, I'll never let you go again."

I got up and went into the bathroom smiling and staring at her naked form glistening under the water, "You couldn't even keep your promise for one day," I joked as I stepped into the shower and brushed my hand against her firm and silky-smooth skin. She looked at me confused and amused in equal measure, "I read your texts. Someone got carried away," I teased and I saw the look of dawning flash across her face.

"Ok, never is impossible, but God babe don't scare me like that again. At least like let me know you're crashing out, k!" She hurriedly explained. I chuckled and leaned into her. Kissed her softly and left her to her shower.

We were getting ready for dinner, and I texted Jacob again, "Things are kind of crazy here so I offered to give a hand. I'll be home in the morning."

I turned my phone off after that and asked Dominique to take a couple vacation days. We took photos after she called in, then posted the photos, "Called in to pamper my boo," she captioned her latest photo bomb and posted it on her public thread. Her phone rang three minutes later. Jacob was calling.

"Jacob, what can I do for you?" She asked in a smug tone and a chill ran down my spine, "No, I'm sure she told you she's at her sisters. Didn't you tell her she can't see me anymore? She's not you, hasn't she always been faithful to you, you cheating dog," she scolded him and I laughed out loud, "No that wasn't her. God, you're paranoid. If you want to talk to her so badly, I'll have her turn her phone back on but are you even going to believe what she says? You're just throwing accusations now," she was taunting him now and I was eating it up. I didn't need to know what he was saying to know how much it was bothering him, "I told you she's not with me, but I have her sister's number. I can call and have her turn the phone back on. I swear it's the truth. Give me five minutes to get a hold of her and you can call or I can have her call you. Sure, sure," she was still talking to him when she lowered the phone, "Turn your phone on, call your old man. God he's so annoying," she said smacking my hip to get me moving.

"Hey, finish your phone call before you talk to me missy," I teased her back and pinched her ass.

"No, I'm still messing with you. You're too gullible. See you round the office," she said and finally hung up, "He's pissed and didn't seem to believe me," she said laying back on the bed next to me, "O yeah boss said he gets how complicated this is, take all the time I need."

I called Jacob while Dominique kissed me all over, he picked up on the second ring, "Kelly, you good?"

"Yes, Jacob and I told you that already."

"What about those pictures of you with Dom?"

"What pictures? My phone has been off."

"Right ummm, you guys together tonight."

"No, it was probably just something from her photo album to rile you up. I haven't seen her since I brought her home. I'm a good faithful partner so surely you aren't going to doubt all the years of loyalty and forgiveness I've shown you, are you?"

"You seem different with her," he replied and for the first time since he had picked this path, I felt a little bad for him. He didn't sound angry, he sounded confused and hurt, but I had been hurt too and I needed him to make the first move.

"Well regardless of how I seem with her, you've taken her from me and I'm at my sister's place," I said, my tone rising and my words rushing as Dominique became more deliberate with her affection and I fought to stifle my response. Finally, I could bear it no more and released a small moan, "Shit, gotta go bye."

I hung up, turned off my phone and returned my full attention to my girlfriend.

FOR OUR FUTURE HAPPINESS

It was two weeks of this cat and mouse game, and I had only returned home twice while Jacob was at work. I was getting impatient when a process server appeared at Dominique's. He had finally made his move. I looked at the papers and honestly, he was more generous than I expected so I signed them instantly.

Dominique came home and we celebrated. It was after all the beginning of our public relationship and now we had to figure out what we looked like outside of the bedroom. While Jacob was still at work we went and packed up all the stuff I cared about. It was surprisingly little to be honest one box and a duffle bag. I had bought a bundle of boxes knowing I owned a lot of stuff, but as we went through the house it all felt like it belonged to someone else.

Dominique gave me access to her entire life to integrate my stuff in as I wished but we had already decided to leave after the dust settled. We were moving closer to her family in Arizona. So, while she worked, I packed and then at night we cuddled and discussed the future. She would be the mother to our children, and I would be the provider in the traditional sense, finally having a career, but we would always discuss things as equals. Something Jacob had never done.

We were a week out from the move, and we had already sent a truck of belongings to auction. Like me Dominique was only taking what truly mattered and we were starting over. That was when Jacob reappeared, at Dominique's door.

“You know I’m a reasonable man. You could have just told me you chose her; you weren’t coming home.”

“She needed me to be free, and I couldn’t divorce you,” I replied calmly.

“So that’s what this was? Your family’s trust. Did you tell her? For that matter why not just ask for the divorce? I would have filed for you.”

“Huh, she really does hate you. I don’t think you ever did anything to her, but you know she was already in love with me when you were parading your mistress around the office. I mean she wouldn’t have made me do it, but she was so happy when she suggested it, I couldn’t say no,” I explained and I could see anger and a sense of betrayal flare in his face. He had come here for answers or maybe closure, but the truth I gave him was obviously not something he had expected. I sighed tired of this dynamic and long past ready to move on, “Look we’re leaving in a week, and I still have a lot to do, so, if there is nothing else,” I said and moved to shut the door.

“Wait,” he said, extending his foot into the doorway, “Why? I mean we were good together.”

“We had an ok life, but then you brought me this gorgeous, captivating woman who was completely in love with me and you let me bask in that relationship and see what being cherished, loved, and protected felt like and then, and then you had the nerve to try and remove that with one simple sentence. Like you had ended all your own indiscretions, but mine wasn’t an indiscretion, it was love. You can’t be rid of love in the same way you can a mistress. I should thank you though. I would've never cheated so if you had used someone else or not been such a pig. I probably would have died still believing what we had was what passed for love in this world. Now, though I know love crushes you to dust and rebuilds you a new a million times every minute. That's the true weight of love, it requires your all, and it gives you everything. Does that answer your question? We were good together for you. Me and Dominique, we are everything for each other. That's why. Now goodbye," I said and went to slam the door. He got the message and pulled his foot back. I knew he was right. I could have asked, and he would have done it, but he would have wanted more of the trust. My grandfather had left each of his grandchildren money. I had not told Dominique about it, but that wasn't why I hadn't divorced Jacob. The trust was nice, but my family's respect meant the world to me. If there was nothing I could do to make them happy that would be one thing but making Jacob file for divorce so they could say we always stuck it out and made it work as long as our partners were willing, that was a small price to pay. Besides Dominique wanted to do way worse to Jacob so I considered it middle ground.

As I was locking the door a text came through from Jacob, "I didn't know she loved you," he said and I realized my girlfriend had played him and he had never asked why a lesbian who still had her virginity and was hot enough to get whoever she wanted was suddenly willing to give it up to him. I had to admit that was just like him.

That week flew by, and Jacob never contacted us again. We moved to a small town in Arizona, where I wrote traffic citations, and she did data analytics from home. I only worked part time, and her work was largely contract and production based. After ninety days at our new jobs, we started looking for a daughter to adopt, and in less than two months we had basically given up. I convinced her to hire a surrogate and pay for in vitro. I used my grandfather's trust. We used a redundancy system to make sure we got a daughter soon, and we ended up with three lovely children. One of them was a boy, which neither of us had ever imagined having, but I loved him from the first moment he was laid in my arms. Dominique seemed equally pleased, she named all of them. Fredrick for the boy, Alice for the first-born girl, her mother had reminded us of Disney's Alice in Wonderland, the baby girl was named Darla as in our Darling baby girl. They went to the best schools, and we afforded them every opportunity and never withheld love, or made it conditional, but true to her word, Dominique doted on me while guiding and disciplining the children. Despite that, they all grew very attached to her.

Jacob, he recovered his position at the company and even has a new wife. He hasn't learned anything, and Dominique joked that she should send one of her single friends to help out. I smacked her and said, "You won can't you let it go?"

She responded swiftly and cruelly, "He hurt you, disrespected you, never."

I didn't say anything else about it, but that line even after all these years had made me blush a deep crimson. That night for the first time in years we did not make love. She ravished me with an intensity and desperation that left me weak for the whole weekend.

Alice married a manager and became a stay-at-home mom in Arizona. Darla married a woman, a tattoo artist. They were both free spirits, so they lived a difficult life, but they were happy and we supported them the best we could. Fredrick never married. He worked hard, built a retirement for himself and then put together resources to help me and Dominique when we got older.

They all three made us proud and we had dedicated everything we had to them. Our live was not always simple, but it was the best love story I had ever heard, but then who wouldn't find their happiness to be the best happiness?

IN LOVE AND DEATH

IN LOVE WITH A KILLER

She stepped from the shadows, the moon glistening off the small blade in her hand. She thrust it up into the man's chin and released the handle. It was such a cold and decisive action. I should have been terrified. I should have fled. I was transfixed, totally obsessed with this warrior angel who had saved my life. Less than two minutes had passed since I had been pushed into this alley. The hungry touches of this lecherous man forcing me to retreat into this dark and filthy place. Two minutes and my life would never be the same.

She glared at me with her dead cold crystal blue eyes. She stepped over the fallen body and reached out to grab my face. She turned it forcefully to the right and then to the left. I couldn't tell if it reminded me more of a mother tending to a child who had fallen while playing or a shopkeeper inspecting goods before signing the invoice. Either way I was certain she was inspecting me for injuries and meant me no harm.

"This city will eat you alive," were the first words she ever said to me and after she turned to return to the shadows she had entered from.

"Wait," I called out weakly, certain she would ignore my plea, but needing to make it anyway. Surprisingly she halted, but I found myself uncertain of what to say. The pause didn't last long, and she was drifting toward the shadows again, “Take me with you please?” I asked, my tone weak and pleading. Even now I don’t know why I made the request. I was safe, she had dispatched my attacker. I had a comfortable life and a caring family, but in that moment it all felt hollow, like it was a blanket that covered the real world I couldn’t unsee and the only place that was definitely safe was next to this woman’s side.

“I’m part of this city,” she responded as she turned back to me, “You can come, but if you do you will disappear,” she said and I could tell she was trying to warn me away, but I was in no state to hear what she was telling me. I nodded meekly and she took my hand. That night I sat on a rooftop drinking coffee while below in the alleys she killed four men and after, we retired to an abandoned warehouse right of the river. She had converted an office on the back side elevated off the floor, probably the old floor supervisor’s office. Inside was a small travel stove, a single pan, sleeping bag, and a small pile of black clothes hanging out of a duffle bag.

“Names, Adriana Frost, you can bunk with me tonight. We’ll get you kitted and fitted tomorrow,” Adriana told me, her tone still cold and distant, but I couldn’t help but wonder if it wasn’t an act. If she had no interest in me being here, then bringing me along made no logical sense. I couldn’t fight, no one would pay my bounty, and I had no connection to anyone with power or influence.

We climbed into the single sleeping bag, and she fell asleep almost instantly. I watched her face turn from cold and calculating to scared and uncertain as her dreams took hold, “Franco, Demetree, Nathan, Conor,” She began and continued for the next three hours. I counted four hundred and seventy-two names. Then she screamed and woke up. She looked at me staring at her and then closed her eyes again. Moments later, she began the list again. This time I wrapped my arm around her, stroking her back and whispering in her ear.

"Don't worry, it's a dream. You're safe with me. Sleep well. I'll shine light on all the shadows," I continued to whisper reassurance and promises, and as I did, she stopped reciting names, and she was beaming with a smile. She curled into me, and I instinctively kissed her forehead. I continued whispering in her ear until I fell asleep.

It was nine in the morning when I finally woke up, and Adriana was still sleeping soundly next to me, "Mrs. Frost, I'm going to get breakfast I'll return," I whispered in her ears and she shot up.

"I'll go with you," she responded and I couldn't help, but wonder how long she had been up. She must have sensed what I was thinking because she responded to the thought, "I'm a light sleeper, comes with the job."

I couldn't help but wonder, "Hadn't I talked to her half the night. I moved her and kissed her. None of that seemed to wake her," but I was too embarrassed to bring any of it up so I figured it would just be an answer I'd never get.

We went and had breakfast. A little hole in the wall dive but according to Adriana, "The coffee was strong, and it had an advantageous viewpoint for maintaining optimal tactical positioning," Her voice had been so robotic about it, but I could tell there was genuine concern for both of us in her thoughts. We then went to a military surplus store. We bought a sleeping bag, some clothes, and a knife. We then headed back to the warehouse and settled into the space. It was an easy silence but breaking it seemed somehow impossible.

"You are from a different world. You must have many questions. Feel free I'll answer what I can," Adriana finally said.

I swallowed hard before I started to speak, "Are you a hitman, a vigilante, or something else?" I asked, it was a shallow question, but it was a start.

“All of that I suppose” she answered unhelpfully and I glared at her as if to say as much, “When I saw you in trouble that was vigilante justice. I didn’t gain anything by doing it but watching such a vulgar and cruel man attacking such a beautiful and defenseless woman.... Well, I couldn’t just stand by and watch it happen. The other men I killed were part of a CIA sanction termination order for members of an international terrorist organization with cells active in the US. When legal contract work is slow, I’ll take hits under an alias. Keeps me sharp and makes it easier to move through the world. Sorry it’s a complicated answer, but I guess I’m complicated,” she answered her typical stoic facade cracking ever so slightly.

“What did you hope to gain by bringing me here?”

“Nothing, maybe everything. I honestly don’t know, but I couldn’t tell you no.”

“I see, who are the four hundred and seventy-two people you list in your sleep?”

“The men I killed. Well not all of them. I don’t know the name of the one who attacked you.”

Again, I swallowed hard and started to speak again and this was our day. Until two in the afternoon anyway, “You can continue when we return. Time for mid-day meal,” Adriana said, rising to her feet and heading out of the building. Same hole in the wall, same mediocre meal. Then back to the warehouse. We did the same again for dinner.

By the end of the day, I knew her better than I had ever known anybody in my life. She was like a mosaic of carefully compartmentalized personas and interests. She had learned to cook for an extended job overseas and she found she didn’t care for the cuisine there, but she liked the regional flavors of a rural village that specialized in seafood nearby. She learned how to make their cuisine for the job instead. She continued to study cooking seafood when the job was done. She didn't like sports, but she loved games that placed you in a match of intellect with your opponent, especially if it provided a chance for deception to determine the outcome. As such she used most of her vacation time to go to poker games. She loved animals and before she started working for the CIA she had kept a bulldog named Scrappy. She didn't have any family, because a black ops group she was with had made her fake her death and sever all ties with her past. She had been an outgoing person once and sometimes late at night she would let that person out and she would cry for her lost friends and the lonely life she felt trapped in. She couldn't leave because she couldn't go back to them and she wasn't strong enough to be alone. There were tons of smaller truths like her favorite this and what she hated most about that, and these were far from the only stories she told, but this was her truest self, and this was who I was falling in love with.

Many would say this was trauma bonding and I would say who cares. It doesn't matter where love begins as long as you nurture it and let it grow.

I asked her as the night was growing to an end, "Why did you save me and let me tag along?"

She responded with abnormal warmth in her eyes and softness I had never heard before in her voice, "My body moved on its own. I felt protective of you. You made me feel a warmth I haven't felt since I left my world behind. If you choose to stay by me then I will make whatever space you want in my world."

"O, and if I said I think I love you? Would you accept that love?"

She looked mildly shocked, but she readily shook her head, "Yes I believe we could be lovers if you wanted," her tone had returned to its flat malonic tone, but there was a sparkle in her eyes, and I leaned forward and kissed her. She returned the kiss with hesitation, but she griped me, as if to make sure I went nowhere while she got past that hesitation. I wasn't sure if she was afraid that she wanted this or if she didn't know if she wanted this, but I would give her time to figure it out.

With the kiss still warm on my lips we laid our bedrolls out next to each other and went to bed. I watched her sleep in her bedroll, the names coming and when she got to the four hundredth name, I closed my eyes tightly and pretended to snore. She woke up with a start, and I waited for the names to start up again. I wanted to respect her choices, and she had chosen to sleep separately so I didn't want her to know I was watching over her, and I didn't want her to feel like I was pressing her.

She had made it clear she wanted me by her side and whatever I wanted from her she would provide, but that wasn't the same as being a couple. I needed to know she was in this not just satisfying me. So, I would let her sleep, and we would hopefully grow closer tomorrow.

"You're terrible at faking you're asleep. Can you soothe me again like you did last night? I slept so well feeling you so close. By the way, the hesitation has nothing to do with wanting this, or if I deserve it, or anything like that. I was just wondering if I should come back to you after leaving this life behind."

"Climb in. I never want to be apart from you."

She climbed in and we huddled close. She was asleep in less than three minutes. When I realized she didn't start the list of names I slowly drifted off to sleep as well.

ESCAPE AND MORE

Adriana had not only basically accepted my confession, but also said she wanted to start a new life with me. I was touched, but also nervous. I didn't know how you quit being a contract assassin for the CIA, but I couldn't imagine it was as simple as a two-week notice. That morning, we washed up in the sink and had breakfast.

"Do you want to start a new life with me," she casually asked as we were sharing oatmeal from the pan it had been made in.

"It would be my honor if you're ready to leave this life," I replied stiffer than I meant to, but more concerned that I made sure she knew my presence wasn't contingent on her giving up her way of life.

"It may take a while and it will be dangerous, but with you I think I could finally face it," she said, looking out over the warehouse as if searching for something. I wished I understood her world. Then I could stand there with her, but if I did could I pull her out of it, and more importantly if I understood her world and could stand on even footing with her what would our relationship look like if we had a relationship at all.

That day she disappeared for an hour and when she came back there was a dark shadow hanging over her features, "If I said life would be harder than you could ever imagine and we might not survive this new start would you still want it?" She asked and I kissed her. She sighed in response, "I need to hear your thoughts."

"I would follow you wherever you want if our story lasts one day and ends in a hail of gun fire then it's better than a hundred years without you," I responded, unsure myself when my feelings had become this deep, but positive they had. The way she protected and prioritized me, the way she let only me get close to her, and this strange feeling of something deep below the surface made me want to always be beside her.

"You are the light in the midst of my inky abyss. I will do everything I can to safeguard that and take you away from here. Is there anyone you need to say goodbye to? Anything you need to take with you?" She asked determined to provide me with what I needed.

I gripped her hand, "Just you," I said. We cuddled close to each other and let the silence hang over us. After a while we made some small talk. Then we ate and went to bed. In the middle of the night, I woke as I submerged into the water of the cool river flowing behind the industrial building we were in. I could feel myself being pulled along. Not by the current, by something firm and real, moving against the current. I could feel its hold on me, and I assumed it was a hand, but I couldn't find the person anywhere and panic began to sink into me. Was it Adriana or was it someone from the CIA I couldn't say. I looked back at the building, it was a raging inferno, and I could see people on the riverbank. All the sudden a mask was forced on my face, and I was dragged under the water. I saw her then, she was wearing a respirator herself, and she would be hard to identify by sight alone, but for me there was no mistaking it. She was my Adriana, and she clearly had a plan. She pulled me to a small out cove in the water and into a narrow cave that became a tunnel she had clearly dug herself. We went a ways in and then she turned back and crushed a support beam, mud and rumble fell into the tunnel, and she finally took off her mask and tossed it behind her.

"We're safe for now. You can take off your mask," she explained to me, and I handed it to her, and she tossed it behind us, "There's a cave at the other end of this tunnel that has supplies for two for a week.

We'll move at night and sleep during the day. When we get to the next major city, we'll disguise ourselves and then I have an island. Nobody knows about it. We'll be safe there as long as we stay off the grid then in a few years, we'll reinvent ourselves and go wherever you want."

"I love you, let's do this," was the only response I could find.

We crawled for what felt like forever. Found the cave and went through the supplies. The sun was coming up, and we camped for the day. For two weeks this was our life. Everything unfolded as she had promised. We were now disguising ourselves to make our way out of the country. We got new identities and we began to travel during the day. We booked passage on a cruise ship that would go close to the island, and we vanished from a neighboring island while we were docked. We were at the island, and our new life began.

She told me about who she was, before the wars, before the violence, and before the nightmares. She told me she had always wanted to leave, but something deep inside her made her stay. She confessed she thought that something was her heart knowing I would come. I personally believed it was fear of doing it alone, but I would never tell her that. I told her about my perfectly normal and relatively happy life. I confessed there had been nothing wrong and I had no real reason to walk away, but my heart screamed every time I thought about walking away from her.

Sometimes we would go days without leaving bed and sometimes we would make love on the beach until the sun came up. The years past and what was supposed to be three became ten before we even discussed it.

"Are we ever going back," I asked one night. I didn't really care what the answer was. It was just the first time I had thought about it in years.

"We can. Whenever you want now. We still need to be cautious. Fake ids and disguises, but I'm sure they've stopped actively looking for us by now," she said smiling brightly. It would be another five years before we would leave the island, but I was always pleased to know we could whenever we wanted.

When we finally did it was for our anniversary, and it was to Paris. The world was so noisy and the people so numerous. It overwhelmed my senses, and I had no fun. We returned to the island. Carefully, methodically, indirectly there we lost ourselves in each other again and we stayed that way until the day Adriana passed away. We had lived on the island for almost sixty years and I was alone. I cannot leave and I do not wish to go on alone. I burnt her and put her out to the ocean on a raft. Tonight, I will swim out and meet her. Someday maybe somebody will find this and know Adriana Frost, a decorated war hero and ruthless killer was the most caring and courageous person I've ever known, and she walked away from the shadows to bathe in the light with a normal everyday girl like me. So, no matter what happens in life, love is always an option.

PIMPED BY MY BOSS
RESCUED BY HER LOVE

DATING MY BOSS

I knew I had to have her the day I met her. She was powerful, confident, beautiful, and had a hunger for life that radiated from her every pour. Her name was Jillian, and I was Erica, a quite mousy intern who hungered for her approval and affection. We were working together for a month when she gave me the first and offered me the second. We were leaving the office when a security guard brushed past me, “She’s not who she pretends to be.”

All the sudden uncertainty swarmed me, and I excused myself to the restroom. This was great for my libido and good for my career. Why was I even listening to some random security guard? As I was splashing cold water on my face and wrestling with these thoughts an impossibly tall blond woman walked out of a stall, “It’s bothering you because deep down it rings true, am I wrong?” She asked and I straightened up.

“Who are you? What are you talking about?”

“She’s not what you think she is. You are amazing, but she will treat you like a thing. A toy for amusement and a prize for those she needs. She will hold you beneath her and make you feel like you always need to earn her presence. Just watch yourself and if you ever need help let me know,” she said handing me a business card, “I know you're not ready to believe me, but if you could keep this meeting a secret from her it would be for the best."

She walked back into the stall and Jillian stepped in a few seconds later, "Come on babe I have big plans tonight."

My heart fluttered at the nickname already. We weren't even together yet. I tried to remind myself some people were just overly friendly, but still I loved it and I wanted more. The next morning, I woke up naked on a strange couch. My mind was blank, and my body was sore.

"Did you have fun? You were pretty good and I'm sure it will only get better," Jillian said as she came out of the bathroom. She was naked and dripping wet from the shower, "Get up and get dressed you can drive us to work today," she commanded and I didn't want to admit I had no idea what was going on so I nodded meekly and headed into the shower. Having no idea what had happened the night before left me feeling dirty somehow and I scrubbed myself until Jillian pounded on the door, "We're going to be late. Rinse off and let's go."

All of a sudden this somehow became my routine. Servant by day and nights I could never remember. A week later I confronted her about it and she chuckled, "Wow you said you couldn't handle your booze, but I didn't imagine it was this bad. You keep asking for liquid courage before we get intimate. Do you want me to stop giving it to you? I can tell you no," she was being so considerate that I couldn't bring myself to give it any more thought. She wasn't wrong. I rarely drank and it was a stronger reaction than I had ever had before, but anything was possible.

I shook my head no and looked at her, "If I'm still not comfortable being with someone as awesome as you and I'm not embarrassing myself while drunk I think we should leave well enough alone for now."

That was that I wouldn't rock the boat; she was too amazing, and she had chosen me. I wouldn't ruin this if I could avoid it. Two months and I still couldn't recall a single night together, but I was living with her now and it was Sunday I was serving brunch for her and some guests. The cooks had prepared everything, but I was serving everything to help out.

"O, you should serve in a naked apron," she teased as she slid on her high heels.

"Not happening babe," I replied chuckling and I thought I saw her roll her eyes before she sighed.

"Fine, just wear this maid outfit for me then," she replied curtly and tossed me a slutty French maid's costume that made my stomach churn, "What you're always saying you want to help and you want to make me happy. This will do both, so I don't see a problem."

"It's humiliating," I responded, laying the outfit on the bed.

"Well, if you don't want to be here with me, I get it. I'm a lot and I can be demanding. It's too much for most people, but I was so happy I thought you were different you'd be there for me. I thought you truly cared and wanted to support me."

Needless to say, I ended up in the maid outfit and a pair of heels taller than I had ever walked in before. The meal was going lovely when one of the men flipped up my skirt and chuckled, "Jill, babe you always have the sexiest help."

The whole table including Jillian chuckled and I thought I would throw up, but for the love of my lady I endured. Somewhere in the after party my mind went blank again, but I did not lose the whole night this time. Somewhere in the early morning hours my senses began to return. I was surrounded by laughing and I felt feverish, and

I felt violated. I could smell the musk of men and the stench of their release. I saw several women in tears and in the doorway Jillian.

“Try not to break her. I know it’s a party, but I have several clients that like her more than any of the girls who have helped me in the past,” she said a sneer cutting across her face, “Here love drink this,” she said handing me a glass of wine that had powder clearly floating on its surface. I rolled off the couch where I was being ravaged and pretended to convulse, “Alright boy’s somethings wrong time to go so I can clean her up,” she said and the crying girls helped her get me in the tub. In the morning, I refused to open my eyes and after she left, I scrolled through my phonebook to a number I had stored not knowing why.

I hit dial and she answered on the second ring, “Hello, I guess you finally figured it out. What can I do to help?”

“She’s a monster. Can we meet?”

We set an appointment for lunch near a clinic so if Jillian found out I could say I was getting medical treatment. I arrived a half an hour early and she was already there.

“Let me tell you about your girlfriend,” she said.

HOW IT STARTED

I was fresh out of college and so was she. We wanted to start a company and we did. It was slow and grueling at first. We had met in high school, and I had picked my major to support her. We were so close in those early days. A small office with one desk and a dream. We took all the client meetings together, came up with all the sales pitches together and put all the money back into the company.

One day she had a late-night meeting without telling me. When I asked about it, she said it was last minute and it was a big contract. No time to consult. I believed her then and it made a big impact at the company. Chump change to her now, but our commission from that one deal would pay to run our small office for a year. In that deal she found a formula to expand the company. We would divide the workload. She lamented we would have less time together, but she swore we'd get bigger and before long we wouldn't have to do any of the deals if we didn't want to. We could just teach other people to deal with clients.

We started our new divide and conquer policy and it was a raging success. I would put together deals and she would pitch them to investors, but all her appointments were dinners, drinks, sometimes even weekend conventions and even when I was free, I wasn't allowed to attend. I trusted her, so even though I was nervous and lonely I watched the company grow. Two years of exponential growth and we had hired Jillian four assistants. They had all started strong then looked like they were going to quit and then got promoted to handle their own client list. They each even had their own assistants at this point, and I couldn't have been prouder of our baby. One night I was working late on an acquisition proposal, and I was headed home to my empty condo to wait for my girlfriend to finish her meetings for the day.

"You have another twenty minutes and then I need to get her cleaned up and put in a cab, boys," Theresa, one of the girls Jillian had personally trained, was saying in a loud commanding voice.

"Sounds good. She's even better than you were. Jillian sure knows how to hire. Too bad she won't let us dig into that wife of hers," A male voice said from somewhere in the room.

"Don't be stupid, they're not even married. Who knows why Jillian keeps her to herself. I mean there is no one else in the company you can't use," another voice argued and my stomach started to churn. I could see the woman with glazed over eyes laying on the coffee table covered in male juices, and I could see the men surrounding her.

"I know she doesn't even get high first anymore. Think she built up a tolerance," The first man replied, and I threw up with that.

I texted Jillian that night, "Where are you? Need to see you ASAP"

She called me thirty seconds later, "What's wrong babe?" She asked, her voice was soft, her tone concerned, but in the background, I could hear the growls and groans of men. I hung up and left.

It took her three days and a hundred and twenty-seven calls to find me, but she did find me. When she did, she looked concerned and heartbroken,

"Why'd you leave so suddenly. I canceled all my meetings to come find you," she explained, clearly irritated that I had cost her so much money.

"You shouldn't have come, go back to your 'CLIENTS' don't worry about me," I replied and she looked sick. I could tell she finally got it.

"How'd you find out? I was so careful. I just needed another eighteen months," that was her response to me. In response I puked all over her shoes.

"What happens in eighteen months," I asked, still wiping the vomit from my mouth.

"I finally will have enough girls trained. I can advance to just supervising them and we can be the happy couple we should be," she said and it clicked. Every deal she had made alone this is what it was. We weren't making deals; we were pimping whores.

I screamed at that point when the realization finally sank all the way in, "The whole time? Every deal? So, this is why we had to divide and conquer? You're a whore."

She flinched at my accusation, "Yes, but I had to make our dream come true and I had to keep you safe. In the beginning I drugged myself, but I could feel myself giving in to the drug induced pleasure and I refused to lose my way back to you. I stopped the drugs, and I've never got aroused during a session since. I love you. I did everything for the company. We can work it out once I stop, right?" She pleaded with me, but all I heard was when I stop. She admitted right there that she wasn't stopping, which was all I needed to hear, but I loved her, so I checked to make sure I understood her.

“What if I said you had to pick today? Be a whore or have me come home,” I asked and she hesitated. Again, I felt like I had my answer, but despite what she had become she was gifted at making deals once upon a time.

“What guarantee would I have that if you forced me into giving up on my dream today, you’d stick around. If you resent me enough to leave. Then I’m not sure changing one little thing is going to save our relationship. Do you?” She asked me, trying to make it sound like I was being petty and manipulative by not giving her just a little more time. Then I asked a follow up question she never saw coming.

“Sit that aside for now,” I said and she looked pleased with herself for navigating this difficult situation, “Do they agree to take the drugs before you let those foul men violate them like that?”

“Somebody has to do it. If I ever want to be able to stop, I can’t be picky about who takes my place or how,” she said so matter-of-factly. I couldn’t believe I had ever loved this woman, but I had. I had loved her, chosen my career path for her, and I had built this company that was used to take advantage of young desperate women with her.

“Well let’s see if you ever stop,” I said leaving things deliberately open, but I disappeared that night and her recruitment changed. She stepped up the pace, and she became cold and calculating. Even actively recruiting sex workers at one point. The office had grown into an office building and secretly a hotel with a bar and twenty well stocked rooms. It offered every luxury you could possibly want, and she collected payments from the clients for all of it.

She kept her word and when the eighteen months were over, she reached out to me. She wouldn’t sleep with any more clients or train any more girls. She wanted me to come home, but Jillian was dead.

Not physically, but in every way that mattered. I tried actually for a month we dated, but the girls would still show up with needs, and the guys would still call with demands, and through it all her face was harsh and cruel, but also part of her relished in the control. She had no sex drive except after discussing her latest acquisition or some truly grotesque request she had facilitated. Then she would want to have cruel and demeaning sex that left me feeling dirty and like I had become the whore.

So, I left and this time I sold my shares and vowed to never look back. She found me again though and she promised she really did love me and apologized endlessly for how her career had ruined her sex drive. She said, "This is why I couldn't quit for you back then. If I had and you left me like this, I'd have nothing," she went on to say how there would always be a place next to her for me and it was only for me. She never recognized what she did was wrong. Only that it played out poorly.

She stayed away from customers but went back to training people the next month. I left well enough alone she had gone to just training low rent hookers to be high class call girls. Then you became enamored with her, and she was intrigued by the opportunity. I wanted to take you away from there, but I didn't know how to get you to believe me. So, I planted the seed and hoped for the best.

A PLAN AND A FEELING

"I see, so she's never cared for me. She's in love with you and using me to make money. You've let her do this over and over again, so you love her too then?" I asked, trying to swallow the hurt and betrayal.

"No and not anymore. The first group of girls were already obsessed with the lifestyle before I knew about it and after, well she hired people who were already used to servicing men for a living. There were no victims to help until you. I tried to warn you, but I'd seen that look on your face before in the mirror, so I knew you'd have to find out before you'd believe me. At this point I want to help you," she replied and something about the way she said it conveyed how much she needed me to believe her, "I don't want to sound creepy, but if you're ready to move on you can crash on my couch while we figure things out."

I nodded meekly and then turned to look at her, "If I'm moving on, I'll have nothing. Her schedule is sporadic so I can't go get my stuff and I can't go back to the office, so I have no job. She'll trash me given a chance so I can't even use it as a job reverence," I confessed to this woman and while I was doing so, I realized I didn't even know her name, "What's your name by the way?"

“Mika,” she replied and giggled slightly. That was when it hit me, she was even more gorgeous than Jillian. I blushed and looked away at the realization. She took notice of my reaction but said nothing. We got up from the table, and she led me to a drug store. We quickly bought all the necessities to last me for a month or so and then we headed for her house.

It was at that time my phone buzzed, a text from Jillian, “Babe, are you feeling better? Where’d you go?”

I sent her back a text without giving it much thought, “No woke up last night. Don’t think I’ll ever be ok again. Goodbye.”

She didn’t text back, so I thought she moved on. I mean I was just a trick to her. She might have lost some money, but she had more money than a mid-size city, so it wasn’t worth putting too much thought into. Meanwhile me and Mika went on and had a lovely dinner, and I crashed on her couch early. In the morning my phone was loaded with texts from Jillian demanding explanations, then compensation, then closure. Then her tone changed. She told me how she just needed my help to get through the contracts that were already expecting me specifically and then she’d welcome me as an equal partner in the company. I could have anything I wanted except her. She even offered to give me other women and said I could stand by her side in public.

I showed it to Mika. I don’t know why I needed to know how she saw the situation and if she wanted to be with Jillian. I feared maybe she’d even sacrifice me to make that happen, but if she would then I could do nothing. In this world I was dependent on her to make an escape.

She laughed and cried in equal measure. She knew, she had told me herself, but to see it written in front of her. The cruelest and most vile woman either of us had ever known loved her with a deep, true, undying, and unyielding love. It should make your resolve waver and your heart thaw. Especially for Mika who had loved her so much, but eventually the tears and laughter both stopped and she puked, "To think some part of her still thinks we can go back. She makes no effort to leave that world behind, she makes no move to change, but she saves herself for me. It's disgusting."

The messages continued pleading and praising. It was almost a month later when she finally let slip the truth. Apparently, the clients hadn't been as fond of anyone since she stopped performing for them. In fact, many of the clients were demanding that if she couldn't return me to them, she would have to take my place, but she had promised her wife she would never do that again. When I showed this one to Mika, she smiled a cold calculating smile.

"We're not married. Never were. Same sex marriage wasn't legal back then. I won't go back to her, but maybe we can give her closure. Would you marry me, so she can finally let both of us go? We can get divorced once she moves on if you want," she asked, but there was a pleading tone in her voice I couldn't deny.

"What if I can never let you go," I whispered in a tone so soft she couldn't hear me. She looked at me apologetically waiting for me to repeat myself. I smiled and said in a loud clear voice, "Could work. Might even be fun." She looked like she didn't really believe that's what I said but chose to let it go.

The messages were relentless, so the marriage had to be rushed, but it still had to be grand. Had to make a statement. That being said Mika managed to put it together in just under a month. The first week was slow. Finding a venue and a caterer to figure out the timeline. At the end of the first week though things started moving quickly. Ten days in, Mika was returning from work and she looked at me relaxing on the couch, "I invited her. If we're lucky she'll stop texting and you won't have to go through with this."

I couldn't help the sadness that struck my heart and painted my face at that. I wasn't sure what I felt for Mika, but I knew I wasn't ready for our story to end and me to never have a chance to find out. As fate would have it though Jillian got more desperate and I got confused, "The love of my life is going to marry someone else if I can't prove I'm past this life. Please we'll start as fifty fifty partners and then you can buy me out. She has her own company now I'll go and support her. It's all I ever wanted anyways. I'm sorry I lied, but I need you to do this or they'll ruin my company."

I read it over and over again but couldn't understand why she still thought she had a chance and how she was unaware I was the girl marrying her ex. Mika got home and it was time for answers. I showed her the text, and she looked even more confused than me, so she showed me the invitation. It was a habit for her. I didn't even need to ask she was always an open book. Always honest above all else. I liked that part of her even more than I liked her model-like good looks and I hate to admit it, but I was kind of shallow, so I really liked her looks. I read it and there was my name right under hers Mika Deluca and Erica Francios. She also showed me her text logs, email, and social messaging apps. She had never reached out to Jillian let alone implied there was a chance they could get back together. Even so with her delusion intact I had no choice but to wait for the day of the wedding. I couldn't block her out of fear with nowhere to vent that she may look for me in person. Which in truth she probably already was.

PREPARATIONS AND DEALS

The time passed by and somehow, somewhere along the way our relationship changed slowly, but noticeably. We went from eating together to sitting at the dinner table together while we ate. Then we sat on the same side of the table and now we brushed against each other sometimes and on occasion we'll share each other's food. Once when we each bought our own individual sliced dessert, I fed her some of my strawberry cake. The same could be said about every other aspect of our life, but it was never more obvious than it was in the bedroom. At first, I crashed on the couch. Then she insisted for the long term it would be bad for my back, so I slept in her bed clothed in layers and under my own blanket and she did the same. Then we wore less until we got down to regular sleep attire. Then we just used one blanket. Now I wake up with her spooning me or my legs wrapped around her leg. We never discuss it and perhaps maybe we never will, but I already feel closer to her than I have with any partner in my entire life. We talked about everything and nothing and we spent time just together, but life wasn't ready to surrender our happily ever after just yet.

"I've put them off until after my ex's wedding. If you come back, you can have the company. If she'll accept me, I'll walk out of my life and into hers," Jillian texted a week before the wedding and I showed it to Mika while we were lying in bed.

She looked at me with a look I couldn't quite decipher on her face, "Wow, that could be a big win for you. Are you tempted?"

I tried to hide the hurt at her question, but I was still lost in my impulsive spoiled phase of my youth, and my hurt was like a second skin. She saw it and frowned, "I didn't mean anything by it, this is different. If she gave you the whole company, you have to go back, not any of that other stuff. I mean you took the job because you wanted to be in that industry, right? This would be a big leap forward even if you liquidated the company and started a new firm."

"Say whatever is going on with us means nothing, which for the record I'm not prepared to do. Say I still wanted that life, even knowing what the people who make those deals are looking for in women they make deals with. Say I believed I could salvage anything worth a damn from that viper's pit. How could I trust her to mean what she's saying? She only needs me to show myself and then she writes all the rules. I'm sure at the very least she would want me to save her from repercussions with her regulars before she gave me the company and what about when you don't take her back and all she has left is the company. Do you think she'd let me keep it?" I was yelling and crying by the time I finished, and I hoped she understood for me the decision was over with the first statement. I may not be ready to say I love you yet and if we were dating instead of desperately trying to escape our shared ex I certainly wouldn't be considering marriage. All that aside I was even less prepared to say we shared nothing, but that made me wonder how she sees things, "Is marrying me an inconvenience for you? Would you rather I take the company? Do you want to go back to her" I asked. I looked at her as if to say *does this mean nothing to you?* but that question I couldn't bring myself to ask.

"I will not go back to her regardless. I want you to do what's right for you. If you stay the person I know and it's what you want I'd marry you even if you took the company from her. So, no I don't consider it a bother. I consider it my joy and privilege. Even if I would have preferred to date, you know at least a little before I proposed," she responded ending with her characteristically light chuckle.

This new revelation gave me something to consider. I could try to take the company and let her walk away, but would it be safe, could I make it work, and would Mika really be ok if I wanted to try. Especially if it was a trap and I had to escape again.

"Send me contracts to transfer the company tomorrow and resign and I'll come back." I texted Jillian three days before the wedding. In less than an hour she had all the contracts e-mailed to me. I felt a little guilty. I couldn't say, me taking over the company would shield her from the contract partners who were demanding favors, and I would not be providing any such thing. All the same I signed the contracts and took possession of the company. Once I received her resignation I began to work. The next two days I locked myself in an office at Mika's company. I even slept there. She wasn't thrilled, but she was supportive. I had decided the only way to be sure this would work was if I could settle all company issues before Jillian realized what was going on. First, I informed all the clients, not just Jillians, there would be no more favors. We were a networking firm not a whore house. We put deals together with finance nothing more. Then I moved on, as expected most partners began pulling their contracts. Then Jillian started texting, I ignored her even when it escalated to calls. I moved on to finding someone to buy all the company's fiscal property. Then I dumped the company. It took the longest to find a company I didn't mind selling a client list that was looking for hookers and a bunch of contracts that would never materialize, but it was done. The day before the wedding I left the office and had breakfast with Mika. She was thrilled to see me and I her, but we were instantly pulled into a day of crazy preparations. It may have been rushed, but she had spared no expense and cut no corners. We did pedicures, manicures, massages, salon for our hair, everything a girl could want and at dinner she said, "I didn't think a bachelorette party was appropriate since you're kind of in hiding so it would just be my friends."

That was the tone of our relationship, she would always consider me even though I had created this mess, by not trusting her in the first place. I had been so enamored with Jillian, looking back now it made me so angry, but luckily Mika seemed to be happy with me and while I still bit my lip every time I considered saying it I was falling in love with her. We drank wine late into the night and then we showered together for the first time. Nothing sexual happened, we just scrubbed each other's back and enjoyed each other's presence. After we went to bed naked and fell into a deep calming sleep, even knowing the storm that was on the horizon. I had turned my phone off as Jillian's text and calls had become non-stop. She would understand tomorrow and then hopefully it would all be over.

AT THE WEDDING AND THEN

We rose early that morning and preparations began even before we had breakfast. I cursed myself for allowing her to decide everything. She had picked a ceremony that would allow the reception to be served for lunch. That meant the venue would start receiving guests at 9 a.m. and we had to be there by 10. We had gone to the salon, but our hair still needed to be styled because we had slept on it. Our make-up had to be done and then we had to be separated and put in our dresses. At that moment my heart sank. We were almost certain this is when Jillian would make her first approach. We had a camera set up in her dressing room so I could watch in case things got out of hand. Jillian was not the most mentally stable person and the pressure of losing Mika was a lot.

We were right. Jillian showed up as Mika was zipping her gown, “You look beautiful,” she said and I watched as Mika turned to face her. The pressure in my own chest threatening to tear me wide open.

“You really came. Part of me had hoped you wouldn’t,” Mika replied and I looked away reflexively. I didn’t know if I could watch this. She looked sad, almost heartbroken, “I told you when I left, the woman I loved is dead, if she ever existed at all.”

“I’m still me. I thought I was giving you the life you wanted. I left that world. I gave it away to some puppy dog intern. Please marry me, forget this passing fancy. I’ve kept an eye on you. You weren’t even dating someone six months ago. It can’t be that serious. I’ve kept my word. No one has touched me since that night when we tried to make it work last time. I know I was a terrible lover back then, but you tell me what you want me to do. Help me remember. I can be that girl again for, no with you,” Jillian pleaded standing there crying in her tailored tuxedo.

“Jillian, I didn’t leave because of the kind of lover you were. I left because of the person you became. You were never building a life for me. You know, right? I chose my major for you. I followed you to this city. This life was what you wanted, and I wanted to help you make your dream a reality. When I realized the nightmare hellscape you had created I couldn’t stay. I tried, but I see the abyss it’s in you Jillian. You relish in it. The crooked deals, and the depravity of it all. I could see the ecstasy after you dealt with clients and when you trained girls. Most importantly, the dreamy eyed eternal optimist I fell in love with is gone. You never shared dreams, you had no ambition, and the way you viewed our relationship made my skin crawl. Lastly, I love Erica more than I knew was possible. So, it is very serious to me. So, no, I won’t marry you. You can stay for the ceremony, but don’t make a scene. We can talk at the reception if you want and if you can be nice to my wife. Honestly though you shouldn’t have given her your company,” my mouth dropped and my heart raced as I listened to all her confessions pile up and I could see in the video that it was having an effect on Jillian as well.

“What do you mean I shouldn’t have given your girlfriend my company? I gave it to that stupid intern who spent two months on her back for me. The men loved her; they couldn’t get enough of her. Though apparently, she’s trying to restructure the company and avoid having to settle with them, but what does any of that have to......” Jillian began and Mika cut her off.

"Like I said, you can stay for the ceremony and reception. Behave, I need to get ready. See you out there." With that Mika had successfully navigated the first encounter with Jillian, but I didn't believe for one minute it would be the last.

Sure, enough after we walked down the aisle and Mika lifted my vail, I heard Jillian, "That bitch. Sorry, continue," she said, clearly remembering her promise.

The rest of the ceremony was lovely, and the reception started well enough. Jillian skirted the reception hall following me and Mika with a look that would kill if it could. As things settled down Jillian approached, "I've been good Mika. For the love of God can we talk? All of us."

So, the three of us snuck away to a small room that had been set up for us to change clothes. As we walked into the room Jillian's rage broke free, "What in the fuck, Mika!"

"May I babe?" I asked, feeling a mix of emotions, not the least of which was protective of my new wife. She nodded and I cleared my throat, "She saved me. Let me crash on her couch, but you wouldn't let me go and kept holding on to her. We decided if we were both off the market, you'd have to let us go. While we were figuring out how to be free of you, we fell in love. In a way so deep, so profound, so ingrained love seems somehow inadequate to convey the whole feeling. However, you still persisted. Even though we sent you an invitation with both our names on it. You never reached out to her, and you never confronted me. You were so confident if you kept your promise she'd come back to you. Even though you kept that promise for years and she's stayed away for years. So, I took the company, dismantled that toxic mess. Now I have savings and I helped pay for the wedding. So, boss, I should thank you. If not for the company, I would feel like a charity case and honestly, I don't know how that would have affected our relationship."

As I finished, I could see all the fight and resolve drain from her face, and she turned and left. We finished the night in peace enjoying the party with all our friends and after cake, bouquet toss, garter toss, first dance, and dollar dance we ran off to a car with all the corny painting and cans on strings that our friends had put together with care. That night with all the months of anticipation and longing released we made love. First with a fevered passion and an urgency that would not ebb until we both reached the climax we craved. Then with a slow reverent exploration of two virgins wanting to know every inch of unexplored territory. Then with a warm embrace and a confidence in our rhythm that honestly surprised even me. The morning would bring the future, but tonight was perfect and we stayed in each other's embrace until it was gone.

It was six months of wedded bliss when we heard about Jillian again. Having lost Mika, she returned to her clients. After she settled the outstanding promises though they disappeared as well and she became just another hooker in a cheap motel. Swept up in a raid she was testifying and sharing her records on all her clients for a new start. I couldn't help but wonder if she really could change with a fresh start and no choice.

Mika also sold her company. She had built the company simply to prove to Jillian given time they could do it the right way. She once told me, until me, she had held out hope that Jillian would see the company she built, and she would repent. Actually, change and prove the girl she had fallen in love with wasn't an illusion. She told me back then she had been prepared to give her the company if she would only be the girl she loved.

We run a non-profit now for abused and exploited women. We help over three thousand women annually. Mika is famous for her fund-raising parties. We have two lovely, adopted daughters and a son I had for Mika with a sperm donor. It was expensive and painful, but if she asked me to, I would do it again even now. Though in our early fifties we are settled into being pretty happy with our life.

BONUS STORY

ME YOU AND PUPPIES TOO

I was by all accounts the definition of a dog person. I had several at all times in every house I had ever lived in since I was a little girl. I lived in a small ranch style home in a small cul-de-sac in a terribly typical town. Stay at home moms bickered on the PTA and dads worked 45-hour work weeks and barely noticed their families. My father spent his work hours traveling mostly and would be home for a couple days a month and a week for the holidays. Mother drank a lot and had male friends that would always be leaving as I was getting home from school. She was not on good terms with the other mothers, and I had no friends because of it. However, I had my dogs. When I was a little girl, there was a dalmatian named Suzy, a bulldog named Bruiser, and a little lap dog that was a mutt named Trixter. Those were my first three dogs. They changed over the years and eventually I moved out, but I took all three dogs I had at the time with me. Recently my baby Trixter passed away. She was the last of my original dogs to go and I replaced her with a teacup terrier and named it Thumbelina. She was a sweet puppy but like an impish fairy she had a free spirit. One day in early Autumn Thumbelina ran away and I searched for her the whole afternoon. I then boarded my other two dogs and called into work and continued looking. I scoured the city until the pounds and shelters opened and then I started personally visiting the next closest one while making calls to others. It took the whole day but finally with only three shelters left I walked into one in a sketchy part of downtown there in a rocking chair in a gorgeous summer dress sat a woman in her early twenties holding Thumbelina and petting her.

"H-hello, um I believe that puppy is mine," I said and the woman looked at me curiously.

"Thumbelina you mean. She really is a mischievous little fairy," she replied and sat her down on the ground. Thumbelina ran over to me, jumped against my shin and darted back to the girl in the rocker.

"I think she likes it here. You can hold her for a bit longer if you like. I'm in no hurry now that I found her," I said, handing Thumbelina back to her. She stroked her and we talked. Her name was Emily, and she volunteered here because she couldn't have pets in her place. She was a student at the local college and she loved dogs. We talked for a while and when I noticed the sky started to darken, I sighed and looked at this gorgeous young woman who had kept my puppy safe and comforted until I could find her and I wanted to spend more time with her, but I had to go get my other dogs, "I'm afraid I've lost track of time. I have to go get my other dogs. Would you join me for dinner to thank you for watching after my newest baby?"

"I would love to meet your other dogos, and dinner sounds lovely, but thanks isn't necessary. I loved having the little guy in my lap," she responded, and for the briefest moment, my eyes flinted down to where Thumbelina was still curled up in her lap. She smiled brightly and we headed out with her carrying Thumbelina.

We ate from a food truck in the park with all three of my dogs. Thumbelina stayed at the table with us while the other two ran around nearby. We had a great conversation covering all kinds of random topics. The park was lit with lamppost lights, but eventually even that light couldn't keep the darkness away. She helped me walk the dog's home and came inside. We had a drink and talked for another half an hour then she prepared to leave, and I gathered my courage.

"Would you like to go on a date? I had a lot of fun and girls who get me and my dogs are rare," I asked, trying to keep the desperation out of my voice, but not sure how I did. Her answer surprised me in the best way possible.

She tilted her head, the genuine confusion obvious on her face, "Isn't that what we just did? Like I said, thanks weren't necessary, and besides, my shift was over at the shelter more than two hours before we left. If you're asking if we can go out again. Then I would love that. If you want to disregard this date and start over next time, that would make me sad," she replied with a warm tone she hadn't used all night.

"When works for you? I work from home on a production-based system, so I don't really have a schedule," I said faster and higher pitched then I meant to and she giggled in response.

"We could do brunch tomorrow. I know a little place with a patio. If they are leashed you can bring everybody," she responded, matching my energy and tone and I smiled back at her and nodded frantically. I barely slept that night, and I was dressed and ready for brunch at 6:30 a.m. We were going at around eleven, but I sat scrolling through my phone waiting and at 8:45 my phone rang. It was an unsaved number, but I recognized it instantly. She had written it on a little slip of paper last night and I had stared at it for hours. I answered, my hands sweating and my throat felt like it was collapsing in on itself.

"Hello," I managed to rasp out, and she chuckled that slight restrained chuckle I had heard briefly the night before and it warmed me.

"Hi, this might sound clingy or pathetic, but, um I've been up for hours I want to see you. Would you like to take a walk before brunch?"

“Yeah,” I managed to reply, and she enthusiastically said she’d head my way. I double and triple checked myself in the mirror before she knocked on the door and I quickly let her in. She was wearing a summer dress similar to the one she had on yesterday. I couldn’t help but muse how well the style fit her. The laid-back grace and effortless beauty made my heart skip a beat. She grabbed one of the leashes from my hand and we headed out the door.

The date was great. We walked and got to know each other. Had brunch and traded even more stories. We talked about trivial things at first, but our conversation depended as we let the dogs run in the park. I told her how I hadn’t believed in love until I walked in to find her holding Thumbelina. Then she looked at me in a sorrowful way I had never seen on her face before.

“I was married once. He was my everything. When he left, he crushed my world. I vowed to never love another man. Who knew this is how I’d keep that vow. I thought I’d die alone,” she admitted and then stared at me with an expectant gaze. She was waiting for my response, and I couldn’t help but chuckle.

“Well, lucky me,” I couldn’t help it. I couldn't stop smiling like an idiot. Again, she walked me home, and we made a date for the following weekend. She kissed me lightly and pulled away and as she did, I whispered in her ear, “Wait.” She did, and I swallowed hard preparing myself for what I needed to say, praying it wasn’t a one-sided feeling. “Can you really wait until next weekend? I never want to let you go,” I confessed and dropped my gaze to the ground, my face turning a dark crimson.

“How about tomorrow then I get done with work at 3 p.m. Then I’m at the shelter until six. We could do dinner, but places your babies can go will be a little tricky. Can you get a sitter for five hours? We can do a movie after.”

"My niece loves them almost as much as I do. She might kidnap one of them for the night as payment, but she'll keep an eye on them," I replied, overjoyed by how quickly she had adjusted our plans, meeting my needs with no doubts or hesitation.

"Good, then, pick me up at the animal shelter. If you miss me come visit early, I get there a little after three," she explained, gave me a quick peck on my cheek, and she was off.

For the love of God, I did my best, but I found myself in front of the animal shelter the next day before four. I went to see Emily; she was in the yard with thirty dogs of various ages and species. She was tossing balls and tugging on ropes, it was obvious how much fun she was having. She was like a child without a care in the world and I wanted so badly to step into that world with her, but I couldn't. I didn't dare disturb the picture-perfect moment with my intrusion. I went back inside and sat with a couple old hound dogs that had definitely seen better days and petted them while staring out the window at the endearing scene. She came in an hour later, and I went to help her feed the dogs.

She said nothing about me being there until we finished as we were cleaning up, she bumped into me and giggled, "I thought you left when you didn't come out to play."

I smiled back at her, "I couldn't disturb you. You looked so beautiful playing with them. I don't want to sound creepy, but I just wanted to watch. You were more radiant than the sun," I admitted the flush on my cheeks darkening with every word.

She just gigged and leaned into me again. We helped clean up the yard and then we prepared to leave for our date. In many ways it felt like our first date. It was the first time we would be alone focused solely on each other and getting to know one another.

"You know I can't help but see this lasting forever. I know it's weird, we've basically just met," she said as we walked, her leaning into me. I had to admit I liked the sentiment, and I loved the easy way we shared intimate space. I kissed the top of her head.

"You know you could stay at my place for a bit if you wanted," I offered. Then I heard myself, and a blush claimed my entire face. I wasn't new to loving women or even to dating them, but I would never use any phrase that implied experience or confidence either. I was prepared for everything I said to be wrong, and I feared the next moment being our last.

"Ok," she replied and again she released that soft restrained giggle that I could tell was the sound she made when real joy collided with her sense of social propriety. She tugged slightly firmer on my arm, and I could feel all the warm places her body pressed against my arm. My blush darkened and I had to look away. Over the course of the next week, we settled into a state of domestic bliss, and I couldn't help but muse at how seamlessly and effortlessly the transitions had been. Our life felt on auto pilot in the best kind of way from there. Not like we didn't have choices, but more like even with the endless sky we had effortlessly found the best course.

She had also been a lesbian for a long time and was pleased to know that she wasn't a whimsical experiment, and I was happy to know we were in similar spaces in our personal journeys. Neither of us wanted kids even though we loved them. We doubted our ability to be enough for a child in a world that placed ever more complications on being a child. Neither of us liked the idea of cats as pets. That was when I knew, pet people had preferences, but I had never met another woman that I vibed with that had disregarded cats as companions the way I did. I asked her to move in with me that night, and a month later I proposed.

After the wedding, using our knowledge of dogs and her connections in finance, we started a dog rescue ranch. We now had more than 30 dogs at any given time and finding funding for it was her full-time job. I still did my job from a home office, though I didn't put in as many hours. We never took vacations, nor did we reach for fame and fortune. We stayed on that little piece of land, and we loved each other. Too many, it might not be much, but to us, it was everything.

BONUS SKETCH BOOK SNEAK PEAK VOL. 2

Kara

Tiaco

www.ingramcontent.com/pod-product-compliance
Lightning Source LLC
LaVergne TN
LVHW020703110826
845149LV00012B/2094

* 9 7 8 1 9 7 1 6 5 9 1 4 5 *